The Sea

of

Travail

Kristin Gleeson

An Tig Beag Press

Other works by Kristin Gleeson:

CELTIC KNOT SERIES
Along the Far Shores
Raven Brought the Light
Selkie Dreams
A Treasure Beyond Worth (novelette)

RENAISSANCE SOJOURNER SERIES
A Trick of Fate (novelette)
The Imp of Eye (With Moonyeen Blakey)

NON FICTION
Anahareo: A Wilderness Spirit

Sign up to my mailing list and get
FREE *A Treasure Beyond Worth*
www.kristingleeson.com.

ISBN: 978-0-9931567-8-6

To Moon

CHAPTER ONE
Bruges, Early Spring 1445
BARNABAS

Margriet pulled at my doublet, unfastening the laces as quickly as she could, but not quickly enough for my own desire. Her breasts pressed against me, large and ripe. I plunged my hands down her front, longing to feel those tender full paps once again. God's breath, but she was fulsome woman.

She moaned at my touch. The laces of her gown were already loosened and ready for me when I'd arrived a short while ago. I eyed the small wrapped parcel of saffron on the table beside us and smiled. Even without the prize of the saffron at the end of these trysts, I would still find them enjoyable. Jehan Baenst was not the only one in this merchant household who was skilled in many areas.

"You are smiling, my sweet," she said. "Perhaps I can make your smile even wider?"

Her hand cupped my codpiece and my reaction was immediate. I gave her an appreciative grin.

"Oh yes," she said. "Just a touch from me is all you need."

I put my mouth on hers and moved down along her neck, kissing, nibbling, and licking, just as she liked. Her lace coif came adrift and fell to the floor as she leaned her head back to allow me greater access.

"My handsome Jacob," she murmured in response. "You do know how to please a woman."

She called me Jacob in her Flemish tongue, which I barely grasped. I, formerly known as Barnabas, and latterly Giacomo, had become Jacob in this Flemish town. But who minded my less-than-fluent grasp of a tongue that I'd only heard these past two months? My lack had done me no harm that I could see.

I pulled her towards the bed and tugged at her skirts while she attempted the laces of my pourpoint. It was awkward, but we were desperate in our need, and in the end we fell on the bed in a heap. With a growl I lunged on her playfully, my laces dangling, drawers adrift, and hiked up her skirts. She spread her legs with a sigh.

"Margriet!" came a voice from below.

Margriet's eyes opened in alarm. "It's Jehan. He's home early." She shoved me away and jumped off the bed, straightening her gown. "Coming, my love," she shouted. She scooped up her lace coif. "Quickly," she hissed. "Out the window."

"The window?" I pulled up my drawers and eyed the opening dubiously. The red tiled rooftops shone slickly against the dark skyline of Bruges.

"There is no choice. You must go." She pushed me towards the window.

With a shrug, I scooped up my leather boots, hat, and cloak. The parcel of saffron was still there, and I grabbed it and tucked it inside my shirt. I certainly wouldn't leave that behind.

Margriet opened the casement and helped me through the opening, giving me a little thrust at the end. Bare feet might have been a better choice for this challenge I faced, rather than hose. I squatted on the ledge for a moment, contemplating my next move. The roofs next door were close enough, but steeply pitched. I had to get onto the roof of this house first, before I could even contemplate them. The shallow gable roof that covered the window where I perched was small enough that I could climb up on top of it. I glanced down at the empty street below, dimly lit from the candles in the window of the house opposite. I risked breaking my neck if I fell, but there was no help for it.

I re-tied my pourpoint laces, shoved my arms through the sleeves of my doublet, gripped my boots between my teeth, and swung up on the little roof. For one short moment, I thought I'd lost my balance, but I recovered quickly enough. Perched firmly now, I slid my soft leather boots on and lamented briefly the inevitable scuffs and scratches that would doubtless come on the expensive red Moroccan leather. They'd been a gift from a Parisian female admirer. I pictured her for a moment, until a shout from within the house prompted me to move.

I surveyed the roofs around me, and with a swift motion, rose and made my way across the tiles to the rear of the house in the direction of the attached outbuildings. The roof ended where the first storey finished. Below it, the house continued on the ground floor, the roof a reasonable drop. I took a deep breath and made the jump, landing with just a slight turn of my ankle. The pain was immediate, but not serious enough that it hindered my progress to the roof's edge. There I managed to find foothold in a small window ledge, and from that position I dropped to the ground. I winced at the impact on my sore ankle, but wasted no time lingering there.

I slipped down the little lane and out to a main street and headed toward the canal. A cool breeze blew off the water and I drew my doublet around me. There was a sliver of a moon out in this March night and it was enough to point me in the right direction. *The Golden Cup*. The watchbell sounded from the church tower. The night was early yet. A little drink to celebrate a timely escape would do no harm. And perhaps a little business as well.

The tavern was noisy and the heat from the press of bodies took the chill from me. I hobbled to my familiar corner and saw that Paolo and Luigi were already there. I was nervous when I'd first met them in the tavern several days after I arrived in Bruges, speaking Italian to each other, until they told me they were Genoese and worked for the Portinari merchant family here in the city. There was no fear they would discover that I wasn't really Giacomo Bonavillagio, son of a minor Venetian merchant, but Barnabas, lately of Eye by Westminster, hiding from the King's men determined to burn me as a witch.

"Ah, Giacomo, *amico mio*, we didn't expect you this night," said Luigi in Italian. He raised a pair of thick brows. "Though we're flattered if you prefer our charms to those of a certain delectable merchant's wife."

"Hands not large enough for her treasures?" asked Paolo, his wide mouth splitting into a grin. He cupped his palms over his chest and looked down. "I'd be happy to take over."

"Ah, dear *amicos*, you are too kind in your concern," I said. "I did go to my tryst and found I was more than capable and she more than willing. No, no, it was only that our time was cut short."

They eyed me lower down.

"Cut short?" asked Paolo. He jabbed me with his elbow. "Not too short, I hope."

I laughed and clapped Paolo on the back. "Ah, never fear for that. I know how to value my jewels. No, I am afraid the lady's husband returned and I was forced to make a hasty retreat."

"How hasty?" asked Luigi. He leaned forward, his straight dark hair falling forward.

I recounted my recent experiences to the pair of them and they howled with laughter. I made an indignant expression. "It is not a matter for fun, rather a matter for a stiff remedy. A pot of ale, I think."

"Oh, several," said Paolo. He motioned to the innkeeper for a jug and tankard to be brought.

"Now, tell us, *amico mio*," said Luigi, once the drink had been brought. "Did you get more than a handful of her bountiful breasts, or was your reward foresworn as well?"

I took a deep drink of my ale and grinned. "Ah, not so fast. All in good time."

"Ah, but Madonna Baenst, her husband's warehouse still has some spices there, no?" asked Luigi.

They knew I had counted on this when I had gone to see Mistress Baenst. Her husband was a clever man who knew when to hold back wares, and with this past winter's floods that had damaged the goods in many a merchant's warehouse and no hope of replenishment until the summer's end, this man still had rare items to sell. At a price.

I took another deep drink. "He does indeed." I slipped my hand inside my doublet, withdrew the small packet and held it up. "*Ecco.*"

I placed the packet on the table and we all stared at it for a moment.

Paolo sucked in his breath. "Oh, *bene*. More sizeable than the last one, is it not?"

Luigi leaned over and gave me a punch in the arm. "Of a certainty," said Luigi. "Signoro Portinari would give much for this amount."

I raised a brow. "More than the last time?"

Luigi nodded. "If the quality matches, there is no doubt, *amico mio*."

"And you will get your usual price," I told them.

Luigi took the packet and opened it carefully. A goodly pile of the fronds of the prized golden spice so carefully stored inside the crocus flower shone brightly inside. He examined it carefully and looked up.

"I should have a care, dear Giacomo," his face serious.

I narrowed my eyes. "Why?"

"Because the woman is clearly in love with you, to give you so much." Luigi laughed and placed the open packet back on the table. "Look at it all. What person in their right mind would make a present of something as rare as that, except a woman in love?"

I shook my head in protest. "Ah, it's nothing like that. We merely enjoy each other's company."

"Gentlemen. Excuse my interruption, but I couldn't help but notice that fine saffron sample."

I turned around and stared in the face of Jehan Baenst's factor. "Mynheere Gruithus, isn't it?" I said in my rough Flemish.

The panic came only for a moment and then it became something else, something mischievous. I rose and bowed as did the others.

"It is," said Gruithus. "I'm afraid you gentlemen have the better of me." He nodded to Luigi. "Though I recognise you, I think. You are with the House of Portinari."

"I am, Signoro. Luigi Salari is my name, and this is my colleague, Paolo Gotti."

"I am Giacomo Buonavillagio," I said.

"And you are with the Portinari?"

"No, mynheere. My father is a merchant out of Venice."

Gruithus considered him. "I can't say that I know the House of Bonavillagio."

"My father is a merchant of select items, only. I am here to see if we might get permission to trade here."

"You are speaking to the Duke of Burgundy's men?"

"I will be speaking to the Duke himself, tomorrow."

Gruithus eyed the saffron on the table. "And that is a sample of your wares?"

I nodded and gave him a pleasant smile.

"May I look closer?" asked Gruithus.

"Of course, mynheere."

Gruithus stepped up to the table and bent over to examine the open packet. I glanced over at Luigi and saw the suppressed humour in his face. I put on a bland expression. Paolo couldn't even manage a look in my direction.

Gruithus stepped back and regarded me carefully. "Mynheere, that is indeed good quality. As good as our own stored in the warehouse. But we have little of it left. Would you be willing to sell this packet?"

I looked over at Luigi and Paolo with a serious expression. "I am afraid these fellows here were expressing their interest on behalf of the House of Portinari."

"Ah, but I would double whatever you were offered," said Gruithus. He glanced at Luigi and Paolo, a sly look on his face. "And guarantee that we would be interested in however much your father could send to us exclusively. If you get the necessary permissions. Which I have no doubt you will," he added.

I named the price that the Portinari would have paid and paused, pretending to consider it. "And the prices you would give us? And I can take your word that they would be...persuasive, no?"

"Oh, very persuasive, if the shipment is of the same quality."

"It will be mynheere, it will be." I reached over, refolded the parcel and tied it up again. "You have the money with you now?"

Gruithus waved his hand. "No, of course not. But if you will wait just a while. I will return to the warehouse to get it." He held out his hand for the packet.

I smiled at him. "My friends and I will await your return with pleasure." I tucked the packet back inside my doublet.

Gruithus gave me a curt nod and departed. When the door had closed on his back I regarded Luigi and Paolo and spoke in Italian. "A fine man, no? With a real eye for high quality wares."

Luigi burst out laughing. "Oh, Giacomo, you are so amusing. It is worth it to give up the fee for selling the saffron to Portinari just to be witness to such a trick."

"Trick? I see no trick. The man wants to keep all the saffron for his master to sell. I only helped in his pursuit."

"You dark horse, I didn't realise you were meeting with the Duke tomorrow about permission to trade," said Paolo. "You never mentioned you moved in such circles. Or was that just part of the joke?"

"Oh, that was no joke. I am meeting with the Duke tomorrow." The matter to be discussed was nothing to do with trade, though. And if it was up to me, I wouldn't be anywhere near the ducal palace, never mind pleading a trade deal on behalf of some imaginary father.

Luigi and Paolo exchanged glances. "So you mean to set up a trading house here for your father?"

"It is only a discussion with the Duke. You have no cause for worry on behalf of your master." He flashed them a smile. "Yet."

I laughed hard and nearly had to stop myself, it became so uproarious. Luigi and Paolo joined in and shouted for more ale. There was much to celebrate. Even if Gruithus didn't return with the money, it was still a good jest. Gruithus and his own packet of saffron, returned to the fold. The jest was shared in Italian over and over.

But the man did return, paid the price, and I left *The Golden Cup* with a purse heavy with coins.

CHAPTER TWO
Bruges, Early Spring 1445
BARNABAS

Master al Qali removed his cloak and draped it across one of the chairs. He'd just returned from one of his many walks along the Bruges docks to glean news from incoming ships.

"Is the translation all prepared?" he asked in Italian. He was always conscious of maintaining the ruse of my supposed Venetian origins.

I nodded and pointed to the table where I sat. The translation, as well as the original codex, was wrapped in an oiled cloth tied securely ready for the Duke. Master al Qali had scanned it the night before, while I was out, and pronounced it sufficient. Even after four years of his tutoring, I still felt anxious that he might find serious fault with my work.

Smoke wafted from the small brazier next to me and clouded my eyes a moment. A chill north wind was blowing off the canal today and finding every crack and gap in the doors and windows of our chambers. Though there were three chambers and a ground level, there were drawbacks to this accommodation, and for a moment, I longed for the smaller rooms in Paris.

"Any news?" I asked. My head and tongue were still a bit thick from last night's caper, but I made the effort. Master al Qali would spare little for what he considered my failings.

Master al Qali made his way to the table in this small chamber that served as our receiving room and examined the wrapped manuscripts. Even now, I couldn't escape the power of his presence. It wasn't just his dark skin, or his flowing robes, there was something that emanated from him that I used to take for strength and kindness, but lately had read as something different.

Master al Qali took his time examining the parcel and then fixed his dark eyes on me. "I am glad to see that you have not let your night of reckless debauchery affect your duty in this regard."

I pasted a grin on my face. "*Mi dispiace*, Master al Qali, you do me a wrong. I did little last night, but have a few drinks with my friends."

"You think I am not aware of your escapades? A merchant's wife, no less. It will not serve. You will not go to her again."

"But what harm can it do? She is willing, careful. There's no risk, I assure you."

Master al Qali stared at me hard. "I will not answer a statement so beneath your intelligence. How many times must I instruct you that you risk all if you are led by your genitals, rather than the mind I have trained with such painstaking care?"

I dropped my gaze. He could do that to me. Reduce me to a child again with a few words and a glance. All thoughts of defending my actions fled. No mention was made of my rewards for these dalliances. I had some shred of hope he might not have heard. The joy that I had felt last night at my great jest of the sale of the saffron turned to anxiety at such a foolish and public gesture that surely would get back to Master al Qali.

"I'm sorry," I mumbled. "It won't happen again."

"See that it doesn't." His voice was sharp. "There are new reasons I would not want to call attention to us." He placed a hand on my shoulder and gripped tightly. "An English ship has just come in."

I tensed, waiting to hear his next words. It had been some time since we'd had any news from England. In Paris, with relations between France and England always in such a precarious balance, it was easy to hear some sort of rumour of the English court and its weak king, Henry VI. The king with whom my former master and mistress both fell afoul with their witchcraft and dabblings in alchemy, not to mention forecasting the future. The dabblings that put me on the run to take refuge with Master al Qali and into my current disguise.

"Any news from the court?" I asked.

"Not the court, no. But about our friend."

I stared at him. "The Duchess?" I whispered. I could hardly say her title without a cold chill running down my back. I had never liked her, not even the first time she showed up at the house of my mistress, Margery Jourdemayne, looking for herbs to help get her with child.

Master al Qali frowned. He never liked to mention names connected to our past. There was always a chance someone, somewhere, might be listening.

He nodded. "There has been a rescue attempt. At Kenilworth, where they're holding her."

"An attempt? It didn't succeed."

"No. But that does not mean that they will not try to unearth all that happened before to see who might be behind this attempt, and any future attempt."

"You think they might make a connection to me? To us?"

Master al Qali shrugged. "It is always wise to be cautious."

"What's your plan then?"

Master al Qali made his way over to the small sideboard, removed a ring of keys from the pouch by his side, and opened the sideboard door. He withdrew a box and placed it on the table in front of me.

I stared up him and frowned. "No."

"I think, Giacomo it is not a question of 'yes' or 'no', in this case."

I folded my arms over my chest and turned my head away. Once again I felt like a petulant child, rather than the man of eighteen I'd been the night before.

Master al Qali leaned over me, his hand at my back. "This is not a choice. We need to know of any danger and this is the way we will find out."

"Can't we just leave Bruges?" I asked.

The pressure on my back increased. "We need to find out enough so that our departure can take us away from any possible danger, not into it. Our destination will depend on what you see."

He released the pressure on my back, lifted another key from the ring and unlocked the box. I didn't have to look to know that the carefully polished showstone sat nestled in its velvet cushioning, refracting the light that shone through the window across the room.

"Go, on. Take it out. Infuse the showstone with your thoughts, your questions, and then see what you find."

I took a deep breath and lifted the showstone reluctantly out of the box. How many months since I had looked in it? It had been longer than that, I realised, because I'd looked last just after my seventeenth birthday, in Paris. Master al Qali had asked me to try to see if the Duke of Burgundy would pose a threat to someone like himself. And there had been no sign of Limpin' Sam, the spirit that would visit me with warnings and messages when I was growing up in London. All of this had led me to hope that I might be done with all of it.

The showstone shone brightly, its prisms of light nearly sparking in the sun. I shifted my gaze and studied its interior, fingertips placed lightly on it. I could see only the clouded core at the moment, but I waited patiently, because the last time it took some while for an image to appear. After a time and nothing had appeared, I closed my eyes briefly to see if that would help. It was as if my great reluctance to look in it provided a barrier to anything I might see. After all, it was this showstone that got me in my current situation. I looked again. Nothing.

"Well?" said Master al Qali.

I shook my head. The impatience in his voice told me how important this was and that he sensed the danger was very real. Would they track me down here in Bruges after all these years for merely being a pawn of Father Thomas and Mistress Jourdemayne in their treasonous plotting? It was the wrong question, I knew, but still it helped me face the showstone again with some calm.

It took nearly an hour, but eventually I got a hazy image of the Duchess. At least I assumed it was the Duchess, because all I saw was the back of an older, greying woman staring out of a window.

"That is all you see?" asked Master al Qali when I told him. "Nothing more?"

I shook my head.

Master al Qali gripped my arm and gave me a direct look. "Are you sure? There is no other image, or even flicker of one, that you saw?"

"No. Nothing." This reaction was so unlike his usual calm. "Is there something more that you heard that you haven't said? Something in particular I should look for?"

"No, no. I heard nothing more of significance." He gave me an odd look and put a hand to my forehead. "Are you well? Your sight seems to be lacking today. I would expect it to come easier to you now, at your age."

I shrugged. "I'm not ill. Just a bit of a thick head, is all."

"Hmm. Perhaps that is it. We will leave it for now."

He scooped up the showstone, put it back in its box, and secured it in its locked cupboard. The keys replaced in his purse, he looked at me. "It is time, I think, to go to the ducal palace."

I stared at him, still as mystified about the danger and our future plans as before. But there was nothing unusual in that.

⚬⚬⚬

The Duke of Burgundy moved his court around throughout the year, though he spent most of his time in Brussels, Bruges, and Lille. It was his extensive libraries, with their hundreds of manuscripts lodged in his palaces, which had attracted Master al Qali's attention and brought us here to stand in one of the palace's grandly decorated reception rooms. Richly woven tapestries hung on the wall showing hunt scenes, one of the Duke's favourite pastimes. The bold and vibrant colours proclaimed Bruges' skilful dyers and the quality of its wool that brought fame and fortune to the Duke and the citizens of Bruges.

The walls not covered in tapestries displayed paintings by Jan van Eyck and Rogier Van der Weyden to reflect glory on the Duke's gracious patronage and his love of the arts. Chandeliers, both gold and silver, dangled from the decorated ceiling and candlesticks rested on tables near beautiful sideboards. Courtiers, some dressed in the velvets of the Duke's favourite black, and others in various hues of scarlet brocade and damask, sat along benches padded with silk cushions to await the Duke's pleasure. There was so little subtlety in the display I expected to have a group from his renowned singing school in the corner of the room praising the Duke's virtues. The power of this man was evident in every detail.

The two of us stood there in one end of the room. Master al Qali, his manner calm, appeared to be oblivious to the curious stares that his presence created. I fingered the wrapped book absentmindedly and returned the stare of one wiry man with a large scar across his cheek. A swordsman, perhaps. His posture and stance seemed to fit the description. I'd taken a few lessons on wielding a sword with a friend at the university in France. I'd done it in secret, knowing Master al Qali, wouldn't have approved. But I had reasoned that a merchant's son would need a few lessons in swordsmanship. Someday I would own a sword and know how to use it.

The far door of the large room had opened many times and various men had appeared, summoning and ushering people to the palace's further reaches, while others had disappeared through the door of their own accord, in search of fellow nobles, or to serve those that occupied other chambers. Finally, the door opened and Jean Miélot, the Duke's secretary, appeared, and with a quick nod, summoned us forth.

"I beg your pardon for the delay," Monsieur Miélot said to us in French. "Other matters kept me."

I doubted very much it was other matters that had kept Monsieur Miélot, but rather his intense dislike of Master al Qali. The feeling was mutual, I knew all too well, and the animosity stemmed from such a seemingly trivial matter as Monsieur Miélot mistaking Master al Qali for my servant on our first acquaintance. Monsieur Miélot clearly disliked making such a mistake, not only for the embarrassment such a mistake created, but also for the fact that he would have preferred that Master al Qali was my servant. Or better, my slave. Master al Qali, though used to such assumptions, didn't take kindly to them, no matter who made them.

"Of course," Master al Qali said, his manner stiff. "You are such a man that matters would keep you."

I winced at the sly undertone of the remark, but knew better than to say anything. We followed Monsieur Miélot down the now familiar corridor to the chamber where the Duke kept his manuscripts.

We entered the room and I couldn't help but be impressed again by the collection housed there. The chamber wasn't as large as the receiving room in which we'd just been waiting, but it was sizeable enough to fit a large table, several chairs. Open shelves and locked cupboards lined the walls containing bound and rolled manuscripts. Some of the bound books were so large they were laid along a shelf with no room for any other book to be stacked on top of it. Others were the very small octavo sized, to be held in the palm and not weigh it down. For me, they all represented a rich treasure of knowledge.

I placed the parcel on the table in front of Monsieur Miélot. "There. As we promised. The book and its translated copy."

Monsieur Miélot smiled and took a chair. He gestured to me to sit. I pulled out a chair for Master al Qali, and when he was comfortably seated, took my own place beside him. Monsieur Miélot carefully unwrapped the parcel, his face full of anticipation. Jean Miélot had translated many works of the Duke from Latin into French, but this manuscript had been beyond his ability. It was an obscure Arab work on medicine that, with Master al Qali's help, I had translated into French.

Monsieur Miélot examined the first few pages of the translation carefully. He looked up at me and smiled. "This appears to be very fine work. I compliment you."

I nodded to Master al Qali. "*Merci bien*, Monsieur. I couldn't have done any of it without Master al Qali's help, though." This was true, but it didn't help to mention it to soothe Master al Qali's sensibilities. Monsieur Miélot would never have awarded the work directly to Master al Qali. I was someone in whom the Monsieur could place his full confidence, and he'd made it very clear that Master al Qali was not. From the first moment we'd come offering to translate an Arab work for the Duke in return for an opportunity to examine the collection, there had been no question of any other arrangement.

"I am glad you are pleased with the result," said Master al Qali, his tone even. "Giacomo is a very talented student. And now that you can see we are both serious scholars who understand the language, you might perhaps allow us to examine some of the other works in the Duke's library."

Monsieur Miélot glanced at me and I gave him my most winning smile. He sighed.

"I'm afraid the Duke is most protective of his collection." He waved his arm at the stacks of shelves. "The Duke will permit you to examine the shelves behind you, though. They are not so precious as the others."

Master al Qali pressed his lips together. I knew he wasn't pleased, but there was nothing he could say to persuade the man. He cast a glance at me.

"Surely if you stay in the room to ensure the collection's safety, the Duke wouldn't mind if we looked at all of it."

"Oh, I shall stay in the room, no question of that. But I haven't the time, and as I said, the collection is too precious, for you to examine all of it."

I gave Master al Qali an apologetic look.

"I see," said Master al Qali, his eyes flashing, but only for a moment. "We must be content, then, with what you have offered."

There was no doubt this was a great setback for Master al Qali. He had pinned his hopes on finding a certain manuscript among the Duke's collections. The only thing I knew about the manuscript was that it was an ancient document, possibly in Turkish, that might have been translated into Latin at some point. He would tell me no more than that, so my help in locating it among the libraries of France had been minimal. I was the translator and the one who bargained. But he was determined to find it and was certain it was somewhere in Europe. It was this hope that had pulled him across Christendom, translating and trading on his wits and determination.

I gave my thanks to Monsieur Miélot, rose, and made my way over to the designated shelves. Master al Qali came up behind me and together we scanned the shelves. There was much to tempt me. Works in Latin, Greek, and a few in Italian lined the shelves. Titles indicating such subjects as mathematics, philosophy, religion, and even some scientific works, but nothing that pointed even remotely to the manuscript Master al Qali searched for.

Still, my curiosity was strong and I pulled out a work carefully from the shelf and held it in my hands. *Livre des Merveilles du Monde* the title read, and the author, one Rustichello da Pisa.

Monsieur Miélot came along side of me. "Ah, you have discovered the work about the travels of one of your fellow Venetians."

I looked through the pages and saw references to places I had never heard of, not even from Master al Qali, who was undeniably well-travelled.

"*Vraiment?*" I said. "Monsieur da Pisa was a Venetian?"

"*Non, non*. Monsieur da Pisa only wrote down what was told to him. The man whose journeys are recounted is a man called Marco Polo. He travelled east through Persia and then on to Cathay and Manji."

I looked at the book with even more eagerness, itching to sit down and read about these far flung places. The door opened at that moment and the Duke entered.

I turned and swept him a bow. "Your Grace."

Monsieur Miélot bowed low and greeted the Duke. Master al Qali followed suit and murmured his own greeting, adding a little flourish with his hands.

"Ah, I see I have caught these scholars before they departed."

Monsieur Miélot moved forward smoothly and stood beside the Duke. "Monsieur Bonavillagio and his companion have just delivered a fine copy of the manuscript. They won't be long, Your Grace, if you should need me for something."

The Duke threw a smile at me and to Master al Qali. He walked over to the table, picked up the newly translated pages and perused them quickly. He nodded several times. He looked up after a few moments and eyed Master al Qali curiously, examining his robes, his dark face and hands.

"I'm sorry I haven't been able to meet with you before," he said. "You are Arab yourself, Monsieur?"

Master al Qali gave a thin smile. "I am from beyond the African desert, a place you would not know, Your Grace."

"And you are a scholar? But how did you learn?"

Master al Qali didn't flinch, but I knew the mark was noted. It sank deep within his mind to join all the other remarks that he'd encountered these past years and informed every gesture and look. This I'd come to realise since he decided to take me on as his protégé.

"I am a scholar, part of a family that are known for their learning obtained in a place that has had learned men for many, many generations."

The Duke nodded and seemed to accept his remarks. "And now you have come here to help us understand the works from your people?"

Master al Qali's mouth twitched again. Hadn't the Duke understood that Master al Qali wasn't an Arab?

"I am here to assist, of course, but also, if possible, to further my own knowledge."

"Miélot, we have other works in Arab, besides the one just translated, do we not?" asked the Duke

Monsieur Miélot nodded reluctantly. "*Bien sûr*, Your Grace."

"Then let this fellow…" I supplied Master al Qali's name for the Duke. "Let Monsieur al Qali and Monsieur Bonavillagio go through the Arab manuscripts and translate what is there. And if you would like to look at anything else, you have my permission."

Master al Qali bowed, his expression neutral. "I thank you, Your Grace. You have been most kind."

I looked at Monsieur Miélot, his face a mottled red, and allowed myself a secret triumphant smile.

∾

Hours later, and we were still seated at the table, piles of bound manuscripts and rolled parchments by our side. I'd sneaked a few long peeks at Signore da Pisa's work and was tempted to secret it somehow in my doublet and take it away with me so I could read it, but Monsieur beady-eyed Miélot prevented any such consideration. The Duke had departed long ago, but had left Miélot there in his suffering silence to assist us should we need it.

The grim determination with which Master al Qali made his way through the various stacks of works was enough to tell me that he was so far unsuccessful in his search. I hadn't found anything promising either, not that I was making the same amount of effort; the subject matters were just too tempting. In some ways I wished I had years to go through and read each one, but there was little time for that.

Finally, Master al Qali looked up from the last stack and rose. "I feel we have monopolised your time far too long, Monsieur. It is time to depart."

Monsieur Miélot gave him a cold look. "Have you selected the next work to translate?"

"I need to consult with my notes, first, to decide which would be the best one," said Master al Qali. "I will send word tomorrow."

"If the work is deemed valuable, I insist that you translate it here, in this room."

"You would have us reside here?" asked Master al Qali.

"Non, non. That wouldn't be suitable. You must make your own arrangements."

Master al Qali nodded and gave a short bow. "We will leave you now, then."

I made my own bow and took my leave, following Master al Qali out of the room and down the corridor. It was later, when we had exited the palace, that I finally asked him the question, the answer to which I already knew in my heart.

"Did you find it?"

"No. There was nothing."

"And are we going to return and translate those works?"

"There is no point. We leave tomorrow."

"For Paris?"

Master al Qali turned to me and gave a grim smile. "No. We go to Venice."

I looked at him speechless. Venice. The home of Master Giacomo Bonavillagio, son of the merchant, Carlo Bonavillagio. But at the moment I felt less like Giacomo and more like Barnabas

CHAPTER THREE
Kenilworth, Spring1445
ALYS

Alys ran the comb through the Duchess' hair slowly. The count was nearly one hundred now, but the time it took to reach that number mattered little when there was all the time in the world. She made it last, not only because the Duchess found it soothing, but because caring for and dressing the Duchess' hair occupied a good part of the morning, and occupation of any sort was treasured.

"Is it still the burnished gold it was?" asked the Duchess.

"It's beautiful, Your Grace, just as it always is," said Alys.

It was a ritual conversation they held every morning, and what harm was it that the Duchess' once beautiful hair was now a dull grey? The Duchess' sight was poor and the one mottled pier glass they had would never reveal the lie.

Alys completed the strokes and carefully braided the once thick hair into two plaits that she wound and pinned to the Duchess' head. She reached for the simple head cloth and fixed it in place. No more expensive hennins and sheer linen veils or riotously embroidered and ermine-trimmed gowns of rich fabrics. Squirrel collars and plain wool was all either them wore now.

Alys straightened the shoulders of the Duchess' gown, noting the angular shoulder blades underneath, part of what remained of a once full and voluptuous figure.

The Duchess sighed and squinted closer to the pier glass. She patted Alys' hand. "You've done a fine job as usual, my dear."

The Duchess had spoken in French, as she did most times to Alys, unless she chose to lumber her way through a conversation in Latin. Though she'd taught Alys Latin as well as French, the Duchess' memory had started to falter of late and Alys found herself the better of the two in both languages.

The Duchess turned to look at Alys. "What shall we do now, Alys?"

"Shall I read to you from the psalter that the pedlar brought yesterday, Your Grace?"

A smile lit up the Duchess' face and for a brief moment the beauty that had once been returned and reminded Alys why she still called the Duchess 'Your Grace' and thought of her as titled, even though it had been stripped from her when she was convicted of witchcraft four years ago. Alys pushed the reminder of that time aside, but not without a twist on the leather bracelet that she still wore.

"The psalter is in my small coffer, I think. I placed it there before Monsieur Gaoler returned from his hunt."

Alys repressed a grin at the reference to Sir Thomas Stanley, the man who oversaw the Duchess' imprisonment.

"I remember. Shall we go into the other chamber where the light is better?" Alys asked.

"Oh, but it's so cold there. Perhaps we can manage here."

"I'll fetch your thick cloak, Your Grace, and build up the fire."

She mentally cursed Sir Thomas' miserly attitude toward their comforts here at the castle. Today she sent him to the devil and vowed any tongue lashing would be well worth it. She wouldn't strain her eyes in this dim dungeon of a bed chamber.

"Very well," said the Duchess.

Alys led the Duchess into the adjoining chamber and settled her in close to the fire with the thick cloak around her shoulders. Alys fetched the book from the small coffer beside the Duchess' bed and took the seat by the mullioned paned window. She drew her wool shawl tighter, feeling the draught. She knew she'd traded warmth for greater light, but she would manage.

She flipped open the bound manuscript. It was her first chance to see exactly what kind of psalter it was, so quickly had the pedlar pressed it in her hands and made his excuses to go. He'd barely taken the time to accept the small sum he'd named to purchase the book before his bag was shut and he was back on his horse.

At first glance, though the leather was thick and new, she could see it was poorly made. The stitching was already coming adrift and the title page badly lettered. She thumbed through a few of the pages. As with many psalters, there were illuminations and elaborate figured letters, which, eager as she was for anything related to art, always caught her eye. But again, these were not of the highest quality. She inspected the Latin words of the first page.

"Are you going to stare at it all day? You can read it, can't you? I thought the man said it was in Latin." The Duchess' voice was full of impatience.

Alys cleared her throat and began to read. It began as usual, the words of this particular psalm familiar enough to her that she could read it easily, despite the sometimes misshapen letters. Towards the end of the psalm though, she stumbled across one word and realised that it wasn't in Latin, but Greek. How could that be a mistake?

"Well? Why have you stopped?"

"The ink is faded in places, Your Grace. It's difficult to make out at times."

"Are there pictures? Describe the pictures, I know you love them. Surely they're not faded."

Alys looked back at the image across from the first page of text and began to describe it. "It's a man riding the back of a lion. A golden lion drawn like the lion couchant. You recall, Your Grace, like those in the King's crest."

"What? Let me see."

The Duchess rose heavily from her chair, made her way to Alys, and peered over her shoulder. The light was good enough, but still the Duchess brought the psalter close to her and squinted hard.

The door was thrust open and Sir Thomas entered. Alys and the Duchess looked up.

"Madam, where is the psalter?"

The Duchess drew herself up to her full height and faced Sir Thomas, putting herself in front of Alys. "If you must burst into my chamber like some wayward boy, at least have the courtesy to pay your addresses first."

Sir Thomas looked sheepish for a moment and then stiffened. "Madam, I am charged with your wellbeing, and not as some fangled courtier to dip and bow at every turn."

"I am not asking for the moon or the stars, Sir Thomas, but common manners."

Sir Thomas frowned. He gestured to the chair by the fire. "Please, take a seat. I have some questions I wish to put to you."

The Duchess turned to Alys and glanced at the psalter. "There's no reason for you to stay, Alys. You may wait for me in my bedchamber."

"No, the girl stays."

The Duchess sighed and made her way over to her seat by the fire, pulling the cloak tightly around her. Alys hid the psalter in the confines of her shawl and gave Sir Thomas a look of polite interest.

"The servants said a pedlar came here yesterday selling wares. He said your waiting woman purchased a manuscript."

"She might have done, I don't recall."

Sir Thomas directed a look at Alys. "Did you purchase a manuscript?"

"It was nothing. Just a poorly made psalter."

"Yet you chose not to inform me of your purchase. You know you aren't allowed to have any contact with outsiders, let alone receive any goods without my permission."

"I saw no harm in it. You weren't available, and I thought it would entertain the... Mistress Cobham." She'd only just avoided saying, 'The Duchess', which she knew would only anger Sir Thomas.

"It is not for you to judge what is or isn't harmful. You obey the rules or you're no longer allowed to attend Mistress Cobham."

"I'm deeply sorry," said Alys. "I promise it won't happen again."

"Now, where's the psalter?"

Alys glanced at the Duchess and could see the stubborn set to her face.

"There is no need for you to have the book. As Alys said, it's harmless," said the Duchess.

"I'll be the judge of that. Hand over the psalter."

The Duchess waved her hand. "I'm not quite sure where I put it."

Sir Thomas made his way to the Duchess, his eyes flashing in anger. He slapped her hard across the face. "Don't play coy with me, madam."

The Duchess put a hand to the livid mark on her face, her eyes clouded with tears. "How dare you strike me." Her words were brave but her voice was thread-thin.

Alys rose and for moment was tempted to hand over the book, until she saw the slight shake of the Duchess' head. "Please, leave her alone. She forgets sometimes."

Sir Thomas gave her a hard look. "Do you think me a fool?" He went over to her and seized her shoulder, pulling her up from the chair. "Very well, you tell me where the psalter is."

He shook her hard so that the teeth rattled in her head. He shoved her across towards the window and she banged her head and slipped to the floor, the psalter falling from her hands. Sir Thomas bent over and picked it up, leaving her sprawled, stunned by the bang to her head.

He grimaced. "A harmless psalter. Well, I'll be the judge of that."

Alys watched him stride across the room, psalter in hand. Dismay filled her as she thought of the peculiar placement of the Greek word and the puzzling picture. She prayed the psalter was as harmless as she'd claimed.

Rough hands jerked her from her sleep. She opened her eyes and made out a large figure looming over her. She recognised Sir Thomas' shape in the murky darkness. Though it had been several nights since Sir Thomas had seized the psalter, she thought of it instantly.

"What is it?" she whispered. She didn't want to wake the Duchess if she could help it, the poor woman slept so badly.

"Get up." Sir Thomas pulled her out of bed. He made no pretence at quiet and a moment later she could hear the Duchess' feeble voice on the other side of the bed calling her name.

"Sssh," Alys whispered. "It's alright. Sir Thomas just wants to speak with me. Go back to sleep."

Sir Thomas gave her no time to put anything over her night dress as he dragged her from the bed and through the door. She managed to keep her footing while he made his way down the stairs to the hall below. There she saw a roaring fire and a figure seated in a high backed chair, sipping from a goblet. Sir Thomas threw her in front of the man. His doublet was finely made and his cloak lined with expensive fur. A nobleman.

"Sir John, this is the waiting woman. She was the one who spoke with the pedlar."

Alys gave a belated curtsey. "My lord," she murmured. She drew the neck of her night dress tighter and tried to assemble some sort of dignity in front of this man. Her hair was woven tightly into a braid that hung in front, covering at least some of her immodest apparel.

Sir John appraised her, but it was more calculation than lust that she could detect in his close scrutiny. On the table next to him she could see the psalter, its leather cover still bright and unscarred in the firelight.

"What was this pedlar like, mademoiselle?" He spoke to her in French, unlike Sir Thomas, and that in itself told her he was part of the King's court. It seemed foolhardy to pretend ignorance of the language, since Sir Thomas would no doubt know that she and the Duchess spoke French together, even though he couldn't speak it.

"An unremarkable man, my lord," she replied in French.

"Unremarkable." He pointed to the table. "And he sold you this unremarkable psalter?"

"Yes, my lord."

"A psalter so unremarkable that it contains treasonous information?"

She allowed the shock to fill her face. "Treason?"

There was no need to feign the shock. She had seen what hints of treason could do to even a person of powerful influence. What chance had she against such a charge? Alys from the docks of Queenhithe.

He held up the book. "Don't play innocent. The pedlar was no pedlar, selling his wares, but a man commissioned to pass on the plans for Mistress Cobham's escape."

"I assure you, my lord. I had no idea. I thought only that the psalter would give Mistress Cobham comfort."

"Oh, comfort her, indeed. Of course a plan to help her escape would comfort her."

"N-no, I didn't mean that."

"I'm sure you didn't mean to reveal your part in this plot. Who would want to make their part in treason known to the King's man?"

31

Alys cast around for words to defend herself. "Surely, after all this time, there can be little harm in such a plot, even if it did exist?"

As soon as she saw Sir John's angry face, she knew she'd chosen the wrong approach.

"This woman has been placed under my charge, by the King. If she were to escape, become involved in any plot that would threaten the King, I would answer for it. I won't allow it."

Alys looked helplessly at Sir John. "What would you have me do?"

Sir John narrowed his eyes. "You will tell me all. Any hint of a plan, an idea that might endanger the King."

"But I know nothing."

"She lies, Sir John. I hear them babbling away in French and Latin. They could be up to all sorts, for all I know, though they say it is only a discussion of prayers and psalms."

Sir John regarded Alys speculatively. "Hit her. Hit her hard and see what she'll say."

Sir Thomas stepped forward and struck Alys across her shoulders with the back edge of his sword. She fell to her knees under the force of the blow. A sob escaped her.

"I know nothing," she said. There is nothing to tell. We haven't been plotting and we received no messages at all about any plot."

There was another blow, only this time she hit her head against the stone floor and she fell unconscious.

~

She awoke and found herself lying in a narrow cot in a small chamber, light streaming in through the tiny window across the room. The bed curtains were faded and ragged. She raised her hand to her head and felt the small lump on her forehead. It was sore and she winced at the touch.

Gingerly, she swung her legs to the floor. Her limbs were stiff with cold. She was still in her night dress and there was no sign of any heat to take the chill from her. The coverlet that spanned the bed was thin, but it would have to do. She scooped it up and wrapped it around herself and carefully made her way over to the window.

Looking out, she could see she was on the same level as the Duchess' chambers except this window overlooked the narrow courtyard. There was little activity below at the moment. Her stomach grumbled. There was no telling when or if she would get a meal.

She went over to the door and was unsurprised to find it locked. She sighed, took a seat on the bed again, lifting her bare feet off the floor. There was no choice but to wait.

The sun had moved from the window by the time the door was unlocked and Sir Thomas entered with a servant behind him. The servant had a bundle of clothes draped across his arm and held a loaf of bread and a flask in his hands.

"Toss the clothes on the bed and put the food in the window," Sir Thomas said to the servant.

The servant did as he was told and left. Sir Thomas turned to Alys.

"You are to dress and eat quickly," he said. "Sir John wants you ready to leave with his men before midday. He wants to reach the town of Lamuntone before nightfall."

"I'm to leave with Sir John?" Alys was stunned. This was the last thing she'd expected.

"You are dismissed from Mistress Cobham's service."

Perhaps it was the blow to the head, but Alys found it difficult to take in his words. "Leave the Duchess? What will she do?"

"Mistress Cobham will manage with the servants that remain. Servants that are loyal to me and my overlord, Sir John."

"But what does Sir John want with me, then? It's as I said, I know nothing."

"Sir John doesn't care what you do now. He's merely taking you to London with him, from whence you came, and far from the Duchess."

She stared at him dumbly. After four years of little action and nothing to occupy her thoughts except the past, her present and future were changing at lightning speed.

"Come on, get moving."

She stared at the clothes on the bed and glanced at Sir Thomas. He was obviously determined to remain while she dressed and ate. Resigned, she took up the clothes and donned them quickly over her nightdress, gratified that at least they had given her the warmest gown she owned. She wound her braid into a knot and tied the white linen cloth around her head, twisting and tucking the ends to cover her hair.

Sir Thomas stood there impatiently while she completed her dressing and she gobbled the food laid on the sill. When she was finished, Sir Thomas grunted and led the way out of the chamber and to the stairs.

"Can I at least bid Mistress Cobham farewell?"

Sir Thomas paused a moment. She pressed her case further, searching for a thread of decency in him.

"Please. Only a few words. We'll speak only in your hearing and in English."

"A few words only, then."

He changed direction and led her back along the corridor and to the familiar door of the Duchess' chamber. He entered, Alys close behind, anxious over what she might find within.

The Duchess lay sprawled across the bed, half-dressed, her hair in disarray. She looked up when they entered and when she saw Alys, she gave a cry of delight.

Alys rushed to her side and took her hands.

"Oh, madam, madam. I'm so sorry this has come to pass."

"Oh Alys, my Alys." The Duchess stroked Alys' head. "My dear Alys. You are well? Come, give my hair a good combing."

Alys kissed the Duchess' hand. "I'm so sorry, madam, but I cannot. I must take my leave of you, instead." She looked around at Sir Thomas.

"Leave? But you cannot," the Duchess wailed. "What will I do without my Alys?" She stiffened and stared over at Sir Thomas. She pulled away from Alys and rose from the bed. "Sir Thomas, I demand that you return Alys to my service."

Sir Thomas grunted. "That, madam, is not for you to demand, or for me to grant. I have Sir John's orders and it's to him I owe obedience."

The Duchess remained silent and stared at Sir Thomas. She pulled herself up and reached out for Alys. "Then the least you can do is to allow me to pray with Alys one last time."

Without waiting for Sir Thomas' refusal or approval, she took Alys' hand and led her over to the prie dieu at the far end of the chamber, where she pulled her down to kneel. It was a tight fit, but Alys managed to kneel on the hard bench and clasp her hands in front of her in a praying pose. The Duchess began to recite the Lord's prayer loudly in Latin and nodded to Alys who echoed her words, while Sir Thomas looked on dumbly. He wouldn't dare interfere with a moment's worship, she hoped.

They were halfway through the prayer when the Duchess grabbed Alys' hands and clutched them tightly. Alys could feel a small pouch in the Duchess' grasp. Alys' hand folded around it.

Soon the prayer was over and the Duchess rose. Tearfully, she grasped Alys to her chest and gave her a kiss on both cheeks.

"May God go with you, child. I shall never forget my dear Alys."

Alys gave her kiss back. "Oh, madam, I shall miss you terribly. Keep well and may God keep you in his care."

The Duchess gave her a weak smile. Sir Thomas pulled her to the door and Alys had one more glimpse of the Duchess, her face drawn and her faded grey hair spread out along her shoulders.

CHAPTER FOUR
London, Spring 1445
ALYS

It was when they reached the outskirts of London that Alys' anxiety returned. Sir John had said nothing about where he was taking her. In fact he'd said little at all since they'd left Kenilworth all those many days ago. He'd just shoved her in various rooms at inns along the way, ordering food and ale for her, and then taking himself off to be with his men. She hadn't minded until now, when she began to recognise the landmarks in the distance.

She moved her horse alongside Sir John's. "Are we to stop soon for the night or continue on?"

He turned a grim face to her. "We'll continue on."

"Am I to be taken to Westminster Palace then?" The palace was to the west of the city and would mean an extra hour of riding, but it was also where the King spent most of his time.

"The King has no interest in you, nor do his councillors. You're my responsibility alone."

"May I ask where you intend to take me?"

He studied her carefully, eyeing her up and down so intently that she was eventually forced to look away in embarrassment. She had no doubt what was running through his mind.

"I have no lady wife, so there is no need for a waiting woman in my household, but perhaps that would be the best place. I can keep an eye on you then." He smiled suggestively.

"I could return to the Duke's household, my lord. I'm sure they would have a position for me there."

"I think not." He reached across and laid a hand on top of hers. "I wouldn't have you return to that nest of plotters. You're better off with me."

Alys remained silent, choosing not to argue. She had a completely different opinion about how safe she would be with him.

Alys stared at the locked door, her mind working furiously. She had no idea how much time she would have before Sir John returned from his meeting with one of the king's councillors, but she knew she must take advantage of the general turmoil of preparation for the King's impending marriage and find a way to leave.

She tried the door once more but the lock was firm. Frantically she looked around the room for something that might force the lock. There was only a small brazier in the room and no sign of a poker. She went over to the chest at the foot of the bed rummaged through it, looking for something small and sharp to fit into the lock. It was filled with doublets, hose and other assorted clothes, but nothing that would suit. The bed and table at the window held nothing either. She moved over to the window and looked down, hoping that she might find a way down there. The window was small. If she forced herself she might get through, but the drop was long. The bed sheets would cover only half the distance.

There was little for it, but she must try it anyway. She put her hands on her hip and sighed. Her fingers brushed the small scabbard at her side that contained her eating knife. How stupid of her. She reached for the knife and made her way to the door. She inserted the knife and jiggled. There was no movement. She inserted the knife again and tried more firmly. On her fourth try, the lock shifted and released. She allowed herself a triumphant smile before opening the door quietly and peering outside. There was a young squire going down the corridor, his back to her, but no one else.

She slipped out of the room and worked her way through the maze of corridors of the palace. She finally found a door that led her to the courtyard and the stables beyond it. She walked deliberately towards it, forcing herself to walk slowly in order to avoid any attention. When she arrived at the stables she was glad to see that a groom hovered by the door, a lad younger than her. She ordered her horse be saddled in the most imperious tone she could muster. Thankfully it didn't take long.

"Should I come with you, my lady?" asked the tow-headed groom.

He led the horse to the mounting block and she shook her head. "I shall be fine. I'm not going far."

Seated securely on the horse, she urged it on. It wasn't until she was safely outside the gate and on the road that she allowed herself to breathe a sigh of relief. She patted the pouch tucked securely in her bodice. When the Duchess had pressed that small pouch into her hand back at Kenilworth, she could only imagine it was a few coins to help her find safety. It was only later, when she was preparing for bed in the small inn chamber that first night and examined the contents, that she found a sizeable sum of money, a small note, and an old letter, folded many times. The note had been from the Duchess and instructed her to use the money to go to the Duke to ask him to plead with the King to permit her release from her awful imprisonment. Alys was headed there now, determined to honour the trust the Duchess had placed in her. Especially since the Duchess had thought to include Alys' precious letter that had been among her possessions she'd kept in a small chest.

The letter was one small page, containing only a few lines, but it was from Barnabas. Or Giacomo, as he'd signed it. All it said was that he was well and hoped she was too, and that he'd enjoyed meeting her when he'd visited London. She'd known he'd added those final words as a ruse to fool any others who might have read it. The letter had come from Paris and she'd received it two years ago. It had been dated six months before that. Its contents, though, were enough to send a rush of joy through her and kiss the leather band the writer had given a young girl what seemed a lifetime ago.

Now she urged her horse on to a quicker pace, determined that she reach the palace before nightfall. The dusk was gathering quickly and the trees loomed with some menace. There were other riders on the road, as well as a number of people on foot, which gave her comfort. It seemed many noblemen, merchants and common folk were heading towards London to make the most of the occasion of the King's wedding.

She arrived at the palace, made her way to the side, and dismounted at the block. A groomsman took her horse, a man she didn't recognise. She inquired after the Duke.

"He is here, my lady," he said. "The steward will take you to him."

He pointed to the steward who approached her from the door, his face arranged in a welcome. He wasn't familiar either, but perhaps that was a good thing. She would play her role as a lady and there would be one less servant who might remind her of her former place. Hopefully, she would find her way to the Duke without any bother.

The steward gave a slight bow. "Welcome, my lady."

She noticed his doublet was faded and worn in places. Had such hard times befallen the Duke? She drew herself up and gave him a gracious smile. "Sir John Middleton has sent me with a message to the Duke."

The steward nodded and led her inside, depositing her in the small receiving room. There was no fire lit and the room was draughty. She withdrew the purse from her bodice and pulled her cloak around her more tightly. A moment later the Duke entered.

Alys curtseyed low. "Your Grace."

The Duke gave her a puzzled look.

"It's Alys, Your Grace. I was in the Duchess' service. I mean Mistress Cobham's service." Had he married again since the King had dissolved the marriage? There had been no word of a marriage at Kennilworth.

The Duke's face cleared and he moved to her and took her hand. "Yes, yes. Alys."

She looked at him carefully. He'd aged considerably since she'd seen him last. It wasn't just his grey hair and lined face. There was a definite stoop to his posture.

"I come from Kenilworth, Your Grace. From the Duchess."

"Eleanor?" A spark of pleasure flickered in his eyes for a moment and then was gone. "You have news of her?"

"Yes. Eleanor."

"We had good times together, Eleanor and I." He smiled weakly and looked beyond her into the distance.

"You did, Your Grace, without a doubt."

He shook himself a moment and straightened with visible effort. "How is she? Have you just come from Kennilworth?"

"She is well enough, Your Grace, though she finds her situation difficult."

"I am glad to hear she is well, though I can imagine how frustrating it is for her."

"Her health would be better if she weren't confined to Kennilworth. Do you think it's possible the King would permit her release? She bid me ask you to plead her case."

The Duke sighed. "I fear any pleading from my lips would only result in further and more severe punishment. The King has no dealings with me now."

Tears filled Alys' eyes. Was there no help for the poor Duchess? "I'm sorry to hear that." She reached in the pouch and withdrew the note and coins and handed them to the Duke. "You must read her words. Surely something can be done for her."

The Duke examined the note. "My poor Eleanor. What have things come to?"

Alys watched him stare at the piece of paper. The fiery tempered man she remembered seemed to have disappeared, to be replaced by this feeble person.

He folded the note carefully and returned it to Alys, along with the coins. "I only wish there was something I could do for her, but there is nothing. Any contact I might have could only make things worse for her. I'm sorry."

Alys bowed her head so he wouldn't see her tears.

"But I must and will do something for you, Alys. You've been such a loyal servant to Eleanor." He gestured to a nearby chair. "Sit here a moment and wait until I return. I'll have some refreshments brought in the meantime."

Alys took the indicated seat, her mind whirring. What would she do now? Should she ask the Duke if she could return to his household? But it was the obvious place for Sir John to seek her, and the Duke appeared to have little enough influence to prevent Sir John from retrieving her for his own purposes.

A servant entered with a platter of some cut meat, a cup and a flagon of ale. It took Alys a moment to recognise the full figured young woman.

"Joanie."

Joanie looked up at her, puzzled.

"It's me, Alys."

Joanie's face cleared. "Alys. Oh, Alys, I haven't seen you in an age, I'd 'ardly know you."

Alys rose and moved to give her a kiss on the cheek. "It's good to see you."

Joanie pulled away. "But you've changed. You've become grand." She paused a moment, her brow darkening. "The Duchess? Are you still in her service? 'Ave you come from her? Is she well?"

Alys bit her lip and nodded glumly. "She's well enough, but much disheartened by her imprisonment at Kenilworth."

"I can well imagine. Oh what a shame it all is, and 'is Grace no better than a shadow of 'is former self." Joanie shook her head. "But you, look at you. You're all grand now. Like a proper lady."

"The Duchess has been very kind to me."

Joanie snorted. "I'd say more likely she's 'ad you at her beck and call and no one else to bear her company."

"She can be kind, Joanie. But what news of you? Any husband?"

There was a sound at the door and Joanie stepped back and curtseyed to Alys. The Duke entered, a large pouch in his hand.

Joanie curtseyed to the Duke. "Your Grace. I've brought the food and ale you requested." She gave Alys a brief glance and left.

The Duke made his way to the table and placed the pouch there, beside the platter of food. "There. That's for you. It's some money and a few items of jewellery that belonged to Eleanor. It's nothing of value, you understand. Just some trinkets I gave her that no one would think of any account. Since she cannot have them, I'm sure she would wish you to."

Alys stared at the large pouch, speechless for a moment. "But I can't take that. There is no need for your thanks. I've served the Duchess willingly. She did so much for me."

The Duke shook his head. "Please allow me to assuage some of my guilt over the events that have taken place these last few years. Since I cannot help Eleanor, I can help you, at least."

She stared at the Duke dumbly. Eventually, she found her tongue, but emotion choked the words. "Oh, Your Grace, I would trade any of this if it were to put things to the way they were before."

The Duke patted her hand. "As would I, little Alys."

It was less than an hour later that Alys found herself back on her horse and heading to the road, her mind in turmoil. At the crossroads she paused. In one direction lay the way to Westminster Palace and beyond it, London.

In the other direction was Eye and the Jourdemayne household. Barnabas' former home. It was the thought of Barnabas that gave her the beginnings of an idea.

❧

The inn was smaller than she remembered it, but that might have been because it had been some time since she'd seen it last. It would suit her needs, though. She dismounted her horse with the help of the young boy, the owner's son most likely, and made her way inside. Once in the main room, she brushed off the dust off from her cloak that she'd sprinkled there earlier to create the appearance of a wearied traveller.

The innkeeper's wife issued forth from a backroom, straightening her headcloth, and stood in front of Alys.

"Ooh, my lady, you look 'alf parched, so you do. Come in and sit by the fire and take the chill off you." The woman looked behind her. "Is your servant behind you?"

Alys put a hand to her head and sniffed dramatically. "My serving woman died only yesterday."

The woman backed away slightly. "Nothing catching, I 'ope."

"No, rest assured. She caught a chill, and suddenly it worsened, until there was no rousing her. She passed away quietly." Alys crossed herself. "She was never very strong. We buried her yesterday, the poor woman, but I had to press on to meet my brother in London. He's been called there for the King's wedding, but I only dared to journey this far without a servant."

"You aren't from London?"

"I was, but I moved to Warwickshire a few years ago, when I married."

"Your 'usband will be coming soon, then?"

Alys looked away, sadness filling her face. "No, alas. My poor husband, God rest his soul, died some months back of an apoplectic fit."

The woman clucked her sympathy. "I'm right sorry to 'ear that, my lady…."

Alys smiled. "Mistress Merton."

The woman gave a quick curtsey. "Mistress Cotter, madam. I 'ope you don't mind putting up with my niece as your serving girl tonight."

Alys gave a sweet smile. "Of course not. And in the morning I shall send to my brother for one of his servants to fetch me."

Mistress Cotter nodded. "I'll just see to some ale. I'm afraid all I 'ave to eat is a small pigeon pie, being the time of year it is."

"That will do nicely, thank you."

Alys took the seat by the fire and let her cloak slip from her shoulders. She was grateful that her travel stained dress reinforced her story of her long journey, but was also sober enough to pass for mourning garb. She stared into the fire contemplating her daring plan. Would she have the nerve to go through with it?

CHAPTER FIVE
London, Spring 1445
ALYS

Alys paced the small chamber downstairs where she'd sat by the fire when she'd first arrived the night before. Half the morning had gone, and still no sign of the boy she'd sent, or anyone else. It was the *anyone else* that she'd set her heart on, and now all manner of scenarios were crowding her mind. Had the boy delivered the message to the right person? Was it possible that Sir John had waylaid the boy and determined that she was here? She glanced out of the window once more, and willed the boy to materialise.

"Can I get you a 'ot cup of ale, Mistress Merton?" asked Mistress Cotter. "The morning is chilly and it will warm your bones and perhaps settle you."

"No, thank you." Alys forced herself to stop her pacing and take a seat. "I'm well enough. Just anxious to be on my way."

Mistress Cotter retreated and left Alys to her thoughts. Eventually the numerous times she twisted her fingers and wrung her hands were rewarded with a sound outside. A moment later, Mistress Cotter entered again and escorted the new arrival.

"Joanie. I'm glad you came." Alys rose and stretched out her hands in greeting.

Joanie curtseyed. "Thank you, mistress."

Alys looked up at Mistress Cotter and nodded. "I'm obliged to your boy and you, Mistress Cotter."

With that note of dismissal Mistress Cotter left the room. Alys stared at Joanie for a moment, the gratitude evident in her eyes. She led Joanie to a seat and took the one opposite.

"It's so good of you to come, Joanie."

"Where is it you want to go, Alys? The boy only said that he was requested by Mistress Merton to come help her to complete her journey. I came because I thought you might be in trouble, calling yourself Mistress Merton, and all."

Ays bit her lip. "You're not far from the mark, Joanie."

"Is it to do with the Duchess?"

"There's a connection." Alys took a deep breath. "I must leave the area. It's not safe for me. The King's man who brought me away from Kenilworth, Sir John, has decided that I should remain within his household to keep an eye on me."

Joanie gave her a knowing look. "'E wants to keep an eye on you in 'is bed, more like. And so you left."

Alys twiddled the leather bracelet at her wrist and nodded. "It's not something I wanted to do, not if I could help it. And besides, the Duchess asked me to see the Duke if I could and request him to secure her release."

"There's nothing 'e can do, I'll warrant. The King has turned his back on 'im." Joanie shook her head, sadly. "But what will you do? Where do you mean to go?"

"Paris."

"Paris?" Joanie stared at her in shock.

"Yes. I have a good friend there. But I need a travelling companion and I was hoping it could be you. Someone who could pretend to be my servant."

Joanie gave a wry smile. "Pretend?"

Alys leaned forward and took Joanie's hand. "I would be travelling as a widow on pilgrimage with you as my servant. In private you would still be my dear friend."

"But 'ow will you manage? You have no money, no one to protect you."

Alys smiled. "The Duke gave me some, in gratitude for my service and loyalty and perhaps to salve his conscience. As for the rest, we'll travel with fellow pilgrims. We'll be safe enough, then."

Alys watched Joanie absorb the information and hoped her plan would appeal to Joanie's adventurous spirit.

"Is there someone you would rather not leave? Have you an attachment?" asked Alys.

Joanie gave a peel of laughter and then clapped her hand over her mouth. "Sorry. It just struck me funny 'ow you said that. If you mean do I have a fella, the answer is no. Not anymore and a good thing too. I've had enough of 'em to last me a lifetime, say I." Joanie sighed. "I'll tell the steward that I need to go 'ome to my sister who's dying, and that I can't say 'ow long I'll be."

Alys leaned forward and hugged her. "Oh, I'm so glad you've agreed."

"Now, first we 'ave to get you away from 'ere to a respectable inn in the city, which will be no easy thing, given that so many are 'ere for the King's wedding. She touched her nose. "But I have my friends, too, you know."

Alys felt a huge sense of relief. Joanie had helped her before, all those many years ago, and she had confidence that her help now would be worth her weight in gold.

～

In the room next door, Alys could hear the bustle of this busy London inn. She smoothed her drab brown gown and forced a smile. The man standing before her in his sober cloak and shapeless hat that marked him as a pilgrim was kind enough, but his questions seemed intrusive. She tried to remain calm. She needed him to permit her to join his small company of pilgrims, and he was taking the responsibility seriously.

"Your husband was a godly man, then?"

She could almost hear Joanie's laughter from her place in the corner near her, plying her needle on some piece of clothing with earnest industry.

"He was most certainly, Mister Benyngton. He was never without his psalter and attended mass daily. The cathedral in Warwick was not far from our home."

Mister Benyngton nodded. He was a wealthy merchant, the same occupation as Alys' imaginary late husband. She only hoped that his dealings hadn't taken him to Warwick, because she had no more than passing knowledge of the place, and remembered only that it contained a cathedral.

"Traded in wool, you say?"

Alys nodded. "He rarely confided to me the details of his business, and now his nephew has taken it over so that I can devote myself to more spiritual concerns."

"Your husband was wise in making such arrangements." Thin and wiry, Alfred Benyngton drew himself up and towered over Alys. "You are young, madam, and it's fitting that he should protect you. And you and your nephew can rest assured that we take seriously this responsibility of your physical as well as spiritual care while you journey with us."

"So you will accept me into your good company of pilgrims, sir?"

"We will indeed, Mistress Merton. If you and your servant can be ready, we propose to leave in five days' time. The passage is already arranged, but I'm sure it will be no trouble to add two more. There are few enough travellers leaving London and going across the sea. Most are coming to London. In the meantime the days before we leave will give you time to get acquainted with the others. I'll let them know that you're joining us. Perhaps you can return to this room at the noon hour? You'll be able to meet them then."

She gave her thanks again and Benyngton departed. The room was warm from the hot sun that streaked through the window and the sudden spell of heat that had taken hold in the last few days since she'd left Mistress Cotter's inn. Joan had been canny enough to find her accommodation here in this respectable inn, where pilgrims gathered before taking ship to France and destinations beyond. It was her good fortune that the impending celebrations for the King's marriage meant that fewer people were willing to make a pilgrimage this year.

"Joanie, we must find a small psalter and a cross for around my neck. And one for you as well. It won't do for these pilgrims to think we're not as godly as they are."

Joanie made a face. "A psalter and a cross mightn't be the easiest things, not from my sorts of friends."

"You managed so well with the clothes." She touched the headcloth, wrapped into a stylish enough shape by Joanie under Alys' guidance. "The plain dark gowns and sturdy shoes speak every bit the pilgrim widow."

"All our things are packed in the chest the innkeeper got from the cooper up the street. He makes them for pilgrims because they often want good chests when going on pilgrimage. The cooper might know where I can get you a cross. I'll say you lost yours."

Alys nodded. She would have liked to have something religious in her hand or around her neck when she met the others. If it couldn't be arranged in time, there was little she could do about it, she reminded herself.

In the end, it was a wooden cross hastily fashioned and strung on a leather cord that she had tied around her neck when she met the others. They were already assembled in the room when she entered, her expression serious. Joanie followed closely behind, her neck bare, but her gown as sober in colour as Alys'.

Alys nodded to Alfred Benyngton and greeted him formally. He bowed slightly, his greying hair and beard catching the light. He turned to the others and introduced them one by one. The first man, John Lyttleton, was a London goldsmith who travelled with his wife, Mary, in the hope that the pilgrimage would bless them with the child they longed for. Lyttleton's eyes flickered over Alys and Joanie impatiently, but his sallow-skinned wife studied the two of them, her expression carefully neutral. Harold Kemp, a long-nosed man, and his daughter Margery, had a manor farm near Killingsworth, a small town in the Cotswolds. The final member of the group was Sir George Sydmouth, an aging knight with kind eyes.

"Mister Benyngton tells us that your husband is dead," said Sir George. "I'm sorry to hear you had such a loss."

"You seem very young to be on such a pilgrimage," said Mistress Lyttleton.

"The loss of a husband and becoming a widow can give any woman experience beyond her years," said Alys calmly. She bowed her head and recited the words she'd rehearsed earlier. "My husband was a good man, and I count myself fortunate to have had the few years together that we did. And it is because of his goodness that I wish to go on this pilgrimage and offer prayers for his deliverance to heaven."

Her reply seemed to satisfy the woman and most of the group, all except for Kemp's daughter, Margery, who examined her curiously. She was thin and pale and fine lines gathered at her mouth and eyes. A not very young daughter, thought Alys.

Sir George nodded and gave her an encouraging smile and Mistress Lyttleon gave a small shrug.

"I've arranged for us all to go to the church at Queenhithe for the blessing tomorrow. I ask that you all wear your grey pilgrim hats and gowns."

Everyone murmured their assent, including Alys, though the name of Queenhithe rang through her mind. There was little chance, she comforted herself, that anyone at Queenhithe would recognise her for the young girl who used to go almost daily to stare at the paintings on the church wall.

∾

It had been eight years since Alys had been to Queenhithe church, and she found it unchanged for the most part, despite the faint mustiness in the air that the perfumed candles and incense couldn't disguise. The paintings on the walls that had once captured her imagination were still as beautiful as before. Even now, she couldn't take her eyes off of them. Alys blinked back the tears that came, remembering the innocent hope and joy she'd taken from them. The Madonna, with her shimmering halo so serene and full of love, looked at her with the same kind eyes.

The priest came towards them and Alys held her breath. Like the rest of the pilgrims, she was dressed in a plain grey gown and simple hat with a red cross embroidered on it, but risking nothing, she bowed her head and stood to the back. The priest greeted them all and murmured something to Benyngton, and he nodded. He spoke again and then they all made their way down the aisle to the nave of the church, Alys and Joanie bringing up the rear.

At the nave, the priest stopped and turned to them. The group spread out in front of him. An assistant came along side of the priest holding a small bowl filled with holy water. The priest intoned words in Latin, signed the cross over the group and moved forward to Benyngton. He rested his hand on Benyngton's head and said a few words more in Latin. Benyngton looked up at him and responded with 'amen.' The priest moved on to Sir George and repeated the words and motions. Alys, kneeling at the other end, watched him make his way slowly on to each person, until he was next to her, giving Joanie the blessing.

Alys licked her lips and tried to remain calm. The priest stood in front of her and she felt the weight of his hand on her head. She said her own prayer as he spoke the Latin words. Instinctively, she looked up into his eyes and mouthed her response, before bowing her head again quickly, with a sharp intake of breath. It was pure foolishness to think he might recognise her, but she had come too far for anything to go awry now.

The priest stepped back, took the small brush, dipped it in the bowl and shook over the group, a final blessing for the whole group. Alys felt a droplet of water on her nose and hoped that was a good sign.

A few moments later and the ceremony was over. The newly blessed pilgrims rose from their knees and solemnly made their way to the door. Benyngton remained behind for a few moments, exchanging words with the priest while Alys hurried after the group.

Benyngton caught up with them near the door. He pulled Alys aside. "The priest would like to have a word with you, Mistress Merton."

"Me?" said Alys. She gave Joanie a nervous glance. "I can't think why."

"Nevertheless," said Benyngton. He nodded toward the priest who stood in the middle of the church sanctuary, waiting for her.

Alys murmured her thanks and moved slowly towards the priest. Joanie followed her close behind and for that she was grateful. She stopped a few feet away.

"Master Benyngton said you wished to speak with me, Father."

"Yes, daughter. Only for a moment." He smiled at her, his deep-set eyes showing only curiosity. "Can you come a little closer? My eyesight isn't what it used to be."

"Of course," she said. She moved nearer and lowered her eyes.

The priest put a hand under her chin and lifted her face to him. "You remind me of a child I used to know. A child who loved art."

Alys felt herself redden. "I've been living these last years in Warwickshire, Father. I'm sure you must be mistaking me for someone else."

The priest looked at her closely and then gave a sad smile. "Perhaps. It was long ago and many things have happened in that time that wrought changes on us all."

She looked into his eyes. "That is certainly true, Father."

He stroked the side of her face. "And now you're to go on pilgrimage. A journey that can present many challenges and perils. May God walk beside you all of the way." He looked beyond her to Joanie. "And beside your servant as well."

"Thank you, Father."

There was something about his voice and the way he looked at her that made her wish she could tell him all, so that his blessing would carry the weight of the truth. She bowed her head once again. It was a temptation that she couldn't afford.

∿

"How will you tell 'em that you're not going to Tours, or Rome? That you'll desert them at Chartres and 'ead for Paris?" asked Joanie.

Alys sat on the edge of the small cot built into the one side of the small cabin that had been her home for the past day, her head hovering over a bowl. She fought the retching that threatened to seize her once again and looked at Joanie. She would have preferred to have this discussion later, when she was on dry land and felt better. But Joanie, whose knowledge of geography outside of London was only vague, had asked enough questions of the other pilgrims to put the facts together. Though some pilgrims might journey from Paris, it was not one of the main direct routes to Rome, or Tours, or any of the destinations their group had marked as worthy of attention.

"Chartres is only a day or two's journey from Paris. I'll say that I've promised to go and see a relative of my husband's family there and will meet up with them afterwards."

Joanie's mouth formed a grim line. "And 'ow will you manage? Will there be places safe enough for us?"

"Don't fret so, Joanie. I speak French and we travel as pilgrims and are guaranteed protection from harm, like anyone wearing that garb. But, if it makes you feel better, I'll hire a man to escort us, if I can."

Joanie shook her head. "I don't know. I just hope you're right."

The door opened and Margery entered. She frowned at the sight of the bowl and sniffed.

"Are you sure you have the health for this journey, Mistress Merton?"

Alys straightened and put the bowl aside. "The sickness is passing now. I'm fine and well able for this pilgrimage, I assure you. I would inquire about your father, though. With you in attendance, I'm sure problems he might have will be quickly resolved."

Margery moved to the small cot opposite and removed the rosary from the small box in her chest. There was barely enough space for Joanie and herself, but Margery's presence made the cabin seem impossibly small. Alys prayed that the weather would hold and it would be only a few days at sea as promised. She could put up with the nausea, but Margery was another thing. Pilgrim life had as many tensions as any royal household, it seemed. She longed to be in Paris, with Barnabas, and hopefully would be so before the month was out.

CHAPTER SIX
Venice, Late Spring 1445
BARNABAS

I tapped my fingers on the table absentmindedly. As much as I tried, I couldn't focus my mind on the text in front of me. It was a work on medicine in Arabic, something that would ordinarily hold my attention, but this late in the afternoon, my mind wandered to other things. Master al Qali, or just al Qali, as I was beginning to call him in my mind, stood at the window gazing out on the canal below. The window was open and the stench from outside wafted in the room. Venice was a city of smells and not all of them sweet. It was one of the first things I'd noticed upon our arrival a fortnight ago.

Al Qali suddenly turned to me. "Did your acquaintances mention any other text or manuscript at Padua?"

I shook my head. We'd been over this before a few times. "They completed their studies, but that's not to say they applied themselves while they were there. Though they might be Venetian patricians, they are, after all, destined to go into trade."

"Yes, yes. I know. But among them there might be some who are inclined toward knowledge of all kinds." He softened his voice. "As you are, my dear Giacomo."

I eyed him warily. I'd begun to view his kind moments with a degree of suspicion, since they seemed to involve me in activities I didn't like.

"Well, among the young scholars that I met with the other day, I must say the subjects they discussed weren't particularly academic in nature," I said.

I recalled the seven young men draped along the steps of the small palazzo on the Rio Marin, near the church of St Simon. Dressed as they were in their voluptuous colours, they were like exotic birds among the dark sober pigeons that were the businessmen and their black-clad wives. With flagons of expensive wine in their hands, the seven young peacocks ogled the passers-by in their gondolas and barchettas, hoping for a glimpse of an ankle, neck, or hand from some unwary woman, and if they were lucky, a courtesan.

"You said they meet most evenings," said al Qali. "Go then, and see what you can find out."

I raised my brows at him. I had thrown that comment out to him after he'd pestered me for details. What did he know of the life of a young man of the merchant class in Venice? Very little, despite his knowledge of the world. Venice, for all its splendour and cosmopolitan outlook, its republican values and luxury, was a nervous city. One in which excess went alongside trade and commerce in a near fever pitch, while the Sultan and his vast Turkish armies crept ever closer.

"You want me to seek out their company this evening?" I asked.

I knew the answer, but I was stalling for time. How could I manage to avoid this request? Meeting the young merchant men fresh from their studies at Padua the previous time had set me on edge in a manner that I hadn't experienced in a long time. I met these men in the guise of one of their own, fresh from my studies in Paris and now returned to my home of Venice and the bosom of my family. A family no one knew, least of all myself.

"Of course. Didn't I just say so?"

"And what would you have me say to these young men about my family, my home? They'll know all the prominent merchants of the city and their families, like the Contarini and the Bembo."

"But of course, you are not a Contarini, nor a Bembo. You have a resourceful mind. What would you tell them?"

"That my father has only a small merchant business and is at present one of the consuls in Alexandria, trading in cloth. Or should he be in Bruges?"

"The Venetian community in Bruges is too small. You should know that." Al Qali sighed. "No, alas your father is in Alexandria, with your brother, and unable to welcome you back home after so many years abroad. He sent me, a good friend he met in Alexandria, to collect you and bring you home safely to your home."

I gestured around the room. "And this is my home?"

The *sala* was spacious enough, though the plaster was cracked in places and the tiled floors were in some disrepair. Old tapestries, threadbare in places, hung on the walls, and the few pieces of furniture, though good, were scarred. There was one more room that contained our sleeping quarters. We rented this modest accommodation that cost dear enough from a minor patrician who allowed one us of his servants as well. It was, overall, part of a modest *casa* that was no closer to the biggest and spacious palazzos that overlooked the Grand Canal than it was to the hovels on the danker, darker canals and backstreets of Venice's lower classes.

He gave me a puzzled look. "Do you have any other home in Venice? The servants call you master and await your father's return."

I looked away. There were times when it was useless to puzzle out al Qali's cryptic words. When we'd arrived it was clear that al Qali had these rooms rented long term if only because the patrician and his servants had seemed well acquainted with al Qali. At the time I thought it was only some clever ruse he'd created with his numerous contacts and letter writing, but now, I wasn't so sure.

"You must seek them out this evening. You said you've studied their haunts, know the places they find the most pleasure. Go tonight and find them."

I frowned. He made it sound so easy. Slipping in among them, becoming part of their group. Didn't he realise these young men had spent years in each other's company? "I'll try," I said.

Al Qali stroked my head. "You will succeed, Giacomo. You are wise beyond your years and certainly cleverer than those pampered young men. You are a Venetian. Believe it with all your heart and none can doubt you."

He knew the source of my worry and his words gave me some heart. I sighed and rose from the table to go and change. I would have to dress the part if I was to be convincing.

∽

A few hours later I was drinking with my new friends on the steps of the same palazzo as before, though this evening was cool and one of Venice's famous fogs was descending fast.

"We won't see much now," said sooty-eyed Pietro Voltini. "Come, we will move on."

Pietro rose with an elegant grace. Though small, he had a large personality that could command the rest of them, even Niccolo Paisano, the oldest at nineteen and the bold one of the group, whose aspirations to noble pursuits had carried him within a hair's breadth of the knife on more than one occasion. Venice could be a dangerous city at night; more than one knifed body had been found tossed in the canals during the course of any given year. Or so the others had told me. Whether it was his father's rich purse or his red hair that made Niccolo so brash and self-assured, he certainly didn't balk at any whiff of adventure like the well-fed Marco or shy Antonio.

"*Bene*, I know where we'll go," said Niccolo. He sprang to his feet and turned to me with a grin. "You, my friend, are in for a treat. My uncle is entertaining tonight."

"Your uncle?" said Pietro. A slow smile spread across his face. "He is a man with taste. There will be music?"

Niccolo shrugged. "Of course. But there will also be gaming. Do you like gaming, Giacomo?"

I gave him an indifferent smile. "*Si*, of course."

"Did your uncle invite you?" asked Marco. His red face was full of doubt.

"No, but he won't mind."

"But it would be wrong," said Antonio.

"Oh, come on. There will be many there. He could hardly notice us among the others," said Niccolo.

Vito and Polo agreed. They were brothers, and so closely alike I could hardly tell them apart.

"Your uncle is a kind man," said Pietro. "He didn't mind the last time."

I knew it was the music that had swayed Pietro in favour of this course of action. He'd spoken often enough about his favourite lutenist and composer, and no doubt he hoped that this very same composer or, at least his music, would be played at Niccolo's uncle's place tonight.

I was torn. The music did tempt me, as did the gaming. In fact, I itched to hold a set of the cards in my hand, it had been a long time since the game in Paris. I also wouldn't mind tempting fate on a throw of the dice, but a room full of rich Venetian merchants with a wide circle of friends and acquaintances would be the biggest test since my arrival in Venice. Alexandria, where my imaginary father was currently trading, wasn't far enough away in circles like these, where men moved back and forth across the sea for trade like chess pieces on a board.

I straightened, looked over at Niccolo and laughed. "Yes, I would like to go."

❧

We took a gondola, shoving each other inside it and singing off key as we made our way along the canals. The fog had descended in earnest now and the gondolier lit a small lantern at the prow of the boat, calling periodically in the distance to other gondolas that approached, determining right of way and the others' proximity.

We arrived at our destinations with damp clothes but high spirits, and alighted on the steps laughing hard. I followed the others inside and was greeted by the sound of more laughter, loud voices and music. Niccolo led us through the *loggia* and up the wide staircase to the floor above. Small marble sculptures of figures and an occasional animal were scattered in the hall, and behind them frescoes and tapestries decorated the walls. This was no simple merchant's home.

I took a deep breath and followed the others inside to the large *sala*. As Niccolo had predicted, the room was filled with people, not just men looking for sport of one sort or another, but women too. Perfumes of all varieties filled the air and covered the underlying odour that accompanied even the best dressed in a city heading into hotter weather. I stared at the women, stunned by their clothes as much as their beauty. Venice was a city that protected its women from the gaze of men outside their circle with dark veils and cloaks. Any opportunities for public excursion were limited to attending mass, feast days, and other special occasions.

This was my first real glimpse of the celebrated and stylish Venetian women. It was a cloth merchant's dream. Rich velvets sprinkled with gold and woven silver, deep velvets with gold worked across its surface competed with figured silk damask, and veils of watered moiré finish. All the fabrics were draped loosely over dangerously exposed shoulders and breasts so full they seemed to beg to be handled.

I caught sight of a nipple so delicately rouged that it seemed more shyly peeping from its silk bodice than bold and assertive. The sheerest of scarfs was draped across her shoulders. I glanced at the woman's face. Framed in long dark hair, it shone luminous in the glow of beeswax candles. Pearls circled her neck and hung from her ears. A lute rested on her lap. She caught my look and gave me a slow soft smile before turning back to the man talking to her.

"That is Alessandra," said Niccolo. "She's too rich for your blood, *amico mio*."

I grinned at Niccolo. "But not for yours, I take it?"

"Ah, of course. She pretends she doesn't care for me, calls me a pup, but I know she really adores me."

I nodded and wondered how much of that was truth and how much pure wishful thinking. At the moment she seemed completely taken by the aging man in dark red robes who sat talking to her.

"Who is that with her?" I asked.

Niccolo shrugged. "One of my uncle's friends. A man in the *collegio.*"

I examined the man more carefully. Membership to the Venetian council was reserved for the wealthiest patricians of Venetian society. The rings on his fingers spoke of money, as did the fur and rich cloth of his robes. He was talking earnestly to Alessandra, his hands emphasising his words with an occasional gesture as she listened attentively. Or was it just artifice?

The smallest tip of her tongue ran across her lips. It lasted only a brief moment but the man stumbled over his words. I could tell, for he halted a moment, his hand in mid-air, and a deep flush spread across his face. Alessandra cocked her head slightly and moved her hand to adjust the silk scarf at her shoulders, brushing her nipple in the process. The man shifted uncomfortably in his seat and gazed at it raptly.

A hand fell on my shoulder. "Come, let me show you the gaming," said Niccolo.

Reluctantly, I drew my attention away from the little scene that had played out before me and followed Niccolo to another part of the room to a table filled with men and women. It was then that I saw on the vast walls not just frescoes of Venus and Aphrodite, but also paintings of the Madonna beside those depicting Venice and portraits of men I couldn't identify. They seemed so real that I thought they might step out of the picture.

Niccolo tugged me to the table. Three men and one woman sat there, hands filled with the small playing cards that I'd come to know in Paris. These cards were finely made and hand painted, though each player clutched them casually.

"You play *Triomphe*?" asked Niccolo?

I shrugged. "Only a little."

The man in front looked up at me and winked. I could see the cards he held. The reds were coloured brilliantly. It was a good hand, providing his partner was adept.

"We'll finish this game and you and your friend can join us, Niccolo."

Niccolo flushed with pleasure and dug me in the side. "*Benissimo!*"

"Providing you have the money," said the man.

Niccolo drew himself up. "Of course. I wouldn't sit down otherwise."

The man glanced at me and I nodded. I'd left the room with a small purse of coins, some given to me by al Qali, the rest acquired by other means. With a bit of luck I might leave with the pouch that bit heavier.

We watched the play, while most of those seated tossed their cards in the middle. A woman gave a groan of disgust and rose from the table with a tinkling laugh.

"You will have me leave here without a garment on my back, let alone a ducat or even a soda."

The man who had spoken to Niccolo grinned at the lady while he scooped up the money and stacked it in neat layers beside him. He glanced at his partner and pushed a few coins his way. "You played well enough, tonight, Arturo."

"Without you, Tomaso, I would be leaving here a pauper," said Arturo. "And now, I think it's time for music. The piece they are playing has suddenly become my favourite."

Arturo rose and left the table. Tomaso turned to the remaining man. "And you, my friend, will you stay for another game?"

The man shook his head and sighed. "I am afraid I can play no more tonight. Like Arturo, I think I must find my amusement in the music and the food."

Tomaso gave a slow smile and watched the man leave the table. He turned to Niccolo. "We will find a fourth, don't worry."

"May I be allowed to make up the party here?" came a voice from behind me.

I turned and was greeted by the dark-haired wonder, Alessandra. Her eyes sparkled, filled with mischief.

"Alessandra," said Tomaso. "With your beauty gracing this table we would find no head for cards."

"No, no, Tomaso. You cannot attempt to compose your verses now while you hold cards in your hands and stack money at your side. It all seems like too much work."

Tomaso laughed, but there was an edge to it. "We all find work of some kind here tonight. Is your own not proving successful enough that you must come here, to these young men for their meagre purses?"

I looked at Alessandra again and saw the faintly painted lips, the pearls, the breasts so revealingly displayed and wondered at my earlier ignorance. Of course she was a courtesan, one whose skills encompassed not just those in the bedroom, but also music, poetry and conversation. I studied her again, with new eyes.

"Oh, Tomaso, must you be so vulgar? These young men have their charms that any lady would value."

"It's the value you place on them that I would wonder about."

She patted his shoulder. "Sssh. Let it rest. We will be friends and enjoy ourselves."

She turned to me and smiled. "Now, would you honour me as a partner in this game?"

I bowed to her and smiled. I was close enough to catch the musky scent of her perfume, laden with hints of something else that I couldn't name and seemed even more exotic. She took my hand and led me to the two chairs opposite Tomaso. Even the swish of her gown against the marble floor was sensual. I sighed, revelling in the pleasure of her. I knew, just as Niccolo had said, she was too rich for my blood, but she chose to spend this small space of time with me, and I would make the most of every moment.

When we were both settled and Niccolo in his seat, she reached for the cards, her be-ringed fingers long and graceful. She shuffled the cards with expert dexterity and dealt the hand. I glanced around at the others, trying to read their faces, and scooped up my cards, spreading them out. I studied them carefully, as if I'd never seen them before. They were beautifully printed, the outlines of the block clearly edged and the hand painted colours were lush and vibrant.

I shot a bewildered look at Tomaso. "These cards are very fine."

Tomaso gave me a calculating look. "Have you seen others?"

I shrugged and tried to appear nonchalant. "Maybe once or twice, but they weren't as well made as these."

"Our host likes fine things," said Tomaso. "Isn't that so, Alessandra?"

"He is a man of taste," she said.

Niccolo sniffed impatiently. "Can we get on with this?"

I glanced over at him and watched him finger the cards nervously. I smiled inwardly. This game would be interesting.

"I'm ready," I said.

"Boys," said Alessandra. "They are always so impatient, so quick to act." She gave me a direct look. "Thinking before you act is a rule that should guide you in many things, but especially in cards."

I nodded carefully. Tomaso opened the game and Alessandra after him. Cards were discarded and picked up. Cups, coins, swords, and sticks—cards from all the suits found their way to the table. My bidding was poor at first and Alessandra murmured some advice to me, trying to guide me through the mire of the game, her eyes studying me carefully all the while. After a time, when it seemed that all was lost, we started to win bids more often and a smile lit her face.

We were playing the last hand of that particular game when I felt a foot rest on top of mine for just a moment. I looked across at Alessandra, and it seemed she winked. It was so quick I could have imagined it. Soon after, the game ended and when all was counted, I discovered we'd won.

"Your partner caught on very quickly," said Tomaso, a slight frown his face.

"It is only beginner's luck, I assure you," I said.

Niccolo grunted. "Tomaso could beat the two of you even on a bad day. He was just being kind, weren't you, Tomaso."

Alessandra gave Tomaso a coquettish smile. "Oh, Tomaso, you are being too kind. It is good of you to allow the boy a little win, given that he is new to the game."

Tomaso waved his hand and gave a little bow. "Of course. He is new to the city, I think and we wouldn't want him to be under the impression that all Venetians are only motivated by profit."

I repressed a smile. Tomaso had most certainly emphasised the word 'all.' Was he implying that Alessandra was only motivated by profit?

"I am a Venetian, signore," I said.

Tomaso raised his brow. "Truly? Your accent doesn't quite say that."

"I have been away for some while."

"His father is a Venetian merchant, trading in Alexandria," said Niccolo.

"Have you been in Alexandria, then?" asked Alessandra. "Such an interesting place."

"You have been there?" I asked, surprised. I didn't think Venetian women, even courtesans, would have travelled there easily.

Alessandra waved her hand. "Ah, *sfortunatamente*, I haven't. But others who have been described its wonders to me."

Tomaso gave a small snort. "I'm sure you know many who are well travelled."

"As would you, *amico mio*, if you were cultured," said Alessandra.

Niccolo looked at the two of them and his face reddened. "Shall I deal the cards?"

"Of course, dear Niccolo. Please do," said Alessandra.

Niccolo dealt the cards, slapping them with some force on the table, as if that might keep the acid tongues at bay. The enmity between the two was real, but I felt there was something else there as well.

The game began and Alessandra exchanged some light banter with Niccolo who eventually relaxed under her charm, but Tomaso eyed both Alessandra and I carefully when it was our turn.

"Where did you go on your travels, if not to Alexandria?" asked Tomaso.

"I spent some time in London, Paris, and then lately in Bruges."

"Bruges?" asked Alessandra. "I have heard much about Bruges. A city of refinement, I think."

I nodded. "The Duke has a remarkable art collection."

"You have met the Duke?" asked Niccolo.

I shrugged. "Only briefly."

"Did you see his art collection?" asked Alessandra.

I told her of the fine paintings, frescoes, and tapestries I'd seen on my visits and the vast library he had. The cards, meanwhile, were discarded and the 'tricks' played and taken between both sets of partners. I made a few mistakes in the early part of the game and I gave off an air of distraction as I explained the wonders of the paintings and the complexities of translating manuscripts, Alessandra seemingly enthralled with my words. Niccolo grasped his cards earnestly and his brow furrowed in concentration. Tomaso took to whistling on occasion.

"Must you?" asked Alessandra eventually.

"Must I what?" said Tomaso.

"The whistle. It is most irritating."

"*Scusi*, I didn't realise I was doing it."

Alessandra gave him a doubtful look but said nothing. She looked at her cards and scooped up those on the table. "There. I believe that is mine."

Tomaso frowned. "I see."

"What do you see?" asked Alessandra. "Do you see that we have won?" She looked over at me and cocked her head. "My young *amore* and I have beat you at your own game, I think."

I gave her a grin. "I think I owe it more to you than to any skill of mine."

She patted me on the hand. "Pah, you are too modest."

Tomaso noted the score and conceded the win, despite some protests from Niccolo.

"Was there some trick, some sleight of hand I didn't see, Tomaso?" asked Niccolo.

"No, *amico mio*. I think there are just some days when the luck is elsewhere." He rose. "And for that reason, it must be time I am away from here and on to better opportunities."

Niccolo rose and went after him. "Might I go with you?"

Tomaso laughed and then looked at him. "Ah, of course."

Alessandra watched the two disappear into the crowd then turned to me and spoke softly. "And now, *amico mio*, you might tell me where you are really from and where you learned to play cards so well."

CHAPTER SEVEN
Venice, Spring 1445
BARNABAS

I inhaled the scents from the bedclothes around me. It was a heady mix of skilfully blended spices and musk, well worth whatever fortune that must have been paid for it. Outside I could see the dawn just breaking and casting a golden glow on the tousled long black hair and limbs beside me.

I sighed, not completely at ease. Alessandra was a charming, talented woman, but also very clever and I still wasn't certain I had convinced her of my story. I certainly hadn't convinced her at the gaming table, and it was on the pretence of questioning me away from prying eyes and keen hearing that she took me to her own small palazzo. On the way, we'd sat in the gondola exchanging banter, but her hands had been busy enough with subtle, well-placed caresses.

She'd asked me a few questions again when we were inside, but I had only repeated my story. She'd smiled and ran her hand along my face, before leaning over and

73

kissing me in a most expert manner. Few words had followed, and in the time to come, I'd learned the difference between the awkward tumblings and fumblings of my previous courtships and the truly sensual experience of a woman trained for pleasure.

Alessandra stirred beside me and lifted her head from the bed. The rich cloth that hung from the rails above served as a fitting backdrop for her smooth skin and full red lips. In this light, though, I could see a hint of lines at her eyes and mouth. She wasn't as young as I had first thought. Her beauty was more of her making, too. Her skin was oiled and smooth, her brows finely tweezed, and her hair brushed to a glossy shine. You couldn't escape the large dark eyes, used always to her advantage, either. They were fixed on me now.

"Ah, my fine young man, you didn't disappoint." She smiled and ran her hand along my shoulder and onto my chest. "In body or in actions."

I leaned over to kiss her and she answered with a deeper one, circling her arms around my neck. I moved to cover her body with my own, but she pushed me gently away.

"There is much greater satisfaction for all, if things aren't rushed," she said. She ran a finger along my lips. "Feel the sensation, give yourself time to enjoy each part."

She rolled over. With deft grace she reached for my doublet, tossed carelessly on the floor the night before. I noted the curve of her back, the soft roundness of her buttocks. She was right, there was pleasure there in the view.

She placed the doublet on her lap, near her heavy round breasts, which were like polished ivory. "This cloth, for instance," she said. "It is Kermes silk, no? Its touch against the skin is as sensuous as a kiss."

I nodded, mesmerised by her voice and voluptuous body.

"It's a specialty of Bruges," I said.

"Ah, Bruges. You say you were there for a time?"

I nodded and grinned. I reached over and fingered the cloth. "It's as smooth as your skin." I ran my thumb over one of her breasts and touched a nipple. It responded quickly.

"You were trading there?" she asked.

"Trading and studying. As I mentioned before, the Duke of Burgundy has a wonderful library." I leaned down and kissed a breast, teasing it with my tongue as she'd taught me.

"You learn quickly, I think," she said. "And would be good at trade."

I pushed her back on the bed, crushing my doublet between us. "I am good at a few other things, too."

"But not quick in them all, I hope," she said.

I stopped her words with a deep kiss and then moved my lips down her throat to her shoulder. She caressed me carefully and with great skill as I moved along the length of her body.

"You will get me some of this cloth?" she asked.

"Of course," I said.

She sighed and pulled me deep inside her and I groaned with pleasure. Of my promise, I would worry later, when I considered how to tell Master al Qali that I'd gleaned little information for him.

❧

Al Qali frowned at me and for a moment I saw a hint of anger flash in his eyes, before his face cleared and he clasped my shoulder. A hot spell made the room uncomfortable. The windows were open and I could smell the water from where I sat on a chair by the small table where I usually worked.

"Come now, you only return in the early hours of the morning and you tell me you have nothing of interest to share?"

I shook my head, feeling some of the effect of the drink from the night before. "Really, I spent most of the night at cards…and other things where little or nothing was said."

"Cards?" al Qali's face grew serious. "Were the cards special in any way?"

"No, nothing like that, I assure you." I knew what he was asking. The gaming cards and others, of more mysterious and apparently powerful origin, came from Arab areas, where he'd spent much of his early life. Cards like these might hold a clue to whatever he was after. "They were just ordinary playing cards."

Al Qali sighed. "You must try harder in future. Learn about their professors. Perhaps we can gain some information from them."

"The professors of the university at Padua?"

"Yes. I must be thorough in my search."

"Perhaps if I knew what exactly you were looking for, I could be of more help."

Al Qali waved his hand. "There is no need. And even if I told you the name of the document you wouldn't understand its meaning or recognise it."

"I read many languages well enough."

Al Qali gave me a tight smile. "No more questions. We will make plans to go to Padua. You can mention your friends' names to the professors. They will speak to you."

I groaned inwardly at his words. There were so many reasons I didn't want to go to Padua, not least of which I was certain that it would be a fruitless journey. I would much prefer to stay and do that bit of trading with Alessandra as well as some even more pleasurable commerce with her.

"Can't you go alone?" I asked. "I could remain behind and see what else I could find out from my new connections."

Al Qali's eyes were fully alert at those words. "Men of consequence that might have information?"

I nodded. "People who assuredly have the ear of some of the most consequential patricians of the city." I allowed a considered pause. "Perhaps even the Doge."

Al Qali's face broke into a wide smile. "The Doge? He would have manuscripts. You have done well, Giacomo. All my training has finally begun to pay off. You are no longer the little ruffian you once were, but a young man of refinement who can pass in company with wealthy and influential people. I am proud."

Despite myself I felt a swell of happiness at his words. Who could blame me? I, who had been found on a dung heap and raised as a penniless orphan, only to be parcelled out to serve a cunning witch who nearly brought me to my death, why wouldn't I take pleasure in words that praised my accomplishments. But it was only for a moment, because the praise, I really knew, was directed at himself, at his cleverness for taking the sow's ear that I was and making me into a silk purse. If these years I'd spent in his company had taught me anything, it was that whenever Mustapha al Qali may seem to be taking my welfare into account, his own interests were behind it.

"Who are these men you say are so well connected?"

I sketched out the people I'd seen at Niccolo's uncle's party.

"Good, good. This is very good," said al Qali. "Why didn't you mention that you'd gone to this gathering before, instead of telling me you'd only passed the night playing cards? I thought you meant that you played cards with your young friends."

I shrugged. "They were there, too."

"Yes, yes. But these other people. You made an impression? You might be called upon to go with Niccolo to see these people?"

"I did make an impression, yes." I thought of Alessandra and smiled. "And I think I can safely say that I will be able to meet up with one or two again, one way or the other."

Al Qali gave a contented sigh. "Yes. Well then, given what you say, I think what you suggest might be for the best. You will remain behind and strengthen these connections. Find out about any exotic manuscripts that have come into the city in the last year or so."

"But not in Arabic?" In the past, in Paris, Bruges and the few other university libraries we had examined, it had always been to look for manuscripts in unfamiliar languages, but al Qali had just admitted that I wouldn't recognise the manuscript if I saw it, and the only thing I could think of was that it was written in a tongue I didn't understand. "Wouldn't the merchants you know that deal in manuscripts be able to tell you of any new items recently come in?"

Al Qali's eyes darkened and his face became neutral. "Perhaps." He turned away and looked out the window. Below, I could hear shouts from the various barchettas and gondolas in the crowded waterways. He turned back again and there was a smile on his face, his eyes alight with it. "For now, you must just inquire. I should be able to make my own investigations at the university at Padua without any undue difficulties."

I suppressed all my doubts at those last words and gave a reassuring smile. Venice, usually very open to travellers from all over, no matter how they looked, were now wary enough of men who dressed like a Turk and bore a name that could be easily be taken for a Turk, no matter that his skin was darker than an average Turk's. The Ottomans had just soundly defeated the King of Hungary after the King had attacked the empire. Now the Turks had turned their attention westward. Venice traded with the Turks quite successfully, but that, like all things, could change. Al Qali had encountered dark looks and even a few snubs since we'd arrived, even from people he'd known before, including a few of the merchants who dealt in manuscripts. Who knows how the people at the university in Padua would treat him, especially without me to lend him the appearance of honest intent. Was there anything honest about his intent? Increasingly I wondered. But it wasn't his intent, dishonest or otherwise, that troubled me.

CHAPTER EIGHT
Paris, Spring 1445
ALYS

Alys looked at the others arrayed around her in the sparsely furnished main room of the inn on the outskirts of Chartres and tried to remain calm and keep her voice firm.

"I must go," she said. "I prayed on it as we came closer to Chartres and I feel now in my heart, despite the fact that my husband quarrelled with his cousins, I must go to them and tell them of his death."

Beside her Joanie shifted uncomfortably. The loud objections that had been voiced initially receded into a few murmurs. Alfred Benyngton looked sceptical, but Alys knew he would be glad to be rid of her, if only to stop John Lyttleton's unseemly attentions. In truth, she was happy to be rid of them, too. She could see the disappointment in Lyttleton's eyes. Harold Kemp and Sir George gave her compassionate looks.

"You must of course do what your conscience bids you," said Kemp.

His voice was thin and tired and his skin greyer than when she'd first met him. She wondered if he'd make it to Tours, let alone Rome, or even Jerusalem, a destination to which Margery had lately declared they should all now head. Margery looked almost joyful at Alys' words, if such a thing was possible.

"I can't ignore my conscience," said Alys. "I'll part from you all tomorrow."

"But you haven't even seen the sancta camisa, our Blessed Virgin's robe," said John Lyttleton.

"And you will miss mass," said Benyngton.

Alys bowed her head and tried to look sad. "I know and I'm sorry for that, but I want to complete this task as quickly as I can so that I might rejoin you on the road."

In a way she was disappointed. She would have liked to have seen the wonders that were said to be found in the cathedral at Chartres. Its beauty and grace were famous and the sculptures and stained glass windows were something she knew she would have spent time studying. But Lyttleton's attentions were becoming uncomfortable and she had become impatient with the slow progress of a pilgrims' gait.

"I'll hire fast horses. With just the two of us we will make good time," she said.

"You mustn't go alone. It will be safer if one of us accompanies you," said Sir George. He gave a small bow. "I would be happy to assume that honour. Though I am no longer a man of arms, I can still act as protector when called upon."

Lyttleton opened his mouth to speak for a moment but then thought better of it.

"You are too kind, Sir George," said Alys. "I assure you it isn't necessary."

Sir George patted her arm. "Nonsense. Let no more be said about it."

Alys looked at him. She could see the stubborn set to his chin and decided against voicing any more objections. Perhaps it would be good to have him accompany them to Paris. He would be able to travel at any pace they set, she was certain of that. But once in Paris, what then? How could she shed his company and find Barnabas? She sighed. She had only a few days to come up with something.

"Come, Joanie, we've much to do."

She turned away from the watching eyes and caught Joanie's doubtful look. Alys gave her a reassuring smile. It will be fine, she mouthed to her. Alys only hoped her words were true.

❧

The road was rutted and full of mud. Damp hung in the air and clung to the trees. The spring had been wet in this region and it made travel more difficult than usual. Alys resisted the urge to rub her backside. Any sign of discomfort and Sir George would insist they stop at the next inn, but she wanted to make Paris before nightfall. They had already spent an extra day on the journey than she had hoped, with the condition of the roads. She patted her skittish horse, glad now that she had the confidence to ride her that five years ago she would never have possessed. The horse snorted a reply.

Sir George pulled alongside of her. "Is all well, Mistress Merton?"

Alys gave him a warm smile. "All is well, Sir George. And please, as I mentioned before, call me Alys. We have been too long in each other's company to be so formal."

Sir George gave her a small bow. "Alys. Thank you. I do feel that we have become fully acquainted in these past few weeks."

Had it been weeks since she'd left Queenhithe and set out on this journey? In some ways it felt like years, and in other ways it seemed only a few days.

"Were you long fighting abroad?" asked Alys. Behind her, on the same horse, Joanie shifted uncomfortably. The third horse, a piebald mare, carried the chest with Alys' things.

"I was. I served many years with John, the Duke of Bedford, and then after that his brother, Duke Humphrey."

Alys flinched slightly at the mention of Duke Humphrey, but managed a smile in the end. "Did you know the Duke at all?"

"No, I only saw him from afar. I served directly under one of his men, Lord Percy."

Alys scanned her mind for any memory of a Lord Percy that might have come to La Pleasaunce, until she realised he meant Duke John, not Humphrey.

"Was Duke John a handsome man?"

Sir George laughed. "Aye, passable, I suppose. His lady wife before he died was a real beauty, though. Jacquetta was her name. She's married now, to a fair young soldier of no more fortune than myself, worse luck for me."

"But you have a wife and family back in England, don't you?" asked Alys. "I thought you had mentioned you were married."

Sir George's eyes darkened. "I was, true enough. But fever took my wife and two boys."

Alys saw the pain in his eyes and she reached out a comforting hand. "How terrible for you. I'm so sorry."

Joanie gave her a light pinch at her waist. What was wrong with a little sympathy, thought Alys.

Sir George turned to her and gave her a tentative smile, his eyes seeking hers. "Thank you for your understanding. It's still difficult to believe. My wife was never a well woman, but when the two boys caught fever, she insisted on nursing them herself, rather than a servant. Before she died she made me promise to go on pilgrimage to pray for our two boys' souls."

"May they rest in peace," said Alys. "The boys and your wife."

For some reason she felt it necessary to remind him of his wife. She reached up and tucked a stray lock of her russet hair back under the protection of her headcloth.

"Have you been to Tours before?" asked Joanie. "Or any of the other places on the pilgrimage?"

"I have been to Chartres. But no, not the other places on our pilgrimage. My soldiering took me elsewhere."

He was courteous in his speech to Joanie, but his voice lacked the warmth Alys had noticed he'd used increasingly when he spoke to her.

"Oh, but you seem to have travelled many places," said Joanie. "Where else have you been?"

As Sir George began his litany of experiences in his soldiering days Alys wondered at Joanie's questions. Was she trying to learn more about him, to determine what kind threat he might pose? Or was she trying to distract him from Alys, by drawing his attention to herself? If that was the case, she was failing badly because he directed his narrative towards Alys for the most part. She did her best to pay attention, but his words showed him more for the soldier he was than any kind of storyteller. She tried not to yawn.

Some hours later, she looked up and saw some church spires in the distance. She pointed. "Is that Paris?"

Sir George nodded. "Yes. It shouldn't be long, now."

Alys breathed a sigh of relief. Hopefully, in a few days' time, she would be shed of Sir George and reunited with Barnabas. Then she would have a chance to convince Barnabas she now had enough money that they could both start over, together. She tugged at the leather bracelet on her wrist. Please let it all be so, she thought.

❦

This was not London, Alys reminded herself, though the smells from the river were just as pungent, and the lanes and streets that wound their way along were just as convoluted and confusing. London she knew well, but this city was foreign in ways she hadn't imagined. It was full of tired buildings that had the scars of neglect from war, and a royal family that also fought with each other and drained money away from the city. People dressed differently, the women's skirts were fuller and caught up higher in the waist, at least those of the higher classes that tried to ape the nobility. The men were less soberly dressed, wearing doublets and hose made with vibrantly dyed cloth.

Even the inn where they found themselves housed some while later had customers whose fine clothes made Alys wish for a moment that she hadn't adopted the dull colours of widowhood and pilgrimage. Alys all but smiled as she saw Joanie's eyes sparkle in appreciation at one young man whose deep red velvet doublet and parti-coloured hose covered well-muscled limbs and chest to a distinct advantage.

"I've arranged for the innkeeper to bring us some roast fowl while he sees to our rooms," said Sir George.

"Thank you. You are kind to do all this," said Alys.

Sir George escorted them over to a small table in the corner and Alys took a place on the settle set before it. Before Joanie could, Sir George took the place beside Alys. Joanie frowned slightly and then caught up a stool, placed it by the settle and sat on it.

"The innkeeper also promised us some wine. It took a little persuading, but I think you'll be glad of the effort," said Sir George.

Alys nodded and thanked him. She'd had wine before, in the Duchess' company, but she wasn't overly fond of it. Still, Sir George was trying to be an attentive companion and he'd done much to ease her journey as well as her purse since leaving the others, so she must seem appreciative. Across from her, Joanie frowned.

The food when it came, tasted heavenly. Perhaps it was the weeks on pilgrim fare, now abandoned in this city, which could still produce some nicely seasoned dishes and even, to her surprise, wine that went down all too well. She savoured every bit that passed her lips.

"You must try this wine," said Sir George.

"You seem to know much about wine," said Alys.

"I spent my years abroad doing more than just fighting," he said with a smile. He rested a hand lightly on hers. "I learned much about the areas in which I travelled and came to appreciate some things they did well. And now I am happy to share that knowledge with you."

Alys blushed. She didn't dare snatch her hand away, for fear of giving offence. She used her other hand to straighten her head cloth, which she knew teetered too much to one side and was in danger of coming undone altogether. With only one hand free she seemed to make more a mess of it than it was before and it tumbled from her head to rest on her shoulders, as she feared might happen.

"I'm sorry. I think the wine and the journey have made me more tired than I realised," said Alys.

"Nonsense," said Sir George. He lifted a lock of hair from her shoulder. "It is a shame to cover such beauty. Leave it for now, tonight. Tonight is special."

"Special?" Alys asked weakly. She was conscious of his hand brushing her chin before he let the lock slip from his fingers

"My lady, it isn't seemly to have your hair uncovered like that. Folk will get the wrong idea. And your husband, God rest his soul...,"Joanie crossed herself elaborately, "would never have approved."

Alys gave Joanie a grateful look. She withdrew her hand from Sir George's and tried to reassemble the headcloth. When she looked up, a dark haired man with swarthy pocked skin loomed over them.

"Benyngton?"

A surprised look spread across Sir George's face. He grinned. "Westford?" He rose and made his way around the table to clap the man on the back. The man, Westford, was dressed in a worn but well-made doublet of deep green and parti-coloured hose to match. She could see now there was some grey threaded through the dark hair and lines around dark eyes that were almost black. His bearing and scarred hands marked him for what he was. A soldier.

While the two men exchanged greetings, Joanie leaned over to her. "Have a care, Alys," she whispered. "He wants you for his bed, one way or the other."

"Surely not," said Alys. "It is just a little harmless flirting on his part. Nothing I can't handle."

"You don't believe that. You know 'e wants more than just a chat." Her London accent came on heavily in her agitation. "I fink it'd be best if I sleeps in your bed tonight."

"Well, we'll be parting with him tomorrow, all being well," said Alys. She patted Joanie's arm.

Sir George turned to her. "I must introduce my friend, Sir Cuthbert Westford. He holds lands in the north, near my own. We fought together some years ago in France." Sir George presented Alys to Sir Cuthbert.

Sir Cuthbert bowed. "Mistress Merton. The pleasure of meeting such a companion at this moment is something I can only say is Fortune smiling on me yet again."

"You're too kind, Sir Cuthbert," said Alys. "I would say that Fortune favoured you in reuniting with Sir George in a place far from both your homes."

"Indeed, you're right on that point," said Sir Cuthbert. "Fortune is smiling doubly, then, Mistress."

"Join us here, if you will, Cuthbert, and tell us what brings you to Paris." asked Sir George.

"I will and thank you," said Sir Cuthbert.

He slid another stool over to the table and sat on it, ignoring Joanie entirely. Joanie gave him a careful look while Sir George called for more wine.

"I'm not on pilgrimage like you, George," said Sir Cuthbert.

"No, I can see that," said Sir George. "I can only imagine that you're still plying your sword somewhere."

Sir Cuthbert nodded. "For the King of Hungary. Though it didn't end well."

"You were at Varna?" asked Sir George. "But our King didn't fight, why would you offer your sword?"

Sir Cuthbert shrugged and gave a grim smile. "Needs must, George. Not all of us are lucky enough to have lands that yield profit. I offered my sword and was lucky to escape with my life. The Turks weren't merciful. But I'll spare you the details." He gave Alys a warm smile. "It's not something I would share in such lovely company." He took the newly refreshed flagon and poured wine into the goblet provided. "And there are so many better things to do than remember unpleasant battles."

He raised the goblet to his lips and drank, staring at Alys. She found herself blushing under the scrutiny of the dark magnetic eyes and touched her headcloth once again. He lowered his goblet and gave her a slow smile.

"Mistress Merton, George mentioned you're a widow. Surely one so young and beautiful cannot have been married for very long. Have you children?"

"We were married long enough, but alas, no children came of the marriage. My husband was a good and generous man and I am grieved at his parting."

"But young hearts recover from such losses," said Sir Cuthbert.

Sir George patted Alys' arm. "She has had companions to comfort her and the pilgrimage will do much to help with the loss too."

"It's true that these past weeks with my fellow pilgrims have done much to keep me distracted from my grief," said Alys.

Sir Cuthbert looked around. "And where are your fellow pilgrims now?"

Alys explained the situation. "I hope to contact my husband's relations first thing tomorrow to let them know I've arrived." She signalled to Joanie and rose. "And for that reason, I must take leave of you both and wish you goodnight. There is much to do tomorrow."

Sir George rose. "I'll see you to your room."

Alys shook her head. "That won't be necessary. Joanie will be with me and the woman and her daughter I'm sharing with are harmless enough."

Sir George looked disappointed but Sir Cuthbert only nodded and offered a pleasant farewell. "I hope I may see you then, tomorrow," he said.

Alys gave a sigh of relief when she reached the room. Climbing the stairs had made it clear that the wine had gone to her head more than she'd thought. It was only Joanie's steadying hand that had kept her from tripping.

The room was empty. It was small, and the idea of a mother and daughter sharing it had seemed laughable, but not completely out of the question, given the past few days where cramped beds found her next to an overly large women one night and numerous giggly young girls another night. It was also not entirely out of the question that a mother and her daughter might present themselves, but given the late hour, she felt it unlikely.

"Aw, Alys," said Joanie. "I 'ope you know what you're doing. And I 'ope this man of yours is better behaved than those two down below."

"Sir George has been fine," said Alys. "There's nothing in his behaviour to complain about."

Joanie snorted. "Aye, and I'm the Queen of England."

Alys frowned. "Well, first thing tomorrow I want you to go to the university and see if anyone knows where Barnabas lives. I'll write it down for you to show them."

"The university? 'Ow can I do that? You knows I don't 'ave much of them French words. Not enough to go asking after someone, leastways."

"No, I suppose not. I'll have to do it then. I'll wear your clothes. That should be safe enough." Alys bit her lip. She would do this. She'd been a servant. She knew how to act, knew the risks. What harm could happen if she pretended to be one again? Especially if it could bring her to Barnabas.

CHAPTER NINE
Paris, Late Spring 1445
ALYS

A lys scurried along the narrow lanes past the shops, churches, and homes that made up the section of Paris that contained the university. Her clogs were slippery in the mud and partial cobbles, and it made her feet sore. She wasn't used to wearing clogs in bare feet anymore, she realised. And certainly not at a near run. Her haste was instinctive and not just because she'd left Joanie behind to mind the chest and ward off any questions Sir George might have. No, there was something more hurrying her along and she didn't quite know what it was, but it fed a kind of panic inside of her.

She spied a gawky youth in the dark gown and hat that marked him for a scholar.

"*Excusez-moi*, monsieur," she said. "You are a scholar, *ne c'est pas*? My mistress has asked me to find a particular man who is a scholar such as you. Would you perhaps know him?"

The young man stopped and gave her a speculative look. Her hair had escaped from her cap long ago and a large tendril hung down along her face. She blew it aside with her mouth.

"I might, my fair maid. But will I do, instead? If not for your mistress, for you?"

Alys gave a pretty sigh and shook her head sadly. "Alas, I'm afraid my mistress seeks a young man named Giacomo Bonavillagio and she would be very cross if I brought anyone for me."

"I'm sorry, I don't know the name. I've only just come here." He leaned closer to her. "But maybe, if you were willing to give me a kiss, I might take you to someone who would know."

She forced a smile. "A kiss, only. But only after you take me to this person."

His face lit up and he grabbed up her hand. "It won't take long. I've just left his rooms. He's one of the tutors."

He dragged her along the streets and into a passage way that for a moment left Alys wondering if it was all just a ruse to get her into some dark place where he could take all the liberty he wanted, without any interference. But a moment later he stopped in front of a scarred wooden door and raised his hand to knock. He turned and looked at her.

"The kiss?" he asked. He licked his lips and leaned once more towards her.

Resigned, she accepted his mouth on hers and endured for a moment the wet tongue that thrust itself in her mouth. She pulled back.

"Enough. You've had the kiss. That was our bargain."

Disappointment filled his face for a moment and then he shrugged. He knocked on the door and waited. An older man, his hair skimming his shoulders, answered. He wore a black robe down to his ankles and his eyes looked worn and tired.

"Yes, Henri? What is it now?"

"So sorry to bother you once again, monsieur, but this young woman is asking about one of the pupils at the university and I thought you might know him."

The man looked at Alys quizzically. He eyed her gown, cap, and bare legs.

"I've come on behalf of my mistress, monsieur. She is inquiring after a young man named Giacomo Bonovillagio."

"Giacomo? You want to know about him?"

"You know him, monsieur?" asked Alys, her heart giving a leap.

"I know him, of course. I wasn't his tutor in any formal way, he had his companion, that blackamoor, for that. He attended my lectures on many occasions, though. There was much to like about him." He frowned. "And some things not to like. Always at the centre of any little joke."

"Please, monsieur, can you tell me where I might find him?"

He gave her a puzzled look for a moment. "Find him? Didn't I say? He's gone. Left Paris a month or so ago."

Alys' heart stopped and for a moment she could find no words. "Do you know where he went?" she whispered finally.

The man thought for a moment. "I think it was said he was going to Bruges. Or was it Venice?" He frowned. "It was Venice, now that I think of it. He and his companion were in Bruges but they came back briefly before travelling on to Venice. Shame, really. Giacomo would have made a great scholar. He has a head for it. More than just the numbers his father wanted him to study. I'm not sure he'd make a good merchant, though. Too much mischief in him."

Alys heard the remainder of his words only distantly. Her mind raced and she fought back the tears. Venice. He was in Venice. What was she to make of that? She wanted to wail with frustration. She'd come so close.

∽

"We must return home, then," said Joanie.

Alys had finally managed to make her way back to the inn and the room where Joanie sat waiting for her impatiently.

"Home?" said Alys. "What home is that?"

"La Pleasaunce. I'm certain you could get a place there again. Duke Humphrey has a soft spot for you."

Could she return there, take up her place among the other servants? "I think I'll go on to Venice," she said after a little while.

"Are you mad? What do you know of Venice, or their lingo? And 'ow will you know where to find this man, Giacomo, or whatever he calls 'imself?"

She knew Joanie was right. And truth be told she was terrified of the thought of journeying to this place with no idea what it was like, or if her French or the little Latin she did know would be enough. Or how to find Barnabas. But would it be that difficult to find Barnabas? As the tutor had pointed out Barnabas was at the centre of any mischief. She had only to inquire, surely. Venice couldn't be so very big of a place.

"No, I understand your concerns, Joanie, but I'm determined to go. If you wish, though, you can travel back to London. I'll ensure you have enough for the journey and try and hire someone to accompany you if you wish."

Joanie stared at her. "If you thinks I would abandon you now, after all we've been through, you're madder than I thought. I'm going nowhere, Alys. Besides, you need someone to keep an eye on you and make sure you don't do even dafter things."

Tears pricked Alys' eyes at Joanie's words. She leaned forward and gave her a big hug. "Thank you, dear friend. I shall always be grateful for all that you've done for me."

Joanie hugged her hard and then pulled away. "I suppose I 'ave some packing to do while you do some explaining."

Alys gave her a puzzled look and then she remembered Sir George. She frowned. What would she do about Sir George?

∼

"It certainly is a shock to find that they'd left Paris," said Alys. She'd hastily cobbled together an explanation when she arrived downstairs dressed in her own gown and found Sir George waiting for her, Sir Cuthbert at his side.

"That is a pity," said Sir George. "Have you left word with the household?"

She shook her head. "The house is shut up."

Sir George patted her arm. "Never mind. You did what you could. Now we can journey on and join the others."

How could she say this? "But they've gone on to Venice, you see," was all she could manage in the end. Her head still was fogged with the earlier disappointment. "I must go after them."

"Venice? Why have they gone there? Are they embarking for the Holy Land? Are they on pilgrimage?" asked Sir George.

She gave a small smile of relief. She could nearly hug him for providing the reason. "Yes. It seems they were moved to go. Perhaps they heard of my husband's death and wanted to atone for the quarrel they'd had."

Sir George shook his head. "I don't like it. Why must you go to Venice after them?"

"If they are going to the Holy Land on pilgrimage, then I would like to accompany them. I can join them in Venice."

"You shouldn't feel that compulsion, my dear," said Sir Cuthbert.

Alys looked at him. Unlike Sir George, whose eyes were full of alarm and concern, his were calmly assessing. Did he believe her? She gave him a warm smile.

"Thank you for your concern, Sir Cuthbert. I know you must think me a foolish woman, but really, I'm here on pilgrimage already, now I've only changed my destination slightly."

"True enough, mistress, but the new destination you've selected may not be the safest place in which to make a pilgrimage at this moment."

"This is about my husband's soul, and my own," said Alys. "If I was concerned with safety, I would have stayed home."

Sir Cuthbert laughed, but Sir George frowned.

"Let me take you to join the group again. We can go to Venice and see you safely there." His face lightened. "Perhaps we can convince some of the others to go on to Jerusalem instead."

Alys took a deep breath and gave him a grateful look. "As much as it might be appealing to travel in the company of the group again, I think, if I hope to join my husband's relations before they embark at Venice, I fear I must make greater speed than the group would achieve."

"I cannot allow you to journey on your own," said Sir George.

"I won't be on my own. I'll have my servant with me."

"But that's not sufficient protection," said Sir George in a kind, firm voice. "There are to be no arguments about it. I'll take you to the group and you'll journey with them."

"Perhaps I might offer a solution," said Sir Cuthbert. "At present I have no commitments. I'd be happy to escort Mistress Merton to Venice, or as far as she wishes."

Sir George frowned a moment and gave Sir Cuthbert a considering look. "I don't know."

"That's very kind of you, but unnecessary, Sir Cuthbert. I assure both of you I am fine travelling with my servant."

"No, that isn't sufficient and I can't permit it," said Sir George. "Either you allow me to take you to rejoin the group and on to Venice, or Sir Cuthbert accompanies you to Venice."

Alys pursed her lips briefly, frustrated by Sir George's stubbornness. Who would be the better choice to eventually slip away from or convince to leave her before she reached Venice?

"Thank you, Sir Cuthbert. I accept your offer."

Alys gave her horse another reassuring pat. It was the third time in less than an hour that the horse had tried to shy. Now it pranced distractedly along the road. The day before, the horse had behaved as it always had, a little frisky and nervous, but nothing Alys couldn't handle.

"I think there's a problem with the horse," said Alys to Sir Cuthbert. "Perhaps we should dismount and examine her. There might be a stone lodged in her shoe, or something else."

Sir Cuthbert gave her an easy look. "Of course."

He swung down from his own horse, a tired-looking animal that was nothing like the large battle worthy horse she'd expected from a soldier. But it had stamina, she could see that. Like Sir Cuthbert. In the days and nights that they had been on the road she'd found Sir Cuthbert something of a puzzle. He behaved well, except for a few harmless flirtatious comments. His manner though, veered between the rough soldier she expected, and a very polished courtier's.

He lifted her down from the awkward side saddle that he'd found for her. He turned to Joanie and offered her a hand. She'd ridden behind, her skirts spread along the back of the horse. Alys hated the side saddle and wished for the security of riding astride, but Sir Cuthbert had explained that this was a saddle used on the continent that allowed ladies to preserve their dignity.

She straightened her skirts and gave Joanie a tight smile while Sir Cuthbert deftly lifted up each hoof of the horse and examined it.

"You look tired, mistress. Are you feeling well?" asked Joanie.

"I'm fine, Joanie. I didn't sleep very much last night."

"I knows that, mistress. I could feel you tossing in the bed." She slipped her hand into Alys' for a moment and gave it a comforting squeeze.

"I can see nothing," said Sir Cuthbert, lowering the last hoof of the horse. "The horse is fine. She probably has scented a wolf or some other animal and it's made her skittish."

Alys nodded and hoped that the wolf was now on his way somewhere else. She accepted Sir Cuthbert's help to mount the horse and felt better when Joanie's comforting arms were around her waist once again. Sir Cuthbert climbed on his horse and took up its reins and the reins of the horse that carried her chest. He urged the animals forward. She followed on behind him.

They proceeded in silence for some time. Alys could sense that her horse still wasn't happy. It pranced and circled a few times and it was all Alys could do to bring it back in line. Sir Cuthbert rode on, oblivious to her struggles, his own horse behaving well. Alys frowned and tried to urge her horse on to a quicker pace to come abreast of Sir Cuthbert. Instead of complying, the horse rose up with a cry and Alys tumbled from the saddle, landed on the ground with a heavy thump, and hit her head.

CHAPTER TEN
Venice, Summer 1445
BARNABAS

Alessandra twirled slowly once more, the kermes silken gown floating out like the undulating motion of the sea. The red cloth shimmered in the candlelight and illuminated her ivory skin, so striking in contrast to the dark hair that cascaded down her back. Her heavy musk perfume hung in the air and clung to the cushions that were scattered on the chairs and benches that filled her *sala*.

"What do you think, Giacomo?"

Who could help but admire the vision that stood there in front of me? And any full-bloodied male couldn't help but notice the full breasts that threatened to spill out of the low-cut bodice.

"No one could set off such cloth so well, but you with your luscious beauty," I said.

My own reaction was fairly evident and it wasn't the cloth that was at the heart of it. I eyed her slowly, noting every detail of her body. Her long fingers, so graceful on the lute, were a source of pleasure in other ways that I only experienced on rare occasions. Her lips, which shaped words that told tales and poetry of the highest order, could send a man places he wished to remain forever. It mattered not to me that in the harsh light of day those lips and fingers showed lines that hinted at the age her skilfully dyed hair and tinted brows belied. She was a jewel of a woman.

Alessandra glanced down at my groin and noticed my reaction. I made no effort to hide it, hoping against hope that she might take pity on me and ply her skills without payment. She threw back her head and gave a long tinkling laugh.

"Why Giacomo, I think I can take your compliments as truth." She gave a sly smile. "At least as far as my attractions go. Would you prefer some personal recompense for the cloth instead of the sum we agreed upon?"

I tore my eyes away from her generous proportions and tried to think with the head on my shoulders instead of the other one that was struggling for control.

"No, we'll keep to our original agreement."

It was a hefty sum and I couldn't afford to let that go. It would more than pay for the goods I'd arranged to have come from Paolo and Luigi. They had been happy to supply me with more cloth, in return for the spices, oils, and dyes I had sent them, purchased through Alessandra with my own money.

She frowned for a moment and sighed. "Just as well, *mi amore*. That is the way a good businessman should be. Though I must say, I would have preferred it much more if you had chosen to take my offer."

I laughed. "I have no doubt of that, *bella madonna*, since you would not only have the cloth without paying anything, but also have the pleasure of my body in addition. There is no loss on your part."

She blew me a kiss. "You can get more of this cloth? And other cloth? As much as I might want?"

I gave her a nod full of confidence I didn't feel. I knew I could supply her with cloth, but the special kermes silk was another thing. That might be difficult since the bolt of cloth that I'd given her for the gown had been a special gift from a grateful woman back in Bruges.

She came over to me and sat on my lap, folding her arms around my neck. Her perfume filled my nose. She kissed me lightly on the head.

"Luigi Bembo remarked on this gown when I wore it last night."

I feigned a hurt look. "You mean I wasn't the first to see how it sets off your glorious beauty?"

Her eyes twinkled. "Ah, he was the only one to see it before you. So you see, you are still special to me. He paid to see it, whereas you did not."

"Oh, I think I've paid," I said. I thought of the card games we'd played with others and how the few times when I did win, my money seemed to find its way into her purse and me in her bed.

"Do not pout, my dear friend," said Alessandra. "You will be repaid in full for any losses you may think you've incurred. My dear Luigi asked if I could get more of this type of cloth for him, he admired it so much. You will be well paid for that, I assure you."

I blinked at her words. Luigi Bembo was one of the most prominent men in Venice. A member of the collegio's inner council and a distant relation of the present Doge, Foscari. This was an important connection indeed.

"Would he like me to call upon him?"

She tilted her head. "I think that wouldn't be wise, don't you agree? There are many…complications with that approach. Leave it to me. I will make the arrangements."

I nodded. I had no choice really, but to trust Alessandra. For the most part, I didn't doubt her. She'd been so helpful in making suggestions on how to expand my dealings and so far had asked nothing in return. Well nothing much.

"I should go soon. Niccolo is expecting me."

"You won't stay? Niccolo's uncle, Valentino, is coming with a few friends. Perhaps he could come as well."

I smiled at her and gently pushed her off my lap. "I'm afraid our purses aren't as full as Niccolo's uncle, or his friends."

"I'm sure Niccolo could persuade his father to give him an advance on his allowance."

"That might do for Niccolo, but I have no rich father or uncle to fund my extravagances."

"What about that Arab who is your companion? Wouldn't he give you some money?"

"My companion isn't Arab. Well, not really."

"But his name is Arab, is it not?"

I thought about how to explain al Qali. I knew little, really. He came from somewhere in Africa. I'd observed no affinity for any religion, which surprised me. Other than that, I knew nothing of his family, background or place of birth. Any questions I'd had in the beginning of our acquaintance he'd dismissed one way or the other. I'd stopped long ago on such a fruitless pursuit and now I no longer thought about it.

"Master al Qali would strongly disapprove of my attendance at your intimate gatherings, Alessandra." Of that much I was certain.

"But how can he judge unless he attends one?"

I grinned. "I think he would probably imagine accurately enough what they're like. But in any case, he's still away." I had begun to wonder at his absence. He'd been gone at least two months with only one letter and that had said he'd found something of interest enough to detain him further.

"All the more reason to come tonight."

I sighed. "You know I'd love nothing more than to be at your side, Alessandra."

Her expression softened. "Then come. We'll play cards and you will be my partner and we'll win so much that you will have no need to think of payment."

I looked again at her body. Her neck and shoulders were bared so that there was little enough of her breasts to leave to the imagination. I sighed and nodded. How could I help but agree? She smiled and came to me, folded her arms around me for a brief moment and I applied my lips to her breasts.

~

Men draped themselves languidly along chairs and benches. A few stood near the open windows, trying to catch any stray breeze that might waft in. Lucia weaved in among the men offering drink and food. Alessandra sat in the centre of the room, a lute on her lap, her fingers poised delicately above the strings before she strummed the final phrase of the music. All eyes were fixed on her.

Niccolo sat beside me, his eyes fixed not on her hands but a little further up her body. His face was red and sweat beaded his upper lip, even though his doublet was open against the heat of the room. Niccolo's heat was evident, no matter that he crossed his legs in a nonchalant manner.

Alessandra's scent hung in the air and mingled with the expensive perfumes of the men who filled the room. I noted among them was Luigi Bembo, whose lazy smile had shifted little during the performance. He glanced at me briefly and gave me a nod. Alessandra had introduced us earlier, before the card game, and had spoken of the cloth. There was no formal transaction, but enough had been said to give me hope of even more trade than I expected. More than the casual, backhanded methods I'd employed in Bruges and Paris. Would I dare apply to establish a small trading house on my own? But I had to remember I wasn't a patrician of a known merchant family. I would be useful only as a tool. A profitable tool, though. Whose contacts were Genoese supplying a Venetian merchant family. How long before I'd be found out was anyone's guess. No, I was still backhanded in my trade, but at least the amusing twists were still present.

The music ended. Niccolo's uncle clapped and complimented Alessandra's playing. Alessandra gave a gracious smile.

"Gentleman all, you have been such good company tonight. The poetry, the song, have flowed from wellsprings of inspiration, most assuredly. You're all to be commended. My own little talents are nothing in the sun of your gifts."

"The lady is too modest. Your gifts are legendary, Alessandra," said Luigi.

"Oh, no. I'm too young to be a legend, surely," said Alessandra.

The men laughed.

Niccolo rose. "If you aren't a legend, you should be. You're too beautiful to be anything but a legend."

Alessandra looked at him and smiled. "Such fine words from a fine youth."

"When I've made my fortune, you'll be the only woman I will choose," said Niccolo.

Alessandra gave her tinkling laugh. "I'm sure your future wife might have something to say about that."

The others joined her laughter and Niccolo reddened even further. Alessandra came over to him and kissed him briefly on the mouth.

"A kiss for such gallant words, a reward that no one could dispute."

Niccolo's face lit up and for a moment I envied him.

"Now everyone, I fear the hour is late and I must retire to my bed."

The men rose from the seats, Niccolo's uncle suppressing a yawn. He cuffed Niccolo and drew him towards the door. The other men followed suit, but I lingered behind, thinking of her earlier words.

"A word, Giacomo, before you go," said Alessandra.

I nodded and remained by my chair, Niccolo casting me an envious glance as he vanished through the door with his uncle. Bembo and the other men left a moment later. The door shut and the maid set about clearing up the beautifully wrought wine glasses and plates.

"Leave that, Lucia. It can wait until morning."

The servant nodded, curtseyed, and left the room. Alessandra turned to me, reached for my hand and brought it to her mouth, kissing my fingers.

"A good night, tonight, no?"

"A very good one for you. Your winnings alone could provide you with a dozen more of those wine glasses you prize."

"They are beautiful, aren't they?" She picked one up, twirled it in her hand and set it down. She smiled again and put a hand to my face. "Did I not tell you I would see to it the night would be profitable? Normally I would allow some winnings for my poor friends who can afford only to visit on occasion, but tonight I chose to favour you. I hope you are appreciative."

I could only laugh. "Somehow I think you're the one who is profiting above all. But I assure you, tonight, I don't mind."

I leaned down and kissed her, something I'd wanted to do all night. Her lips parted and I drew her close to me. I slipped my hands around her back and worked at her laces. She pulled away.

"Not so quickly, or so urgently. Remember, this gown is expensive."

"Who better than I would remember?" I said.

She took my hand again. "Come, we'll go to my bedchamber. I'll remove the gown there slowly, with the ceremony befitting its splendour."

We spoke few words as she drew me across the marble-lined corridor to her bedchamber. Candles had been lit and enhanced the richness of the velvet drapes and brocades that adorned the windows and bed. Above the bed hung a painting of two cherubs whose puckered mouths and generous limbs seemed filled with as much lust as I possessed.

I lay back on the bed as instructed. Alessandra stood before me and slowly removed the gold and pearl encrusted netting that encased her hair. There were no false pieces braided and inserted among her hair to give it more fullness. Every thick lock and braid was hers. Carefully, she loosened each strand, her eyes fixed on me and full of desire. When she'd finished, she shook her hair free and it fell along her back. She lifted up its bulk and turned.

"Now you can untie the laces. But have a care."

I worked at the laces, my fingers trembling a little. When I was done, I pulled her towards me and inserted my hand inside her bodice, cupping her left breast. She groaned and I rubbed lightly, in the manner I knew she liked. She gave a little gasp and pulled away.

"The gown," she said in a hoarse whisper. "Let me remove the gown." She slid the dress off her shoulders, halting a moment, all her breasts and skimpy chemise exposed, while she unfastened a lock of hair that had caught up in her gown. It was an action that in itself that held its own measure of eroticism. She stepped out of the dress and I took it from her, tossing it onto a chair. Enough care had been taken.

I don't remember when or how we found our way to the bed, but it was a good while later. The candles still burned, providing light enough to cast sensuous shadows on her skin so that there was nothing but for me to find new ways to delight her once again.

Exhausted, we both fell into a sleep afterwards. I knew nothing of my dreams until a wailing song wended its way into them. It took me some time to realise that it wasn't in my dreams and I roused myself and looked around. A draught blew in from the open window. Alessandra was leaning against the railing, the curtain wrapped around her, her hair hanging free. She was laughing and shouting to someone below.

"It is late. Go home to your bed," she said to someone below.

A muffled voice came up from the water. Niccolo?

"There is time enough for that in the morning. I must get my rest. Go, I say." She blew a kiss. More muffled words that receded gradually. She shook her head and turned to me.

"Such a silly young man. But so endearing."

"Niccolo?"

She nodded. "It is his first *amore*. He must be treated tenderly."

"But I'm a youth, am I not to be treated tenderly?"

She laughed at me, the curtain still clutched becomingly around her, leaving her legs and shoulders bare. The candles in the candelabra on the nearby table burned still and illuminated her body so that it glowed. "I am certainly not your first *amore*. Besides, do I not treat you tenderly already?"

I grinned. "Oh there is no doubt that at the moment I'm feeling tender enough from your treatment."

She giggled and leaned back against the window frame. A gust of wind blew in and the candelabra on the nearby table toppled over and fell against the curtain. The curtain caught fire, its silver thread feeding the flames heat and strength. Alessandra stood paralysed as the flames engulfed her and set her hair alight. She opened her mouth to scream but no sound came out.

Horrified, I jumped out of bed, tripping over the dress that hung from the back of the chair onto the floor. I cursed as I hit the floor and quickly got up again, heading towards Alessandra. I grabbed the bowl that earlier I had used to relieve myself and tossed it on her, the only liquid to hand. I snatched at the other window curtain, threw it over Alessandra and pulled her down on the floor, wrapping her up in the cloth. After a few moments, the flames were out, smothered by the cloth. I patted out a few stray cinders before turning to a groaning Alessandra.

Carefully, I peeled back the layers of cloth. Even as I removed the first layer I could see she was badly burned in places. Pieces of the curtain fabric adhered to sections of her skin and in other sections the skin was livid, angry, and blistering. I tried to remove parts of the cloth that came away easily. She opened her eyes and looked at me. Her face was wracked with pain.

She moaned. "Oh, Giacomo," she whispered. "It's bad, isn't it?"

I hushed her. "Don't try to speak. I'll call Lucia and she'll help me get you comfortable. Then we'll get the doctor to attend you."

She moaned again. "I'm finished, I know. My body, my looks, they are ruined."

"It's fine. You'll be fine," I said, though I knew it was a lie.

She closed her eyes and a tear slipped down her face. "You're a very bad liar, Giacomo. But I love you nonetheless for it."

"Say nothing more. Don't move. I'll get Lucia to go for help."

I dressed quickly, found Lucia and sent her for the doctor. On my return I managed to get Alessandra on the bed, though the pain I knew from moving her was terrible. I covered her gently with a sheet and dressed quickly in my own clothes. I fetched a bowl of water and cloth from the kitchen and began bathing Alessandra's face and hands as best I could. I didn't dare try to do more than that, for fear of doing further harm. Large angry weals bubbled along one side of her face and by her ear the skin was nearly black. Her arms and hands were just as bad.

When the doctor came and tended to her he made little pretence at any hope of an unscarred recovery. "She'll live," said the doctor, his voice grim. "And perhaps thank God and you that her life was spared. Or perhaps not. She'll never again be the beauty that was her fame. Such a shame."

He gave me instructions for her care and I relayed them to Lucia. It would be a long a gruelling recovery, that was clear. Later, before taking my leave, I went to look at her, sleeping heavily under the effects of an opiate. The remains of her hair, clipped close to her head by the doctor to better tend the burns on her scalp, looked like a distraught crow's. Her lips, once so full and inviting, were dry and chapped. The rest of her face I couldn't make out under the dressings and salves the doctor had applied.

Sadly, Alessandra had voiced the truth of her future as a courtesan. That was the reality, though there was nothing fair about it. But I would still come, regardless of her appearance. I wasn't Venice, though. I wasn't the power and influence that ran this city and put Murano glasses on her table. I glanced over at the gown that not so long ago had adorned a legendary beauty. Would she still want to wear it? Somehow I doubted it. Nor would she want the other bolts of cloth she'd insisted he get for her.

I sighed. Well for one night at least, I'd felt like a success. A success apart from any of the ambitions Mustapha al Qali might have for me.

CHAPTER ELEVEN
Venice, Summer 1445
BARNABAS

I opened the door quietly, so as not to wake anyone in the house, and was greeted by a figure coming down the stairs into the narrow *loggia*. My heart sank.

"So, I hope seeing you up at this hour of the morning means you have been already out and about working on the tasks I set for you."

I eyed al Qali blearily. He was back and with no word of warning. This was an encounter I would give anything to avoid just now, but I knew he would take none of my evasions.

"It's been a long night," I said in weary tone. "I'm sorry, I'm fit only for my bed. I promise I will tell you everything after some rest."

"I can see you are tired from your nocturnal efforts, but I'm afraid I must insist that you tell me about all your activities since I left."

With a resigned nod I followed him up the stairs to our small *sala*, hoping that at least I might request some food from a servant before I began my explanations. But I was disappointed.

In the *sala* he turned to me expectantly. "Well?"

"But don't you have news?" I asked.

"It can wait. What have you been doing, or more to the point, what have you accomplished while I was away?"

I paused a moment, wondering how best to phrase my words. "I've been active among my contacts and working to make more."

"Contacts?"

"Patricians. And those who know them. Some of great influence, like Luigi Bembo."

"Good. Good. And have you discovered anything?"

I glanced at al Qali, his face intent and alert. I let a small sigh escape before I spoke. "An old manuscript came into Venice, recently."

"When?" Al Qali's voice was curt.

"About ten days ago."

"And?"

"It's foreign, Arabic, I think, but I'm not certain. It was sold for more than 500 ducats."

Al Qali raised his brow. "That's not so very much in these times."

I'd been surprised when I heard the sum mentioned during the party last night. An event that seemed to have taken place ages ago, rather than only a few hours.

"Who bought this manuscript? Tell me more."

"A Venetian. That's all I know."

Al Qali frowned. "It is probably nothing. Anything else?"

I shrugged and shook my head. "And you? You mentioned something of interest in your last letter."

Al Qali waved his hand. "Nothing so much, only that there are many manuscripts now in the new universities eager to establish libraries. We must establish contacts there and keep apprised of any new books and manuscripts they add. One was promising at Padua, but it had been sent on to another university, I don't know which."

"Is there some way you can find out?" I asked.

He tilted his head and gave me a direct look. It was a look that made me go cold.

"Interesting you should ask, Giacomo, since you are the very one who can help me with this."

I turned away. It had been months, now, since I'd last looked into the showstone. So much time had passed that I could almost convince myself that it was done. That part of my life was over. It was a foolish idea and the set of his face and dark cold look in his eyes told me there was no hope I could refuse to do it.

He moved over to the cabinet against the wall and withdrew the familiar box from it. He placed it on the table in the middle of the room.

"You would have me do this now? Can't it wait until later? I've had little rest, for reasons that are complicated, and frankly, all I think I can manage now is to make my way to my bed." It was a feeble excuse, but I had to try.

"There is no better time. And with your mind drowsy and uncluttered by daily worries you will have a better chance of a good result."

I gave him a sceptical look and took a place at the table. He opened the box and removed the showstone, placing it on a velvet cloth tucked in the box. There was no other ritual, he knew that I needed none. I frowned, took a deep breath and tried to clear my mind. A moment later I looked up at him.

"Since the matter pertains so closely to you, it would be best if you sat and placed your fingers on the showstone," I said.

He gave me a quizzical look, uncertain if I was speaking the truth. I wasn't sure myself, but felt I would need every bit of extra help. I recalled the Duchess placing her hands on the showstone and hoped that such a move wouldn't yield something dangerous.

Al Qali gave his assent, took a chair and placed his hands on the showstone carefully, the long brown fingers nearly spanning the orb. I looked past them, into the stone, and studied its various prisms. I looked for a good while and there was nothing. Had I lost the ability? I almost felt triumphant at the thought.

Just as I was about to lift my head and shake it, my mind shifted and the sounds of water boats outside the window faded and it was only my breath I could hear. The milky colour of its centre slowly dissolved and images began to form. Rolling waves in an endless seascape appeared and finally, in the distance, a ship. I tried to make out the type of craft and saw it was a galley, one heavily laden with goods, by the way it sat low in the water. I blinked and the image cleared. I muttered a curse, because I'd had no chance to get close enough to the galley to see if I recognised anyone on board.

Another image appeared. It was a figure, but it was difficult to make out because I was nearly dazzled by the bright sun that appeared behind it. Eventually, I could make out a man with an intricately woven headcloth and jewels on his fingers. He was mounted and other mounted men surrounded him. A moment later, the image was gone. I waited, but nothing else appeared. With a sigh I looked up.

"Well?" said Al Qali. "What did you see? You did see something."

I nodded slowly, still trying to understand what kind of person the man who'd appeared was. His dress and manner were unfamiliar, like nothing I'd ever seen, though if my fears proved correct, I'd certainly heard tell of him and his people. I began slowly recounting the first image and then the second only in general terms at first, delaying the moment of confirmation.

"Tell me about the headcloth," said al Qali when I told him of it.

I described it as carefully as I could and at his insistence told him in detail about the rest of his clothes, the rings and even the horse he was mounted on. Al Qali grew agitated as I spoke, which made me even more uneasy. He quizzed me further on specific aspects of the vision and I did my best to answer.

Al Qali gave the table a short thump. "It cannot be. After all this time."

"What is it?" I asked.

He turned and stared at me for a moment. "Nothing." With a visible effort he rose from the table. "You are free to go your bed, now."

He left the room and I heard him go to his own bedroom. I sighed, puzzled at his reaction and what it would mean for us. I didn't have to wait very long. That evening, after I had my own rest and sat at the table copying a manuscript, he appeared, his expression calm.

"You must pack. We are going on a journey," he said. "I will make the arrangements in the coming weeks with one of the trading vessels."

I looked at him apprehensively. "Trading vessels? Where are we going?"

He gave me a studied look. "East. To a land you have never been to before. A land very different from what you've known. You will like it, though. There is much to learn there, many manuscripts of the kind you will have never seen before."

I paled. "East? To the land where headcloths are folded intricately?"

Al Qali gave me a broad smile which I remembered so well. "You will enjoy it, *amico mio*. So much to see. Was it not your wish to travel to far places?"

I gave him a weak smile. It had been my wish, I couldn't deny, but that had been years ago, before I'd known Mustapha al Qali.

∽

I stared out the window of the *sala*. The view, so much improved from the one from the small house al Qali and I inhabited, was obscured today by one of the thick fogs for which Venice was so famous. A fog as thick as the one clouding my own future, it seemed at this point. But it was here I'd come, to Alessandra's villa, in the hope that she might help ensure I had one bit of firm ground, one certainty that would keep me steady as I sailed away with al Qali to places unknown.

Part of me, if I was to be truthful, was a little excited at sailing on a ship again heading towards new and exciting destinations. It still held an appeal I couldn't explain. But to do such things in the company of al Qali, I knew, meant a journey that would have hidden secrets and objectives that wouldn't be revealed until later, if at all. It was just as well I took these steps here with Alessandra, though there was no guarantee she would be interested in my proposal, or even able to help me.

In the weeks since her accident I had called many times, only to be refused entry by her servant, Lucia, who'd given me sorrowful looks. I'd written as well, but I'd had no answer to my inquiries, not even a verbal message. I'd asked no one else about Alessandra's condition, since no one I knew had spoken a word of what had happened to her and I had no idea what explanation she would want to give everyone. I took care, then, to keep the knowledge to myself.

Now, with only a few days left before I was due to depart with al Qali, I had come again, imploring Lucia to explain my imminent departure. This time I'd not been turned away at the door, but escorted to the *sala*, to await her decision.

Anna entered her face full of smiles. "She will see you."

I nodded to her gratefully and gave a playful tweak to her headcloth as I was wont to do in the past.

"Be careful not to tire her," said Lucia.

I followed her through the door and across the marble hall to the door beyond. Lucia opened the door for me and I entered slowly, assembling a cheerful expression in anticipation of what I might see.

Alessandra was there in a chair near the window, but the curtains were half closed and she laid cast in shadow, away from the dreary light that filtered in. Though the weather was warm enough, she wore a dark, loose-fitting gown, with sleeves that hung past her hands. A dark veil covered her head, so thick that I could only see a vague outline of her features.

"Giacomo," she said. Her voice was slightly hoarse and there was little pleasure in it. "Come in. Lucia has provided a chair for you."

I responded to her formal air and avoided any of the greetings I might have made in the past. No sweeping bow over her hand and certainly not a light flirtatious kiss on the cheek. I gave her a slight nod and took the chair she indicated.

"I am glad to see you've recovered," I said, my voice neutral.

"Recovered?" There was a hint of bitterness in her voice. "I'm afraid I wouldn't go that far. I am here, possessed of all my limbs."

"And your sharp wit," I said in a soft voice.

She sighed. "Yes, my wit is still intact, though sometimes I wish it wasn't." She straightened a moment. "I haven't thanked you for your part in saving me."

"I wish I could have done more," I said. I wouldn't waste breath on telling her falsehoods. I'd seen the burns and knew her skin would never be as it was before. She understood that.

She waved her hand. "You did more than many would have, Giacomo. And the fact that I can count on your honesty instead of lies about my recovery is the only reason I allowed you in."

"Are you in pain?"

"What pain I have is distracted by other things."

"Yes. I can imagine. I'm sorry," I said. "What will you do?" She was too clever and accomplished to languish away in some small room, but what patron would sponsor her now?

"I don't think I have the temperament for religious life, though I'm sure the dear sisters would welcome my money and possessions. I'm considering various possibilities, but that isn't one."

I gave a small smile at the thought of Alessandra as a nun, under the supervision of an abbess, a situation Alessandra would find extremely irksome rather than secure and comforting. Though some religious women could wield much authority within the community,

Alessandra wouldn't tolerate anything less than total authority over her own will.

"I could search for a new, untrained courtesan and perhaps take her under my wing," she said. "For what I know many would give a hefty price. And if there was a particularly suitable girl," she shrugged, "who knows, she might earn me a fortune."

"She could never be what you are. Were." I paused. "It's for that reason I've come."

"You know of a suitable girl?"

I shook my head. "I know nothing of suitable girls. No, it's an entirely different proposition that I have for you." I'd come to ask a favour, but the favour had now blossomed into an idea.

She leaned forward for a moment in eagerness, but then forced herself back. "What is it?" The calm in her voice was an effort.

"Before, you had expressed interest in the kermes cloth and wished for more. I have contracted to have more of that cloth and other types to be sent here, along with a finely made clock and a few other items."

"Yes, alas. But I'm not certain I will need them, now. And you, I understand, are about to depart."

"Would you reconsider taking the cloth and the other items? Perhaps there is someone among your contacts and acquaintances who might be interested in purchasing them? You did mention Bembo."

"But would I have to buy them from you?"

I shook my head. "No. I propose that we do this together. I've paid for the goods already. Any profit you make we can split between us."

She gave a sigh. "That's very kind of you, but one transaction will hardly support all this." She waved her hand around.

"No, it won't," I said. "But if we establish a small merchant house, geared towards women like you, to provide fine things for their homes…"

"Ah. I see what's in your mind now." Her tone was brighter, hopeful. "Perhaps, this might work."

"I have contacts in Bruges. I could arrange to have regular shipments of goods. It will be a small enough enterprise, but one that should see us both independent of others."

"And perhaps we could send goods back to them?"

I considered this a moment. Would my friends be willing to sell goods I might send them? "It's possible," I said. "If they are exotic enough that they could act for their masters. I don't think they would risk selling goods privately on their own. In time we might arrange for a man of our own to sell them."

"Then, Giacomo, you must find the exotic on this journey of yours and send it to them."

I laughed. "I can make no guarantees."

"Where is it you go and when?"

I grimaced. Al Qali had still to tell me the exact place. All I knew is that we were going in a ship, heading east. And if my vision was anything to guide me, my guess is that it was among the Turks.

"Oh, my destination is exotic enough. We go in four days' time."

She nodded. "I'll have the papers drawn up immediately. I know a notary who will be glad to do this favour."

I nodded. "I'll be back in two days, then." I rose and bowed. "I'll take my leave, now though, for I know I've tired you."

"You haven't, Giacomo. You've given me life. And for that I will be forever grateful. But go, I have much to think about and things to do."

She extended her hand to me and I made my way over, leaned and kissed the gloved hand. At this distance I could see her face through the veil just enough to detect the livid skin only beginning to heal into scars. But her mouth was smiling and it was that which gave me cause to smile back.

"Goodbye, until I see you again."

I left, feeling a small sense of satisfaction that in solving my own problem I had in fact solved hers. If all went well I would have enough money on my return to leave al Qali and establish myself independent of him. And perhaps then I might consider the dream formed so long ago to go back to England and get Alys. It was possible she'd probably forgotten me, but I would chance it. I thought of the drawing of me she'd done and given me. I'd tucked it away in one of my few precious books. I hadn't looked at the drawing in a while. In some ways it reminded me too much of that innocent boy I'd been, a tool of the powerful. I was still a tool, only it was al Qali who used me now. I wanted to break from that. Perhaps I would be able to if the venture with Alessandra proved successful.

CHAPTER TWELVE
Mantua, Early Summer 1445
ALYS

Alys kept her eyes shut against the dull thud in her head and moaned. She could smell the dampness in the room, fusty and earthen, as if it had been there for many more years than she had been on this earth. Was she still on this earth, or had she died on the road and was now awaiting her time in purgatory?

A hand rested on her head. "Mistress?"

It was Joanie, her voice tentative. Alys opened her eyes carefully and saw two pairs of dark eyes staring at her. She blinked and realised that they were children, one seemingly a girl with her hair plaited and pinned to her head, and the other a boy with a scrape on his chin. Beside them was Joanie, a cloth in her hand. They were all in a small damp room, with only a small window for light and a small chair next to the cot where she lay.

"Mistress. You are awake." The joy in Joanie's voice was real.

Alys smiled weakly. "Yes. Where am I?"

"We're at a miller's house, not far from Mantua."

"A miller's house?" She tried to recall the events that might have brought her here, but the last thing she remembered was falling from her horse. "How did I come to be here? Did Sir Cuthbert bring me?"

Joanie gave a small snort and glanced at the small children. "No, Sir Cuthbert took leave of us outside of Paris, with Sir George. The fall must've made you confused about what 'appened. We left the two of them and went on. It was many, many days later, as we'd neared Mantua, that a wolf startled the 'orse and we both fell."

"Yes. I remember the fall," Alys said carefully. Clearly there was some reason that Joanie had to lie and it made her even more uneasy. "Did you manage to bring me here on your own?"

"We were lucky. I only suffered a few bruises and I was able to catch the horse. I tried to get you back on it, but I couldn't. It was then that the miller came upon us and offered 'elp. He brought us back here. I've been nursing you ever since."

"H-how long has that been?" Alys had no sense of the passage of time. She only knew that she was a little hungry.

"A few days."

"A few days?" She'd thought maybe a day at most. She tried to sit up in the bed and a searing pain in her leg seized her. She cried out.

"Careful, now," said Joanie. "You mustn't move just yet, you'll do more damage."

"Damage?" Suddenly she was conscious of the bandages around her left leg and the splints on either side.

"Your leg. You broke it. It's bad."

She grimaced at the pain that shot through her as she shifted slightly. "How bad?"

"It broke the skin. I did the best I could, but I don't know enough about them things and no one 'ere did either."

Alys saw the concern in Joanie's face. "You did your best, I'm sure."

"I 'ope my best is enough. But you must remain still and allow the bones to knit." Joanie looked at the two children and motioned them away. "*Mange*," she said and pointed to Alys.

The two children grinned and scampered out of the room.

Joanie sighed. "You can't imagine what it's like trying to manage around here. I don't have that lingo. Only a few words of the French you taught me."

"But why the lies about the wolf and Sir Cuthbert?" Alys whispered. "We were speaking in English."

"I don't trust any of 'em," said Joanie. "Especially now. That bastard Sir Cuthbert left us on the road for dead after putting a thistle under your saddle. 'E took off with our other horse and chest."

"The chest?" Alys' heart sank. She felt all her hopes slip away. "It had everything in it. All our money, the jewels—they're all gone?"

Joanie pursed her mouth. "Well, not everything. I hid a few coins and a jewel on me. Just to be safe, you might say."

"Oh, Joanie." Tears filled her eyes and she turned her head away for a moment, overcome. So much lost, but perhaps not everything. "What would I have done without you?" she said finally. "How can I ever repay you for your help?"

Joanie sniffed. "You don't owe me nothing, Alys."

A grey-haired woman with a severe expression appeared at the doorway carrying a small earthenware bowl and a wooden spoon. She spoke a few words that Alys couldn't understand that well, catching just a phrase or two that sounded similar to the French she knew. Alys tried a bit of French on her as she took the bowl from the woman, but the woman frowned and shook her head. Alys switched to Latin. The woman's brow furrowed in concentration, but she eventually she shook her head again. She held up her hand and then disappeared from the room.

"Where did she go?" asked Alys.

Joanie shrugged. "Damned if I knows. That woman is a sour old thing, so you can bet it won't be good."

Alys took a few sips of the broth. It was tasteless, but she supposed it was some nourishment. She was about to ask Joanie more about the woman when the woman appeared with a man in tow. He was no more than thirty, with dark curling hair and grey eyes. His doublet was undone and his shirt, though clean enough, was old and worn.

"I am glad to see you are recovering," said the man in Latin. He examined her carefully, taking in every detail of her face and then the rest of her body. She resisted the urge to pull the coverlet closer about her.

"Yes. I'm so thankful you can understand me so that you can thank your mother for me for her hospitality. And...,"she made a guess,...."your father for rescuing us?"

"My father is dead," said the man firmly. "It was I who came across you and your servant on the road."

"Then it's to you I must give my thanks directly. I-I would wish to pay you for your kind hospitality, but—"

"You have no need to explain and you owe us nothing. Your servant has told us the story already. I can only express my sympathy that you have met such an unfortunate accident while you are on pilgrimage." He nodded slightly and gave a slow smile.

"Thank you, sir. I'm deeply grateful."

"Please. Call me Jacopo. My mother is Julia, and my two children are Giuseppe and Carlotta." He came closer to the bed and took up her hand. "We are only too happy to help a woman in distress such as yourself."

"Mistress, I think it's time 'e left you to finish your broth so you can get more rest," said Joanie in English, moving towards her.

Alys withdrew her hand from his grasp and placed it back with the other around the bowl. She forced a smile. "My servant tells me I must take more nourishment and then rest."

Jacopo's eyes flickered a moment before he nodded. "Of course. We want you restored to full health. But you must remain here as long as it takes. Be assured of that."

He left and Joanie muttered under her breath.

"What was that?" asked Alys.

"I said, I don't doubt they want us to stay for as long as possible. Don't I do all the work, now?"

"What do you mean? Don't they have a servant?"

Joanie gave a dark laugh. "She might've been once, but she's too old now to do anything but stir a pot or sit by the fire. And the mother is twice as useless. Just dotes on her son, fussing over 'im and ordering me to get 'im things, like I was her servant, never mind that I don't speak her lingo. She makes it clear quick enough what she wants."

"Oh, Joanie. I'm sorry. I had no idea."

Joanie smiled at her and patted her arm. "Never you mind, Alys. Better that, than spending what little money we 'ave on paying those folk. Let them think we 'ave nothing and when it's time to go, we can leave with a clear conscious. We've paid them enough with my labour."

"How much do we have?" It was a question she was almost afraid to ask. Would it be enough for her to get to Venice and find Barnabas? And then what? She no longer had the money for them to use to start over. She forced these thoughts from her mind.

"Not much." Joanie told her the sum.

"And the jewel? Which jewel did you save?"

"The small one. Easy to 'ide, you see."

Alys nodded. "You were always better than me at thinking of all these things." With the jewel they would probably have enough to get to Venice, but there wouldn't be much to keep them after that. She would have to find work of some kind, if she couldn't find Barnabas right away. She wouldn't consider the possibility that he might not be there. She gave a deep sigh that nearly became a sob.

"You need to rest," said Joanie. "You'll feel better about things once you've 'ad some sleep, you'll see."

She took the bowl from Alys' hands and settled Alys back into the bed. Alys allowed Joanie to tuck her in and took comfort in this small action. There had been a lot to absorb. So much of her plans overturned once again. She needed her strength if she was to face the next stage of their journey, there was no doubt about that.

～～

The house was quiet. Joanie had gone with the others to see the pedlar in the village to try and find out directions for their journey. With an effort, Alys swung her left leg off the bed and tried to place it on the floor. This time she was able to keep it still while she swung the other leg over and placed it next to the left one. She reached for the crutch that leaned against the chair. She wanted to try this herself, without Joanie's cautioning words and restraining hand. She was determined to use the crutch as soon as possible and walk.

She pulled herself up with a groan and a sharp pain shot through her leg. It took her breath away. It was too soon, she knew, but perhaps once she was positioned on the crutch the pain would lessen enough that she could hobble. She paused a moment and the brief wave of dizziness passed. The reaction was most likely because she'd been abed days now and she wasn't used to being up. Her linen shift was clammy and in need of washing, as was the rest of her. Her russet hair hung limply down her back. She must ask Joanie to give her water for a proper wash when she returned.

"What's this, ho? Out of bed?"

Startled at Jacopo 's voice, Alys nearly lost her balance. He gripped her shoulder, steadying her. She muttered a thanks and attempted to move away from him with her crutch, but his hold was firm.

"I think it might be a bit too soon for that," he said. "Let me help you back to bed, instead."

Before she could protest he'd removed the crutch from under her left arm and tossed it against the wall. He scooped her up and laid her on top of the coverlet, his hands lingering a little too long at her waist. He gazed at her. She could see the flecks of green in his eyes and something else she didn't like. She bit her lip.

"Thank you. I think you're right. I should probably rest."

He cupped her chin and gave her a slow smile. "I agree you should be in bed. But perhaps not alone, heh?" He stroked her cheek with the back of his hand. "You are too young and much too beautiful to be a widow."

"What do you mean?" she asked. She tried to keep her voice firm. "I'm afraid I must ask you to leave now and let me rest. The others will be back soon."

He waved his hand. "Ah, the others. No, they will be too busy oohing and ahhing over the pedlar's goods. And his stories. Usually they don't return until dusk."

He sat down on the bed. "That leaves us plenty of time to get to know each other better."

His hand moved from her cheek along her neck and then her shoulders. She flinched and tried to pull away, but he held her firmly with the other hand. He leaned down to kiss her on the lips. She turned her face.

"Please, I assure you," he said. "There is no need for modesty. We're both experienced and are free to enjoy ourselves. And I promise, I intend to have you stay here as my wife. I only ask for a little sample of the goods ahead of time."

He gave her another lazy and confident smile while his hand slipped under her linen shift to rest on her thigh.

"After all," he said. "Though your clothes and manner show you come from a good family, you have no money. And pilgrimage is surely out of the question now that you're injured. I offer to take you on as my wife, instead. You will have the protection of my home and name."

She pulled his hand away and drew the coverlet along her body and up around her shoulders. "I'm flattered by your offer, but I'm afraid I can't consider it."

His eyes darkened. "Why? If you had any family, they would have arranged for you to be better chaperoned on this pilgrimage. Do you deny that?"

She pulled herself up straight. "I was on my way to my husband's family in Venice. I was to join them there for the rest of the pilgrimage."

He gave her a sceptical look and shook his head. "That's a good story to tell others. But I don't believe you." He pulled the coverlet away from her grip. "Give me a chance and I can show you just what you will gain by marrying me." He drew her to him and she tried to fight him off, but he grasped her wrists and held them in one hand.

There was a shout outside. He pulled away and cursed. The shout came again. His eyes darkened and he rose from the bed.

"I must go for now. But think about what I've said. You could do much worse than marry me and remain here."

He left the room and Alys closed her eyes a moment and took a deep breath. The man was a pig. She could no more contemplate marrying him than someone like Sir Cuthbert. She and Joanie would have to leave, bad leg or not. The question was how she would manage it.

∾

"This is folly," said Joanie. "You'll do more 'arm to your poor leg."

"I must take that risk. There's no other alternative."

Alys took another step and hop with the crutch and winced as the pain surged again. She forced herself to repeat the motion, over and over again until she reached the door of the small stone house that was beside the mill. Even with the door closed she could hear the race of the water and the creak of the wheel as it turned.

It had been three worrying days while she summoned up the strength and the courage to make this journey from the bed to the door and the horse beyond it. It was today or never, Alys knew. Today the family were in the village at mass. It was their only hope of leaving the house without any interference.

Joanie opened the front door for her. She could see their only remaining horse ready and saddled. How would she manage to mount, though?

It took some doing and with much help from Joanie. They placed a bench beside the horse and she managed to balance on her good leg while she hoisted the splinted one over the horse. She cried out in agony but continued to settle herself on the horse. It was awkward at best, but there was no help for it.

"Now you, Joanie."

"No, I think it best if I walk beside you, in case you should fall. At least until you get used to the riding."

Alys nodded through gritted teeth and urged the horse onwards. More pain soared through her as the horse started to move. How long would she last, she wondered? They made their way down the small lane that led away from the mill and the house while Joanie cast her anxious looks. The pain was terrible but she refused to give in. They would finish this journey to Venice, whatever it took.

She wouldn't allow them to stop after an hour when Joanie's worries at Alys' grey face made her suggest a rest. The second hour was no less grim, but the pain was familiar and the faintness passed. It was dusk before Alys gave in and Joanie found a farmer who was willing to put them up for the night. It was not before time, though. Alys felt near to fainting, and the nausea that gripped her didn't disappear after the eating a small chunk of bread and cheese the farmer's wife offered them. The farmer insisted she sleep in the only bed but she refused, preferring to sleep on the floor next to Joanie.

It was the next day that Alys realised how fortunate they were to have stopped there when the farmer said he would take them to Padua in his cart. From there they could take a barge the rest of the way to Venice. Payment was only a matter of selling the horse in Padua, something he could help them with. Even Joanie seemed to trust the man and was happy about the plan. Alys allowed herself to relax a little. Bouncing around in a wooden cart would be painful enough, but at least she could cushion herself against the worst of it and they would make faster progress. The night before, she'd worried that she wouldn't ever reach Venice, now it seemed within her grasp.

CHAPTER THIRTEEN
Venice, Summer 1445
ALYS

Alys sat back against the chair and closed her eyes for a moment. The stink of the canal wafted up and made her nearly gag with the stench of it. The summer months were upon the city now and with it the odours that revealed the city's lack of proper sewers. Most especially, here, in these humble quarters, so close to the Arsenale where Venice's poor lived.

The smell that once told her she'd reached her destination, now reminded her of the poverty of her situation. In the week since they'd arrived, their meagre funds had been eaten up dramatically. Venice, with homes crowded up against each other and bursting with people, was expensive. They'd been lucky to find this room. But she needed to find Barnabas quickly, or some means to earn money.

Joanie had offered to try and take in washing, but with few words of the Venetian dialect, and little enough to be earned, it remained for Alys to find a way to secure an income, if they didn't find Barnabas soon. She cursed her leg once again. Her lack of mobility had limited her ability to locate Barnabas. Joanie certainly couldn't go out and inquire after him. She'd resorted to writing messages that Joanie carried to give to those who might know where to find Barnabas. She'd not expected to find the city so large, and with little of the Italian language at her disposal she was forced to use her Latin and inquire at the churches. And there were so many of them. Too numerous for her to ask at all of them and she'd left it to chance that she would be successful. But she hadn't been, except for a recent message from a priest who had directed her to a man of his acquaintance who had many dealings with outsiders.

She held his note containing the man's name and where he could be found and offered a tiny prayer. Please let him give me news of Barnabas. She'd already sent her inquiry with Joanie, with clear directions on where to go. Now it was a matter of waiting.

Her leg throbbed. It was probably her anxiety that caused the throbbing. The sharp pains had eased this last week. Perhaps because she was no longer bounced on a cart, or was heaved on and off a river barge. She gave a grim smile and thanked God that journey was over.

The door opened and Joanie entered. There was a hopeful look in her face.

Alys smiled. "You found the man?"

Joanie nodded. "He was there. And he took your note and read it and had me wait while he wrote an answer." She withdrew a folded piece of paper and held it out to Alys.

It was her original message with another one scrawled in Latin on the back. *I am afraid to tell you that the man you seek sailed from Venice a few weeks ago. I sorry but I cannot say where they were headed. Tomaso Cortini.*

Alys' heart stopped. She closed her eyes.

"It's not good, is it," said Joanie, her tone flat. She went over to the chair next to Alys' and sat down. "He's not here, is 'e? Either that, or 'e's dead."

"He's not dead," said Alys faintly. "He's gone."

Joanie sighed. "So where are we to go next? I take it you mean to follow him. When you can get enough money to go, that is."

"That's just it. There's nowhere I can follow him to." She drew a deep breath. "He doesn't know where he's gone." She looked at Joanie, her face pale and expressionless.

"Then we go home. As soon as we have enough money. I don't care what you say about washing, I'll do something. Teach me the lingo. Then I'll find work as a servant."

Alys laid a hand on Joanie's arm. "No. Not just yet. Let me see if I can find out any more about where Barnabas has gone. Someone must know."

"But we must eat in the meantime," said Joanie.

Alys gave a wan smile. "I know. And I will find a way to get some money. There's enough for a few more days, at least."

Joanie frowned, but she said nothing more. Alys turned away and glanced out the window that overlooked a cramped courtyard. She fingered the note in her hand. She would find something. She was determined. Carefully, she rose from the chair and reached for her crutch. She hobbled to the door, her progress much more smooth than the first time she'd tried it. This time she opened the door and made her way through the threshold.

"Where are you going?" asked Joanie.

"To church."

"Prayers? Is that your answer?"

"Prayers won't hurt. And perhaps something else will help as well."

"What?"

Alys smiled firmly. "Come. You'll see."

∾

Alys sat on the small bench at the back of the church. She'd come as far as her leg would let her, to a church that was away from the crowded quarters that contained her room and in an area a little more prosperous. The paintings that greeted her here made it worth the pain she was now suffering.

Beside her, Joanie sighed impatiently. "We're 'ere, now. What next?"

Alys opened her purse and gave her the smallest coin it contained. "Take this and offer a prayer. For the Duchess." She paused a moment. "And for my brother."

Joanie gave her a puzzled look. "Your brother?"

She nodded. "His name is Hal. He went to sea, long ago. Before I knew you."

Joanie sighed, took the coin and made her way to one of the smaller altars at the side. Alys turned once more and studied the paintings on the wall, and the one framed, above the altar.

The painting on the side nearest her was dark, the figures stiff and flat, the faces expressionless. It was a scene depicting the flight to Egypt. Mary's mount appeared more like a dog than a donkey. The legs seemed too thin to carry a grown woman, let alone the goods strapped to its back and the babe in Mary's arms.

It was the next painting that took Alys' breath away. The figures were skilfully rendered, so real she could almost feel their presence. But it wasn't just its realism that caught her attention. The colours were vibrant and the manner in which the light was handled was so powerful she had to close her eyes to see if she was imagining it. The scene depicted the Annunciation. The angel appeared in front of Mary, powerful and full of energy, while Mary crouched below it, humble, her face expressive with the wonder at the angel's message. Alys remembered when she'd visited the church at Queenhithe and Mary had been her protector, her beacon of hope. And here was Mary again.

It had to be a sign. This is what she'd come for. In fact, it was more than she'd hoped, to be able to study such beautiful and skilled paintings so that she might learn enough from them to create her own sketches and drawings to show to a painter. A painter who might be willing to have her work for him in some way. Make his brushes, mix his paints, or even prepare his boards for painting. She'd learned something of that from a priest who'd visited on occasion, in the years she'd spent with the Duchess. He had commissioned works for the walls of his church. Her idea was farfetched and had little hope of being realised, but it was all she could think of at the moment.

She rose and hobbled over to the painting, wanting a closer look. Her hands itched to touch the work, to feel for herself that these figures were flat on a large board and standing against the wall, real as she was.

Joanie found her there, a while later, still staring at the figure of Mary.

"Well, I've done the prayers, like you asked."

Alys forced a smile. "I hope that we have them answered already."

Joanie stared at the painting and frowned. "What? You mean this painting? 'Ow is that an answer?"

"It's not the painting, Joanie. It's the idea of it," she said, trying to keep her voice positive.

The doubts she'd fought off earlier assailed her in full force. She turned away from the painting and with determination made her way out. Tomorrow she would send Joanie for some paper and charcoal. It would cost dearly, she knew, but she was certain it would be worth it.

<hr />

Alys looked down at her sketch in dismay. It wasn't bad, but it wasn't good either. The angles were off somehow, but she didn't know enough to fix it. She studied the painting in front of her and tried to decide what it was she was missing.

Behind her a man spoke. She looked up, startled. There were few enough people in the church at this time of the day, after mass had been said. She was certain this morning she had the church to herself. The presence of this slim man with long, dark, unkempt hair and swarthy skin contradicted her assumption.

The man gave her an easy smile. He'd spoken in the Venetian dialect and she'd only just grasped a few of his words. Something about a longer line. Was he referring to her sketch?

She shook her head and spoke in Latin. "I'm sorry, I don't understand."

"Ah, you are not Venetian. You could be, though. There are some with your colouring, though none half as beautiful, I'm sure."

Alys blushed. "You are too kind."

He pointed to the drawing in Alys' hands. "You must pull the line in more and make it longer before you angle it out." He took the paper and charcoal from her hands. "See? Like so."

She watched him in amazement as he corrected her drawing with a few deft strokes. "You can draw?"

He nodded and grinned. "A bit."

She looked at the drawing, his deft lines making her awkward pose suddenly perfect, just like the painting.

"Do you know who created that?" She indicated the painting, so beautiful to her it could only be described as a creation.

"Yes. A fellow of some ability. Or so they tell me."

"He has more than ability. He has a gift from God. This work is wonderful."

He smiled at her warmly. "You think so?"

"Oh yes. What is the painter's name?"

"A fellow you wouldn't know. Carlo Crivelli."

"You're right. I don't know him," said Alys. "But then I don't know any painters."

"But you are interested in painting?" He nodded to her sketch. "You certainly have ability."

She laughed. "I have a little skill, born of years of practice, but I've never had anyone to teach me."

He considered her sketch again. "Then you have talent, there is no doubt."

She felt a flicker of hope. "Do you know an artist who might need someone to assist them, or act as a servant?"

"Few artists make money enough to do more than keep themselves, let alone a servant...or an assistant."

She lowered her head. She had suspected as much, but still she persisted. "But do you know any such artist? Perhaps the artist who painted this work?"

"Are you proposing yourself?"

She straightened. "Yes. I can work hard and I'm eager to learn."

He sighed and shook his head. "There are a number of workshops in Venice who take on students, young apprentices outside of their own family who are talented and eager to learn. But few have women, and those that do, only have them because they are members of the family and there is no son. You must put that thought out of your mind."

She fought back the tears that suddenly rushed in. She would find a way. She had to. A pain, sharp as a knife, flared up in her leg. She shifted. The man looked down. Her skirt hid the bandages and splints that still bound her leg, but he could still see that she put no weight on her foot.

"There is a problem with your foot?"

"My leg. It's nothing." She shifted again and this time she couldn't help the wince.

"I think it is more than nothing. Let me help you to the bench."

She shook her head and reached for the crutch she'd tucked in the little dip in the wall and placed it under her arm.

"No, allow me."

He put a supporting hand under her elbow and took the crutch from her. She could feel his wiry strength as he led her to the bench nearby. He sat down beside her.

"There, now. Rest a moment and tell me how you came to Venice."

She studied him. Took in his kind eyes, the full lips and the concern writ all over his face. Dare she trust him?

"I came on pilgrimage, but my servant and I were robbed on the road," she said.

"You were travelling with just a servant? No other group of pilgrims?"

"We were with a group at first, but we got separated. I was injured during the robbery and my servant nursed me. She's been very good."

He frowned. "And you have no family who can send you funds, or help you in any other way?"

She shook her head. "No, I'm alone. My family are gone." For some reason she'd omitted the detail of her widowhood. Should she mention it now?

He looked at her closely, noting her dress, though travel stained, still finely made. "You must have a care. You'll find there are few women of good families who travel the streets of Venice except for feast days and special occasions." He lifted a strand of hair that had escaped her headcloth. "I might know someone who can help you, though."

"An artist?"

He gave a rueful smile. "An artist of sorts. She is a woman of many talents, cultured and, I think, in need of assistance."

"A woman?" She felt her hopes rise.

"A woman who would appreciate the talents you have to offer."

"She likes art?"

He nodded. "She likes art, music, and literature, and is very knowledgeable about them all."

"I would like to meet her. You say she might need assistance?"

"I think you could assist her, and in return she could do the same for you. Do you know what a courtesan is?"

Alys narrowed her eyes. "I don't think so."

The man gave her a direct look. "She is a woman who entertains men of great wealth with her wit, her looks, and her varied talents."

Realisation dawned on Alys. "You would have me assist a whore?"

"Not a whore. A courtesan. There is a world of difference. The woman I'm thinking of is someone of great refinement and taste. Her house is filled with artwork, she writes verse and plays the lute to perfection."

She looked away, too dumbfounded to speak. Was this what she'd come to? "My servant?" she heard herself ask. "What of her? Would she hire her as well?"

The man shrugged. "I suspect she would. I will ask. Is it agreed then? Shall I approach this woman and see if an arrangement can be made?"

She took a deep breath. "Yes. If you will." With luck it would only be for a short time. Until she could earn enough money to travel on to Barnabas, if she could discover where he'd gone. If not, she would have no choice but to return home.

"Good. I'll send word when I know. Tell me your name and where you're staying."

She told him and then asked, "What's your name, sir?"

He grinned. "I am called Carlo Crivelli."

She looked back at the painting she'd been copying and remembered who he'd said painted it. She wanted to laugh, but thought if she did, she would end up crying.

CHAPTER FOURTEEN
Sea Of Marmara, Late Summer, 1445
BARNABAS

I looked out at the rolling sea and felt the wind whip at my clothes and face. It was glorious, the deck of the galley heaving gently in time to the waves and the stretch of sea all around me, land only an outline in the distance. We'd left the Middle Sea, slipping through the Dardanelles Straits with barely a breeze for a comment. Now we were passing Gallipoli. Ahead of us was the Sea of Marmara, named for the rich marble contained in one of its islands.

Would we continue on to Constantinople, the jewel in the crown of all cities where the emperor of the Byzantine Empire still resided? Surely, with its ancient libraries, that was our destination. It was a thought that had excited me all through our voyage, though I'd had no word of confirmation from al Qali.

Behind me, I could hear the drum beat the time for the galley slaves who rowed us forward, whether the wind appeared or not. I watched them labour, their backs glistening with sweat under the hot sun and their eyes lined from constant squinting against the wind and bright light. Their skin was burnt, blistered or tanned, according to their origins. There were Turks among them, captured during one of the many battles that raged along the seas, as were the others. War plagued these regions, Venetians against Milanese or Genoese, Christians against Mohammedans.

"There is a storm coming soon. You should go below," said al Qali.

Startled out of my thoughts, I looked up at the sky and saw that he was right. The weather seemed more fickle than it was in Venice. A horizon that was azure blue could in one breath turn to a violent purple.

I thought of the larger sea that lay ahead. "Will the sea be this temperamental the rest of the journey to Constantinople?"

"It might. But we won't be journeying there."

I gave him a puzzled look. "But surely that's our destination."

"I never mentioned Constantinople. No, we are not travelling there. Our journey ends before that."

"And will you tell me where?"

He gave me a faint smile. "I have not mentioned it before because I am certain you will not know it. We land at Yaliova."

He was right. I knew nothing of Yaliova, not even where it was. I recalled all those years ago when I had boasted the few names of foreign places that I had learned from sailors arriving at Queenhithe Dock. I felt as foolish now as I had then.

"Where is Yaliova then?"

"It is south of Constantinople, on the coast."

"And we go on to Constantinople afterwards?" I said.

His need for precision in this instance made me impatient. But it made sense we would travel on to Constantinople because it was the only destination in the area not in the hands of the Ottoman Turks.

He gave a dark laugh this time. "You insist our destination is Constantinople, even when I tell you it is not. You are right in that we do travel on, my friend Giacomo, but to Hüdavendigar."

"Hüdavendigar?" Again I felt my ignorance.

"It is a place of great learning. A place of theologians. And the resting place of the sultans."

"The sultans?" I mouthed the words.

He could only mean what my instincts had already told me. What I had known deep inside me since I'd first seen the image of the man in the turban. What else could it be but that we were heading to the land of the Ottoman Turks, to its heart?

∽

It was the call of the muezzin that I heard first, the rhythmic cry from the mosque that signalled the time for prayers. Before we even entered Hüdavendigar, the sound had risen up and the two men who guided us stopped on their horses, dismounted and knelt on the ground, almost in unison. I watched, astonished. Even more surprising was al Qali, who followed suit only a moment behind them.

Al Qali's lack of attention to any form of religion had always puzzled me, but I'd never dared ask. Crossing myself and uttering the odd prayer in times of difficulty were natural to me as breathing, but I'd never detected anything like that in al Qali. Yet now he knelt, like the others, and spoke prayers. To their god. Once again this man confounded me.

He was surely not a Turk. The colour of his skin was darker, his robes long, like some of the Turks I'd seen in Venice, but they were mostly Mameluks, from Egypt. Whatever his origins were, his actions now made me even more uneasy.

The prayers finished, the men mounted again, and we resumed our journey. Ahead, I could see the domes and minarets rise out of the trees clustered on the side of a mountain. It was a city, as big as London, at least, and again I was surprised, expecting tents and hovels, even though al Qali had told me it was a place of theologians. But what kind of theologians? The snow-capped Mount Olympus was nearby, which told me the Greeks had been here at one time. I tried to find reassurance in that piece of knowledge.

We threaded our way through the streets filled with men in bright coloured clothes, some with wide loose breeches and billowing overcoats, turbans topping their heads. Market stalls lined one road we passed through. Fruit and vegetables, some strangely shaped, filled baskets woven in clever patterns. Shimmering silk cloth hung from racks, catching the light. The smell of spices filled the air. I wanted to linger to touch the cloth, sample the fruit and purchase the spices. I caught sight of baskets of feathers in brilliant blue and gold. Peacocks. I smiled, remembering Alessandra's plea to bring back the exotic.

Al Qali urged me forward with a look and a few words, and I paused only a moment longer, before following on with a sigh. It wasn't long before we found ourselves in a front of a small house in the heart of the city. The guides dismounted and disappeared inside. A little while later they reappeared and spoke with al Qali. Though I spoke and read Arabic, I didn't understand the language they were speaking, which left me even more uneasy.

Al Qali dismounted and gestured to me to do the same. He led the way inside the house.

I glanced around the narrow sparse room. A small carpet hung on the wall and few cushions were scattered along a woven mat that covered the floor.

"Is this where we are to stay?" I asked.

"It is only temporary," said al Qali. "Until I get word to the palace."

"The palace?"

He waved his hand. "Never mind. You will see soon enough."

I frowned. I had expected little information when I'd asked the question, but it didn't make it any less frustrating.

"Do you mind if I visit the market in the meantime?"

He shook his head, his eyes darkening. "No. You will remain here until we go to the palace."

I studied his face, trying to extract any information I could from his expression. But even after years of practice, there was little enough I could see. Only that he was determined and in that mood, there was little I could do to change his mind or find more about what might lay in store.

As it was, two days passed before anyone came. Two days of boredom in which I could only listen to the sounds of the city outside the house. There were voices from the nearby market shouting about their wares and later, in the evening, the howls of the jackals as they scavenged the streets, clearing refuse and any other remains. And periodically, the cries of the muezzin issued from the minarets throughout the city. And each time they made their call to prayer, al Qali would stop whatever he was doing, wash himself, take a mat, and kneel down to pray, as did the servant who saw to our needs.

It was curious and unnerving to watch him and I did so carefully each time. Was this his true self? Or another invented part to allay suspicions among a people known for brutality against its enemies?

I still had no answer when the men arrived on expensive horses and dressed in their fine clothes. Before we left, al Qali fussed over me, brushing my hair and insisting I change into my finest doublet, the kermes one that held such memories. When we were ready, we mounted our horses, al Qali holding a curious box that I assumed to be some kind of gift to offer in return for hospitality and a chance to look at the manuscripts.

The men took us to the marble-lined palace, set high up along the mountain and cooled by the breezes from the sea and a cataract of the clearest water that fed its fountains. The palace's curved domes and graceful arches were spacious, and polished to dazzle the eyes. There was no question of the effect on me. I was struck dumb.

They led us to a room with rich carpets on the floor, cushions, and even a table covered in ox skin on the side. Three men sat on the floor, cross-legged. The one in the centre wore a green brocade coat that split to reveal loose scarlet breeches. Gold earrings adorned each lobe and he wore jewelled rings on all his fingers. On his head was a turban, fashioned with complicated folds and a jewel pinned to its centre. I knew that turban and jewel, just as I knew the face beneath them. The man from the vision.

Al Qali made a deep bow and obeisance and gestured me to do the same. "We are honoured that you received us, Lord Candarli Halil Pasha," he said in Arabic.

Numbly, I followed al Qali's example, bowing and kneeling to kiss the floor near this man. Though I knew his name now, I still had no idea who he was, except that there was danger surrounding him. I couldn't ignore my instincts any longer. I glanced at the guards that stood by the door. Black moustaches, sharp, curving swords and cold eyes. Every detail I noted increased my unease.

Halil Pasha eyed al Qali coldly and barely gave a nod. His lips were full and sensuous, his own moustache carefully curled.

"I am not here to do you any particular service, al Qali. Do not waste my time. I must return to my duties in Edirne soon. The Sultan needs me."

"That would be Sultan Mehmet?"

Halil Pasha scowled. "You should tread carefully, al Qali."

Al Qali bowed. "I apologise, lord. I meant no offense. I haven't been in the empire for some time and I am not always in receipt of the current situation."

Halil Pasha frowned. "In these cases it is better to say nothing, until the situation is clear. Or the result can be dangerous."

He glanced at his guards. Alerted, they moved to their swords, but Halil Pasha gave a slight shake of his head and they resumed their positions.

"Truly, I am sorry, lord," said al Qali. His calm was forced, something I had only rarely seen.

"Well, what is this valued item that many would give to possess?"

Al Qali held out the box that was clutched in his hands. "I would offer this, lord, in part. With the hope that you might grant me a boon, one that would mean a mere trifle to you but means all the world to me."

"And what is that boon?"

"A manuscript, lord. A particular manuscript for which I have been searching for some time."

Halil Pasha narrowed his eyes. "What manuscript?"

"Prester John."

Halil Pasha appeared to consider this statement for a moment and then shook his head. "I regret I don't know this manuscript."

Al Qali tucked the box back under his arm and shifted uncomfortably. "Lord, I know that your treasures are so great it would be easy to overlook a paltry manuscript as this. But it is through this gift I have for you that I know with certainty that you have the manuscript."

Halil Pasha raised his brow. "A gift of such power I must see."

Al Qali looked down at the box and hesitated before extending it to Halil Pasha. Halil Pasha took it and after a moment opened the box. The lid blocked my view, so I couldn't see what was inside, but it didn't matter. I knew what was there.

"How pretty. But I have many such baubles, al Qali."

"It's a showstone, lord. A powerful one."

"A showstone." Halil Pasha's tone held a hint of excitement. "And you can use this showstone? You have that gift?"

I felt al Qali's hand encircle my neck and draw me forward. "Not I, lord," he said. "But this youth can."

Halil Pasha turned to me and studied me carefully, his eyes slowly moving along my face and down my body. I flushed under his scrutiny. He smiled slowly.

"This is your servant?" he asked.

"No, lord. A student of mine. Giacomo Bonavillagio. He speaks Arabic."

Halil Pasha gestured me forward. Reluctantly, I did as he bid and on al Qali's signal, knelt before him.

"He is not so young," said Halil Pasha. He lifted my chin and stared into my face. "But perhaps I might call him a youth."

"He is young in some ways, lord," said al Qali. "In ways that matter."

Halil Pasha nodded. "So, you can see into this showstone?"

Unexplained anger rose up inside and for a moment I almost denied it. I set my mouth in a grim line. "Yes."

"I see. And you have done this often?"

"Often enough...lord." I remembered the title and forced myself to use it.

"When did you first use this talent of yours?"

"When I was young, lord. About six or seven years of age."

"What kinds of things have you seen? The location of a lost glove, perhaps? A missing pet?"

I shook my head and sighed. "Nothing like that."

"Yet you have seen this manuscript al Qali seeks. And have discovered it is here?"

I glanced across at al Qali and made a decision. "I saw only a land and people, and upon describing them to him, he understood what it meant."

Halil Pasha nodded. "I see. And have you seen other things that are not in connection with items that are lost? The future perhaps?"

"I see visions of what might happen, lord, but I cannot always be certain what they mean, or if indeed they are the future."

Halil Pasha smiled at me and ran a hand across my hair and along my face. He looked over at al Qali. "I will require a demonstration, of course, but I accept your gift, al Qali."

"And the manuscript, lord?"

"Oh, I'm sure my secretary will locate it somewhere, since you say it is in my possession."

Al Qali smiled and bowed low, backing out. I looked at Halil Pasha and did the same, my heart beating loudly in my ears. A bargain had been made, but somehow, I felt I didn't know the exact terms.

CHAPTER FIFTEEN
Hüdavendigar, Ottoman Empire, Summer 1445
BARNABAS

I eyed the clothes laid out on the carved chest dubiously. There was a pair of loose breeches of brightest blue silk, embroidered with gold thread along each leg and a sleeveless overcoat of gold and violet brocade called a dulimano. Short boots that curved to a point in matching violet and gold lay beside the chest. Behind me, two men waited to dress me. Other than that, I was alone. Al Qali was no doubt in his own quarters donning similar clothes. Would his have the same flamboyance as the clothes arranged carefully on this chest?

Frowning, I submitted to the servants' ministrations. They dressed me slowly, with great care. It wasn't a matter of putting the clothes on my body, but my body must be prepared first. Every part of me was washed, then oiled to the point where I thought I would slip off the bench. They took no notice of my nakedness, or even any slight stirrings in my loins from all their rubbing, their hands and eyes all full of their tasks and nothing more.

When the oiling was complete, they wrapped the loincloth around me and helped me into the loose breeches, overcoat, and finally the shoes. I began to protest when I realised they wanted to circle my eyes with kohl, but they assured me this was the custom and it wouldn't do to argue.

I ignored the polished pier glass that was in the room with even more determination than I'd done the past two days since our arrival. Those two days had been occupied only by reading the two manuscripts that had been sent to me at al Qali's request. Neither manuscript was the one al Qali had mentioned. They were in Arabic and their topic was alchemy. A hint I couldn't ignore.

I hadn't seen al Qali or had any direct word from him since we'd left the Pasha's presence. I could only imagine that the manuscript he'd wanted had been produced and he was studying that. It was the servants and not al Qali who'd told me that Halil Pasha was none other than the Grand Vizier, the Sultan's second in command, and I should have no worries about my comfort. The knowledge made me feel anything but comforted.

Now, I was to be presented to Halil Pasha again and I had no doubt what my role was to be. I was to read the showstone and I would do my best to please. It mattered not whether al Qali was successful in obtaining the right manuscript. It only mattered to me that I keep my head, literally. I understood that Halil Pasha's disapproval would be instant and deadly.

They escorted me to the same room as before. This time a breeze blew through the arched openings and caused the thin muslin curtains to billow. Halil Pasha sat on his cushions, his dark moustache shining with oil and the expensive plume in his turban fluttering. He was wearing a different overcoat than previously. This one matched my own, as did the loose breeches. The coat hung open and his bare chest gleamed in the torchlight. Lying beside him was the carved box containing the showstone and in front of him, on the rich thick carpet, was a small feast.

I looked around. There was no sign of al Qali. There was no sign of anyone else, except for the janissary guard at the door with his curved sword at his side. I took a deep breath and made my obeisance. He laid a hand on the back of my head.

"Come and sit with me, my fair youth."

I raised my kholed eyes to him and tried to read his expression. I could only see curiosity and a faint hint of humour. Reluctantly, I sat beside him where he indicated.

"We will enjoy ourselves a little, I think, before we have this demonstration."

"Will Master al Qali be joining us?"

"Al Qali is engaged elsewhere. But what need have we of his presence? He has no talent for the showstone. He has admitted that himself."

"I thought perhaps he might be required to explain the stone and its origins. It was his, after all, not mine."

Halil Pasha raised his brows. "But it's mine, now. And I have no need to know more of its origins at this time."

I could only nod and say nothing more. Clearly he preferred not to have al Qali present. It made no difference to me in regard to using the showstone, but despite everything, I would have felt easier if he'd been there.

He poured me a cup of a honeyed drink. It was sweet and strong and I sipped it slowly while he picked up a fig. I thought the fig was for him but a moment later he offered it to me. I took it and bit into it. It was heavily sugared and tasted good. There were other dishes which he described and explained, offering portions to me directly from his fingers, often putting them directly in my mouth and licking his fingers afterwards. It was all I could manage not to gag at such an action.

Though the breeze from the window continued to cool the room, I was sweating heavily. Halil Pasha chatted aimlessly while we ate, querying me about my background and my experiences since meeting al Qali. His attentiveness did anything but put me at my ease and the drink was beginning to have its effect. My head was fuzzy and I had some difficulty concentrating. I looked for something substantial among the dishes, something that would help my fuddled mind and absorb all the drink that was being pressed on me.

I reached for the flattened bread and rolled some of the spiced vegetables and mutton inside. I took a bite, conscious of Halil Pasha's scrutiny. After I'd swallowed the last morsel he leaned over, licked his finger and wiped it along the side of my mouth.

"You have missed a small bit," he said.

I reddened, still feeling the saliva from his finger on my face. "I thank you for this food, lord. It was truly a feast. Will I wash my hands and begin the reading?"

He gave me a slow smile. "Ah, we'll get that business out of the way, as you say. And then we'll indulge in some real pleasure, eh?"

I looked away and reached for the small bowl of warm water and the towel that was beside it. Carefully, I bathed my fingers and wiped them dry while Halil Pasha did the same in his own bowl.

When the bowls were set aside, he nodded to his guard, who opened the door and spoke softly to someone waiting outside. Servants entered and cleared away the dishes and food and withdrew as quietly as they had come. I looked at Halil Pasha warily.

He smiled and reached for the box beside him and placed it on the carpet at my feet. "Open it and let's see what we can discover."

I lifted the lid and withdrew the showstone. It felt slippery against my sweating fingers and I put it hurriedly on the carpet, nestling it on one of the cushions Halil Pasha had placed there. I took a deep breath and began to explain what he should do.

He cut me off with a wave of his hand. "There is no need for an explanation."

He gave his moustache a quick stroke and then placed his hands on the showstone. I stared into the stone, looking once again at the familiar depths, and tried to clear my mind of all that filled it. It was difficult. Never had I felt the danger so close and so ominous. Not even when I read the stone for the Duchess, for I was too innocent then. Now I knew the danger of looking into the stone, a danger that could easily mean the end of my life, reading as I was for such a powerful man. Looking into the stone now, I almost hoped that I would see nothing. I blinked my eyes and the reassuring opaqueness remained. I was just about to paste a look of disappointment on my face and shake my head at Halil Pasha when an image began to form. It was blurred and almost indistinct. But though I strained and tried to see it more clearly, I still couldn't make it out. A sudden roar of fear arose, fear that had no connections to any concerns of my own. I shut my eyes for a moment, hoping that it might dispel the image and a new, better one would appear. I looked again and saw Halil Pasha, lying dead on the ground.

I gave a small gasp. I shut my eyes again, determined to force a different image to appear. How could I explain what I'd seen to Halil Pasha? Not without thought to my own safety. I would have to make up something that conveyed a subtle warning of danger, or just say as little as possible. I opened my eyes and looked again. This time it was only a moment before a scene materialised that showed men fighting. Ottomans, by the look of their dress, and at their head was a handsome young man, with a large jewel and feathers in his turban. I still felt uneasy and I searched for some more detail that would help me understand more. The image faded and I sighed. Would I try again?

"What do you see? What is happening?" asked Halil Pasha.

I formed my answer quickly. "A young man, leading soldiers into battle." I described the man and those that surrounded him.

"Where are he and the soldiers? Who are they fighting?"

"I can't really tell," I said.

Halil Pasha gave an impatient snort. "Look again. I need to know more."

I frowned and looked once more into the showstone and waited to see if another image would appear. There was nothing. I closed my eyes, took another deep breath and tried again. Still nothing. I kept staring, willing for something to show itself, but it was no use.

I looked up and shook my head. "I'm sorry. There is nothing more."

Halil Pasha frowned. "Impossible. Look again."

"I cannot command the images, lord. I'm sorry."

He narrowed his eyes and gave me a considering look. "How is it you have no control?"

I shrugged and tried to appear calm. "I don't know, lord. I understand nothing of its source, only that it comes of its own will and not mine."

Halil Pasha stroked his moustache and considered my words. "But we can try again and we may learn more on this subject?"

I nodded. "Yes, lord, but I don't know when an image will appear again and cannot guarantee that it will contain the information you seek."

"I see. Well we must try again. Perhaps tomorrow." He studied me again and eventually spoke, touching a lock of my hair. "You have more to you than just beauty, I see. Al Qali was not mistaken in your value."

I lowered my eyes to hide my alarm. There was something about his words that made it clear there was more meaning to them than what was immediately evident.

"Come, my fair Giacomo. We shall relax now, and leave these serious thoughts for a another time, when we shall try again."

I watched him lift the showstone and put it back in its wooden box, closing the lid firmly. I nearly wanted to insist I could try again. Anything to put off discovering what exactly he meant by "relaxing."

Halil Pasha spoke a few words to the guard and the guard opened the door and the servant entered again. Halil Pasha called for more refreshments and I breathed a little sigh of relief. I was happy to eat and drink if it meant less time to spend talking or whatever else he might have in mind.

The servants came with refreshments a short while later and left, the guard following in their wake. Though I knew the guard would be standing on the other side of the door and could hear if either of us called, it gave me no comfort. I was alone with Halil Pasha. He bid me take off my coat and as I did so he removed his own. Then he poured me a lavish cup of the honeyed drink, nearly spilling it.

He handed it to me. "Drink, please."

I did as he told me watching him over the brim of the cup as I did so. He took a sip from his cup, the same sweet honeyed drink that made him smack his lips with enjoyment.

He set his cup down and turned to face me. I took another deep drink from my own cup and tried to still my nerves. He put a hand to my face and looked into me. I looked away, unwilling to see what was in his eyes.

"Tell me again, fair Giacomo, what brought you into the company of al Qali?"

I swallowed hard and tried to retrieve the familiar story from my fuddled mind. "My father is a merchant who met al Qali in his travels. He asked al Qali to tutor me."

Was that the correct story? Something seemed to be missing from it but I couldn't remember. I tried again.

"I have a brother. My father is in Alexandria with him at the moment."

That seemed it. But there was something about London. Should I mention London? I decided against it and thought of something else instead.

"I was in Bruges. Translating manuscripts."

Halil Pasha laid a hand on my bare arm and gave it a little stroke. "What manuscripts did you translate?"

Suddenly, I couldn't even remember why I was translating the manuscripts, let alone what they were called. I shrugged. "Something in Arabic. I think."

Halil Pasha gave a nod. "Arabic. So you can read it as well as speak it. I'm intrigued." He moved his hand to mine and clasped it. "Your fingers have strength, capable of clasping a sword, rather than writing tools."

I looked at him blankly, his face blurring in front of me. He spoke some more, but I could hardly make out what he said, let alone answer him. His hands stroked my arm once again and then moved to my chest. I felt him pull me down on the cushions, my limbs moving like they were ploughing through a deep river and any efforts to voice a protest seemed impossible, for my tongue was thick and solid in my mouth. The room spun once more and I closed my eyes against it. Halil Pasha whispered in my ear softly, but I could hear nothing of it beyond the soft soughing sound.

The time passed, but I had little understanding of what might be happening, if anything at all. Was I wrapped in cloth, or enfolded in arms? My senses were numb, and all I know is that eventually I slept.

I opened my eyes to bright sunlight and closed them hurriedly, against the throbbing pain in my head. When I tried to lick my dry mouth, I found my tongue was thick as a loaf of bread. Carefully I opened my eyes again, shielding them from the light with my hand and peered out. I was in my room, laid out on the pallet with only a linen sheet between my skin and the bed, but I was alone. I breathed a sigh of relief.

My skin felt clammy and for a moment I thought I might be sick. In slow motion I rose from the bed and forced myself to the window, wrapping the linen sheet around me. I inhaled the air, still cool in the early morning, and shivered. My reaction was not from the cold. What had happened the night before was merely a muddled dream in my head and at the moment I dared not think about it. What I was clear about is that I needed to see al Qali as soon as possible. Somehow, I had to get him to leave. Presumably he had the manuscript, or at least had a chance to look at it. I would go to the market, make some purchases and then we would leave and, once in Venice, we would go our separate ways.

I glanced down at my shaking hands and made my decision. If he refused to leave when I saw him, I would find my own way back to Venice, whatever it took.

A door opened and a servant entered, bearing a tray of food. He brought it over and placed it on a small table near me. I glanced at it and bile rose up at the sight of the sheep's feet with a thick sauce in a finely decorated ceramic bowl. Beside it was a flagon and cup of what I could only imagine was more of the honeyed drink.

"Thank you, but I would prefer something other than that," I said.

The servant gave a small smile. "But it will make you feel better. Please, you must drink and eat."

I gave him a sceptical look, but made my way over to the table and poured the drink. The liquid was thick and golden. A rich drink. I took one sip, surprised that I didn't gag. It slid down my throat slowly, coating it on the way. I waited a moment to see if it would return the way it had come. It settled eventually, without any further threat. I took a deep drink and enjoyed the sensation as I swallowed. I looked at the food and suddenly it appealed to me. I dipped my fingers into the dish a put a small morsel to my tongue and swallowed.

The servant nodded and turned to leave.

"Wait," I said. "Master al Qali. Can you tell me where he is? I must see him."

The servant gave me a puzzled look. "But Master al Qali has left."

Stunned, I stared at the servant. "Left? When? How?"

"Two days ago, with an escort. I presume he has already sailed by now."

"But that's impossible. Why didn't he tell me? Why didn't I know he was leaving?"

The servant shook his head. "I'm sorry, master. I thought you knew. Master al Qali's movements are of no matter to you now. You belong to Lord Halil Pasha. It was the bargain Master al Qali made."

"No. You have it wrong. The showstone was the bargain. I was only there to read it. I was to depart with Master al Qali afterwards."

The servant gave him a reassuring look. "I'm sorry, but you will find that service with Lord Halil Pasha has its rewards. If you obey him. I know he finds you pleasing, so you will see, you will gain much."

"I'm sure your lord is generous, but I have no wish to remain here."

"I'm certain it must seem strange to you, this place, this change of circumstances. But you will grow used to it."

"I don't want to grow used to it. I have to leave. Now."

The servant's look turned to pity. "You mustn't think such things, let alone voice them. You cannot leave. Lord Halil Pasha won't permit it. I must remind you that you belong to him."

My head felt fuzzy again as I struggled to take in his words and their implication for my life. How could I be so tied—tied to a life I didn't want, in a foreign place, with a man who was far more dangerous than any of my other past masters? I cursed al Qali. I wouldn't let this rest. Somehow I would escape this prison, and I had no illusions that it was anything other than that, no matter how luxurious it was. And when I did escape, al Qali would feel my vengeance.

CHAPTER SIXTEEN
Venice, Summer 1445
ALYS

Alys stared at the wall opposite the bed where she was lying, her leg throbbing slightly. A small bead of sweat had formed on her forehead and she swallowed. Her stomach emitted a soft gurgle of hunger and she tried to shift her mind from her empty belly.

It had been several days since that fateful visit to the church and in that time she'd managed to use up the last of their money. She cursed herself for the foolish purchase of paper. What had possessed her to think that she could sell any sketches she might make? Joanie had never said a word of recrimination, something she had every right to do.

Alys looked across at the other pallet where Joanie laid her head at night and thanked God again for such a companion. What would she have done without her? At this very moment she was out scavenging for some way to get food in their stomachs.

She looked down at her leg. Carefully, she pulled the coverlet aside and raised her gown. She could see the suppuration through the linen bandages that bound it still. It wasn't healing well, she knew that. What she could do about it was something she didn't know. Joanie had applied her knowledge and abilities and Alys was thankful for that. But Alys didn't like the discolouration that was beginning to form around the wound.

Alys heard footsteps on the stairs and hastily pulled her gown over her legs again. The door opened and Joanie appeared. Alys studied her face for signs of a successful forage, but all she saw was puzzlement.

"Did you manage to find anything?" Alys asked.

"What?" Joanie said. "Oh, not much. Only a bit of stale bread. But just below 'ere, I met a boy with a message for you."

"A message? For me?"

Joanie nodded. "It was that painter you met. What was his name?"

"Crivelli. Carlo Crivelli."

"That's the one. Master Crivelli wants you to meet 'im at noon in the piazza nearby. Leastways that's what I could make out. What's going on?" Her voice reeked of disapproval.

Alys reddened. "It isn't what you think."

"And just what am I thinking?"

That I would bed him."

Joanie's eyes narrowed. "Just what does he want with you then? I can't see 'im doing much art teaching. Not with a woman. You said yourself there's no women doing painting here."

Alys blushed again. "No. It's not to do with painting. It's a woman he knows. A woman that might want our assistance."

Joanie looked thoughtful. "Servants, you mean? We would serve some high born woman?"

"Yes. He said he knew a woman who could do with our assistance."

"I suppose. Well, we could do worse than be servants again, given what little we have." Joanie frowned. "Though I don't think you can do much with your leg at the moment."

Joanie's remark only confirmed the fear Alys had thought in the back of her mind and with great effort she fought the despair it evoked.

"I'm sure my leg will improve soon. We're both young and strong enough. Perhaps she might let me do light work like sewing or some such thing. Or even writing letters."

Joanie nodded and accepted her reassurance. "Right. We must get you ready for this meeting. With your leg the way it is, you'll need time enough to get down them stairs."

By the time Alys was ready to manage the stairs she was exhausted. Just the effort of rising from the bed and allowing Joanie to brush down her travel-stained gown and comb her hair into some semblance of decency took all the energy she could muster. But she steeled herself to face the stairs, and with Joanie's support she made her way down them, one step at a time with a great pause in between.

She arrived at the bottom in a cold sweat, panting heavily. It was then she acknowledged she wasn't getting better, she was getting worse. She brushed away tears and once she caught her breath, allowed Joanie to help her towards the crowded piazza near their room.

It was filled with market stalls crowded with goods and people when they arrived and for a moment she wondered if she would ever find Signore Crivelli amid all this noise and bustle. At this point she almost didn't care. It was enough just to find a place to rest.

"There, Joanie. Just take me there to that wall and I'll lean against it while we wait."

Joanie did as she was bid. Alys leaned gratefully along the wall and closed her eyes for a moment. She took a deep breath, trying to still the pain that was tearing through her leg.

"Are you well, madonna?"

She opened her eyes and saw Signore Crivelli standing in front of her, his face filled with concern.

She forced a smile. "Yes, of course."

He frowned and nodded. "If you are well enough to make it to the canal, we'll take a gondola. It is quicker that way."

She nodded and steeled herself for the distance she would have to walk to the canal. She explained it briefly in English to Joanie, who gave her an encouraging squeeze and put her arm around her in support.

"We'll get you there," she said. "Never you fear."

Alys gave a wan smile and introduced Joanie to Crivelli. "My servant. And dearest friend."

Crivelli gave a quick nod and motioned them onward. It was a painful journey, one that she wasn't able to recall well afterwards. Somehow, though, she managed to get to the canal and into a gondola where she sank into the seat in gratitude.

∾

The woman studied her slowly and Alys blushed under her scrutiny. She walked around behind Alys, tugged at her dress so that it clung to her in front, and then dropped the cloth. She peered at Alys' face, lifted her chin and pulled her head from side to side.

"Walk for me," said the woman in Latin.

Alys stared at her, speechless. Amid the haze of her pain, Signore Crivelli had escorted her and Joanie from the gondola to the *loggia* of a comfortably sized palazzo, and up steps that were increasingly painful to mount to eventually wait in a beautifully furnished *sala* while the woman in question was alerted to their arrival. When she'd come finally, amid dark veils, gloves and gown, it was all Alys could do to stand without swaying. The woman had made no introductions, nor had Signore Crivelli. He'd only mentioned that Alys preferred to speak in Latin. Following that there was this long, detailed examination.

Alys took a deep breath and began a slow painful hobble away from the woman.

"She's a cripple." The woman turned to Crivelli. "You didn't mention she's a cripple."

"No, madonna. It is only a wound to the leg. It will heal soon enough. Look at the bone structure. That's what you should notice. The face. Did you see the cheeks? The eyes?"

The woman gave a snort. "Of course I did. What do you take me for? But I can't afford to take on a cripple. I must have perfection. I'm known for perfection."

She turned to Alys again with renewed intensity. Alys wanted to protest that she was fit for work, that she would do whatever the mistress wanted to secure a place in such a wealthy household, but her tongue was too thick and her head was spinning. She bit her lip hard and went to open her mouth, but all she could do was fall to the ground.

❧

Alys opened her eyes. Joanie's face loomed over her, filled with concern.

"Oh, Alys," she whispered. "I'm so glad that you're awake now."

"What's happened?" She looked around her. She was lying on a bed covered in rich brocade cloth. Light streamed in from a large window hung with more of the brocade cloth. "Where am I?"

"You're in that woman's home. Mistress Alessandra. At least that's what Master Crivelli called her."

"How long?"

"A good while, Alys. 'Tis almost night. They asked for a doctor to come and 'e's been and gone."

"A doctor?" Alys cried, alarmed at the thought. A doctor meant death. Amputation. She felt her leg and was reassured when she found it was still there. "What did he say? What did he do?"

"Shhh now. Rest. It's fine."

The woman entered at that moment and Joanie drew back to allow her to approach the bed. She still wore her dark veil and her clasped hands were gloved in dark lace.

Alys started to rise from the bed. "I thank you for your kindness. I'm sorry to be a burden. I'll leave as soon as I can."

The woman pressed her back against the pillows. "Nonsense. I have not paid good money for the doctor's services so that you could leave. Besides, you are in no condition to go anywhere."

"I have no money to repay you, but I promise that when I am well enough I will serve you in any way I can, if you permit." She looked at Joanie. "And my friend and servant, Joanie would as well, if you let her stay to help me."

The woman turned and studied Joanie. "Yes. She is good and strong. Does she speak anything but her own language?"

"She has a few words of Latin and French. But she is quick and we will both learn your language quickly. I have some phrases already."

"Good," said the woman. "I will have her here, tending you, until such time as she can follow instructions from me and others. As for yourself, in the meantime, you can begin by learning more Italian, and when your health is better we will begin in earnest with the real work."

"What kind of work?" asked Alys.

"It will take some effort, but I think you have the makings of a notable courtesan. That is if your mind is as quick as Crivelli says."

Alys thought at first that she'd heard incorrectly. Or that she had mistaken the meaning of the term that had been spoken, or that it meant something else entirely.

"A courtesan?" she asked. "But aren't you a courtesan?"

The woman gave a small laugh that had an edge to it. "Did Crivelli say that?"

Alys nodded, puzzled.

"Once, but no longer." She gestured to her face still hidden by the veil. "My situation has changed. But my skills and knowledge should not be wasted. I chose to pass all of it on, if I found a suitable candidate."

"You think I am a suitable candidate?"

"Perhaps. We will see. First, we must get that leg healed. The doctor says you may have problems, though. You must do all you can to see that you do not."

Alys stared at her, stunned, until she caught Joanie's worried looks. She forced herself to put on a calm expression. She closed her eyes a moment to think. What choice had she?

"What do you want from me in return? That is, besides learning all that you teach me," she asked.

The woman stood unmoving. "I would have all your earnings, until you have paid off what you owe and then, after that, a percentage. I will be providing you with a home, clothing you, and feeding you, in addition to my instructions. And when you are ready, I will host gatherings for people I know and introduce you to them."

Alys nodded slowly. "May I know your name?"

"I am Alessandra. You understand and agree to all that I have outlined?"

"I understand. And yes, I agree."

Did she really understand? Did she know what kind of life this would be for her? She glanced at Joanie again and gave her a reassuring smile. She would have to talk to Joanie later and try and convince her that this was the best course for them to take.

෴

Alys stared at the consistency of the paste and grimaced. She stirred it again and tried to remember what Alessandra had explained about the mixture. It was to go onto her hair, to bring out its golden highlights and make it shine. Or so Alessandra said. Alessandra had instructed her the first time and had her explain it to Joanie so she could apply the preparation. Now, Alys was preparing the mixture again and wasn't so certain about the proportions of powder and herbs.

Joanie frowned at her and snorted. "Let me," she says. "It's my job by rights, anyhow."

Alys gave Joanie a weak smile. "Thank you."

Joanie took the bowl containing the mixture from her, added a pinch of the contents in a small twist of paper and gave it a rigorous stir. Alys watched her silently. It wasn't that she hadn't understood the first time, it was more that today her mind wasn't on her tasks and Joanie knew it. This morning Alessandra had told her that Carlo Crivelli was calling to see her and Alys was nervous. She hadn't seen him since she'd fallen ill that first day all those weeks ago. In that time so much had happened she'd hardly thought of Signore Crivelli, until now.

"There," said Joanie, showing her the bowl. "That's how you want it, see."

Alys peered at the bowl and nodded. "Will you put it on?"

"Of course. Didn't I do it before?" Joanie said in a brisk tone.

Alys sighed. Joanie's disapproval over her choice to agree to Alessandra's plan was still evident in her manner. There was no telling how long it would be before Joanie softened toward her, of if she would ever do so, no matter how much Alys tried to placate her.

Joanie settled Alys in a chair on the small balcony. She draped a cloth over Alys' shoulders and spread her damp hair on top of it. Carefully, she applied the paste to Alys' hair using flat wooden spoon. It took time and patience but the result, when it was rinsed out and fully dried, was noticeable. In today's bright sun it didn't take long.

"Ooh, I can see the gold so strong, it does blind me, nearly," said Joanie.

"Let me see," said a voice in Italian.

Surprised, Alys turned to see Alessandra standing behind her, inspecting her closely. She touched her hair self-consciously.

"*Si, bella.* It's as bright as I thought it would be. That's good," said Alessandra in Italian.

Joanie gave a sniff. Though she pretended she knew little Italian, in truth her command of the language had become almost as good as Alys', who had made a point of practicing it every day, conversing with the servants, and increasingly, with Alessandra.

"You should change, now. Signore Crivelli will be here soon."

"Of course. Is it me he wishes to see in particular, or is it just a general social call?"

"Does it matter?" said Alessandra tersely.

"No. No, of course not. I just wondered if I should don a specific gown."

"You must always dress as if every man who visits is of particular interest to you. Remember that."

"Yes, yes. Of course." Alys took a deep breath and with a nod, got up and left the room slowly, making a great effort to conceal the limp that plagued her still. Joanie followed in her wake, muttering.

Back in her room, Alys picked a dress from the three that Alessandra had ordered to be made for her. They were like nothing she'd ever worn. Sumptuous and daringly cut, they were made of worked velvet and silk, with deep necklines and costly trim. They left her breathless at the thought of the expense and made her wonder once again about the kind of life a courtesan led to afford such luxuries.

In the room she now occupied were hung silk tapestries, paintings and costly brocade and velvet curtains, carved chairs. Even the bed was draped in brocade and silk. It was the two paintings that captivated her most, though. She'd been told they were gifts from wealthy patrons and painted by Venetians. One was by Crivelli himself and like the other showed no sign of religious themes. Crivelli had chosen a scene from Greek myth, of Persephone in the underworld. Alessandra had explained it to Alys while she stared at the figures and marvelled at their lifelike quality. The depth and light in the paintings, the vibrant colours, were unmatched by any she'd seen in England. If only she could learn to capture a scene in that manner.

"Which gown is it to be?" asked Joanie. Her tone was short again. The lapse earlier had been just that. A lapse.

Alys considered the three before her. The dark green *brocadello*, the blue *damasco* worked with silver thread, or the saffron *ormesino*?

"The blue one, I suppose."

Joanie nodded. Without further word she helped Alys into her gown, laced her up and leaned over to put the matching slippers on her stockinged feet. The gown's deep slashed sleeves allowed the snowy linen of her chemise to pucker through, the linen so fine and transparent it revealed her skin. But such revelations were modest compared to the low cut bodice that bared her shoulders and threatened to uncover her nipples with the anything but the slightest of breaths.

"Your hair. What do you want to do with it?" asked Joanie.

"Madonna Alessandra says to have it loose, for now."

Joanie gave a short hrrmpph. "And jewels? Does the Madam 'ave anything to say about that?"

"She gave me a small strand of pearls to wear. It's in the coffer on the table."

Joanie nodded and pursed her lips. She went over to the coffer, removed the pearls and placed them around her neck.

There was a knock at the door and the servant, Lucia, entered. "Madonna Alessandra says you are to come now. The signore is here."

Alys nodded and thanked the girl. She took a deep breath. This was her moment. Her performance as a courtesan would begin now.

❧

Alys shifted imperceptibly under Carlo Crivelli's stare.

"Magnificent, madonna," he said. "You have worked miracles."

"Thank you, Crivelli. It is has been a difficult time, but I think I'm pleased with the results."

"And the limp. It is hardly noticeable," said Crivelli.

Alys blushed and saw Alessandra purse her lips. It was the one blemish, the one major issue that stood between them. Alys had tackled all the lessons, the instructions on deportment, conversation, cosmetics, and even bedroom pleasures with as much energy as she could and had been happy with her progress. But as much as she might try, she couldn't eliminate the limp and the shooting pain that accompanied it whenever she walked. Alessandra had said only that she must excel at the lute, if she wasn't to dance. Dancing was out of the question. And, if she was to limp, it must at least be graceful.

"It will be her eccentricity, Crivelli. A woman who is all perfection will seem unattainable. We cannot have that. But in all else she will be perfect and complete."

"Intact?" asked Crivelli.

"Oh yes. Like the Virgin Mother."

Crivelli surveyed Alys once more. "Yes, exactly like the Madonna. It is perfect."

"Did I not say so?"

"I will paint her. As the Madonna, herself. Just look, madonna. Consider."

The two of them studied Alys, now. Alys lowered her head and stared at the floor tiles carefully to conceal her anger. How dare they regard her as some bit of goods, ready for sale? But that's exactly what she was, she reminded herself. And at least they felt she had many fine points and they admired them.

Alessandra clapped her hands. "You're right, Crivelli. Yet again I'm beholden to you. The irony would be perfect. We'll even call her Maria."

Alys' head snapped up and she looked at Crivelli questioningly. "What do you mean?"

"Why, that he will paint you, child. As the Madonna. The Virgin Mother. With Crivelli's talent some wealthy patron will buy it and display it. Your fame will spread. You will become the Virgin Madonna and everyone will want to be your patron."

Alys' head reeled, her emotions confused. In the end, she held onto the thought that Crivelli wanted to paint her. She, simple Alys of Queenhithe was to be painted by Carlo Crivelli of Venice. And perhaps, while he painted her, she might learn something of his skill. And with that skill she might find a way to make her own paintings. Paintings that Crivelli might sell for her. And rather than Maria, she would call herself Alberto.

CHAPTER SEVENTEEN
Venice, Autumn 1445
ALYS

Alys tried hard to resist the urge to scratch her nose and failed. Crivelli frowned, but allowed her the time to ease herself before resuming the arranged position. The moment past, she looked upward again, an expression of wonder once more plastered on her face. She found the ceiling cracks of his studio that had been her focus for the past hour and stared, conscious of Joanie's scrutiny from a chair by the door.

He was painting a scene from the Annunciation and she was the Virgin Mary, stunned at the angel Gabriel's news she was to give birth to the Christ child. Crivelli was working on her face, now. All the sketches he'd tried with various expressions were now applied to the final result. But the details, the fine brush strokes that could make all the difference between an awkward or unbelievable depiction were down to the work of these next days. The weeks that had passed since she first began her sittings were now counted in months and she began to hope that it would soon be done.

"May I see the painting today and ask you questions?" she asked.

He grunted and Alys took that for a yes. Except for the last few days when he'd worked on her head, he'd allowed her to look most of the time. It was a privilege that he gave to few, and not at all to any of his other models. Even Madonna Alessandra hadn't been allowed to see it yet.

In these moments when she'd posed questions to him she'd learned much, asking him about a particular technique or how a certain colour was achieved. If only she could put such knowledge to use. Try it out and see if she could accomplish half of what he did. But getting the paints would be difficult enough, let alone a board to paint upon. She hadn't dared ask Crivelli up to now.

Her eyes slid over to Crivelli and she saw there was a peculiar expression on his face.

"Is something wrong?" she asked.

He looked up at her, startled. "What? No, no." He blinked and his mouth formed a smile. "On the contrary, madonna, it goes well."

"May I see?"

He considered the painting more, his head cocked to one side. "*Sì*. I think this is the time when I must stop."

Alys lowered her head gratefully and rubbed the crick from her neck. She stretched, unwound herself from the position she'd been holding, and rose from the stool. The crimson and blue silk robes she was wearing fell from their carefully draped folds and swept the tiles as she made her way to the easel. Crivelli stood back and allowed her a view of it. She gave a soft gasp.

Before, when she'd looked at the painting, Alys had admired the deft manner in which he painted each fold of cloth and the way he'd created a great balance between the dark of the background and the bright lustre of the fabric. But now, with Mary's face—no, her face—painted in detail, the figure became luminescent. Her burnished hair framed her head and fell loose along her shoulders. The figure looked so real, yet unearthly at the same time. And what was more unnerving, it resembled her to every lash of the eye, tilt of the nose and curve of the mouth.

"Oh, Signore Crivelli, it's a marvel. I've never seen anything so fine."

Crivelli gripped her arm. "It is good, is it not? I think it might be my finest work to date." There was excitement and pride in his voice. He turned to her and gave her a fierce hug. "And you are in no small part the cause of it, *bella mia*. You have been a muse to me, a divine inspiration."

Alys blushed. "It's your talent that has done this, Signore Crivelli."

He cupped her chin. "Please, call me Crivelli. The time has passed for formalities. This will most certainly be the first of many paintings of you I hope to do. That is, if your mistress agrees." He nodded across at Joanie. "Will you take your mistress home now and tell Madonna Alessandra that I'll bring the painting this evening?"

A rush of happiness filled Alys at the thought of spending more time with Crivelli. Time that would also be spent learning more about painting. She couldn't imagine anything more pleasurable.

◈

Alessandra swept in the room and made her way to the easel. Crivelli stood back from the painting biting his lip nervously. He'd spent ages unpacking the painting, taking care over its placement and ensuring there was enough light to see it properly. It wasn't until he was completely satisfied that he'd allowed Alessandra in to view it.

"It's finished?" Alessandra asked.

"I think so," said Crivelli. "Except for the frame, of course."

She nodded and drew back to study the painting carefully. She remained motionless for a few moments then moved in closer to inspect it, her eyes narrowing. Eventually, she looked up and shook her head.

"This is astonishing, Crivelli. You are a marvel. Truly a marvel."

"Do you think so?" he asked, pleasure in his voice.

"This is better than anything else I've seen by a Venetian painter. Few have captured the light as you have done." She took a deep breath. "This painting will most certainly cause a stir. Oh, we must make it a real occasion when we bring this painting out for its first viewing."

"You plan to show it here?" asked Crivelli. There was a small hint of doubt in his voice. "You don't think the subject matter…"

"Oh, here, of course. Just think. We'll spread word that you have created something so fine that few will be able to afford to hang it on their walls. I will invite some particular people to view it and they will confirm the rumours. Then we'll have a gathering and show the painting to the select few who express interest and can afford it."

Crivelli smiled. "Yes. Yes that would be wonderful."

"And when they're all talking about the painting, and the beautiful Madonna in the painting, we'll tell them it is a woman of incomparable beauty. A Madonna Virgin who has talents that are pure and unsullied."

Crivelli glanced at Alys and gave her a reassuring smile. "Yes. This will put her image in the mind of every man who comes to view the painting."

"She will be celebrated, sought after." Alessandra smiled. "This is better than I had hoped. Crivelli, you are a genius."

"It's the model you must thank as well," said Crivelli. "She makes the painting the marvel it is. And, with your consent, it won't be the last time I create such magic with her."

Alessandra nodded at him. "Ah. *Si, si*. In time. For now we must think of getting this painting admired and sought after. As well as the madonna who has modelled for it."

Alys heard the exchange numbly. The past few months, as she practiced the lute, sang the songs, learned the card games, and applied the cosmetics and perfumes as she'd been taught, in addition to conversing every afternoon with Madonna Alessandra on Venetian art, politics and history, she'd lulled herself into a sense of security. She'd thoroughly enjoyed most of these activities, except perhaps the cosmetics, but now she was reminded once again for the purpose behind it all. Soon she would have to put into practice the arts she'd learned so well.

Alys could hear the laughter and chatter as she approached the door to the *sala*. Everyone who had been invited was assembled inside, viewing and discussing the painting that was on display in the centre of the room. She smoothed her gown and adjusted the small pearl-encrusted velvet cap that was perched on her head. She tried to take comfort from the luxurious feel of the gown. It was so beautiful, of crimson kermes and cut in a deceptively simple style. Madonna Alessandra had presented it to her to wear tonight, assuring her its design would allow the difference in their size. The low cut bodice seemed too low on her and she'd pulled the lace edging of her chemise up just that bit to cover a bit more of her breasts. If she was to play the Virgin Madonna, she reasoned, there must be a degree of modesty.

Her pale ivory skin glowed in the candlelight and reflected the subtle warm hues of the crimson cloth. She had hardly recognised the woman she'd seen in the mirror in her room as the same one who'd left the Duchess' care less than a year ago. It was surely a lifetime ago, in more ways than one. She bit her lips to bring the colour to them, steeled herself and opened the door.

When she entered, many heads turned and stared. Eventually, the room fell silent and all pairs of eyes were on her.

"Ah, the Madonna Virgin. In the flesh, as I promised you all," said Alessandra, her voice full of laughter.

Alessandra made her way to Alys and took her hand. Gently, she led Alys to the only vacant chair. It was near enough to the painting that none could mistake the resemblance, but not so close that each exhibit couldn't have its own audience. Alys made her way, careful to go slowly and conceal her limp as much as possible. The distance was deliberately short. Alessandra had tried to account for everything.

Alys took her seat gratefully and arranged her mouth in what she hoped was a beatific smile. She clasped her hands lightly and spoke the few words she'd rehearsed under Alessandra's instructions.

"I greet you one and all and hope that you may enjoy my company in the months to come, as I'm certain I will enjoy yours."

She kept her tone musical, modulated in the manner in which Alessandra had coaxed her. It was a shade lower than she was used to speaking, but Alessandra had made her practice it enough that it was comfortable. In time, Alessandra assured her, she would find it as natural as her prior speaking voice.

There were murmurs and she scanned the room, looking at their reaction. The few women who were present were in the company of several men, their dress, cosmetics and manner marking them for what they were. For what she was. She was surprised to see the men regarded her with deep interest, some with speculative looks on their face, while others stared unblinking at her. Finally, she saw Crivelli, at the back, exchanging a few words with an older, well-dressed man.

Moments passed and no one approached her. The talk resumed, but at a lower level, and when she caught a phrase here and there, she realised she was the subject of conversation.

"You have astounded them all," said a voice beside her.

She looked up and found a handsome man with a slightly rakish air regarding her. "Signore?"

He bowed. "Forgive me. I am afraid your beauty has caused me to lose all sense of my manners. Allow me to introduce myself. I am Tomaso Cortini."

She smiled. The man was charming and she felt more at ease with his little joke. "Signore. You are too kind."

He gestured to the chair nearby. "Do you mind if I sit beside you?"

"Not at all. I would welcome some company. I seem to be the only one who has none at the moment."

He took the chair, placed it beside her and sat down. "That's because they are all in awe of you. It will take them time to get the courage to approach you."

"But you felt no such awe," she said and gave a little tinkling laugh as she'd practiced.

"Ah, but I did. I just worked to overcome it as quickly as I could, before anyone else could steal your attention."

"You are flattering me."

"How can you say that? You are the object of great curiosity and not just because you are Madonna Alessandra's new protégé."

Alys gave a tight smile at the reminder of her purpose at this gathering. "I know people will be curious about me."

"Curious yes, but they also marvel at your beauty. There is a quality about it that's unique."

She forced another laugh. "There is no question now that you are flattering me. No, I am new to Venice, and my appearance may be different to what might be common here, but I assure you it isn't in my home country."

"And where is that?" Tomaso asked.

She hesitated a moment, wondering if she should be truthful. "England."

"England? How interesting. I cannot believe that there are many like you, but I have never been there."

"You must meet Giacomo when he returns then," said a voice behind Tomaso.

Alys froze at the mention of the name Giacomo and then looked at the source of the voice. A tall, red-haired young man hovered at Tomaso's shoulder. Tomaso turned and put a hand on his shoulder.

"Ah, Niccolo. You have dared to approach the fair maiden."

Niccolo reddened. "I was hoping that you would introduce me."

"Of course, *amico mio*."

Tomaso performed the formalities and Niccolo gave a deep bow. "You are beautiful, madonna," he said.

Alys murmured her thanks and tried to calm herself. There were many men, she was sure, called by the name Barnabas now used. But she couldn't help herself. She had to ask.

"You mentioned I should meet someone named Giacomo who has been to England?" she said.

Niccolo nodded, all eagerness. "Ah, certainly. His father sent him there to learn something of the trade practices and the language. Though I am much more interesting than Giacomo."

"I know a Giacomo who spent time in England," she said. "Perhaps this is the same person."

Tomaso narrowed his eyes and studied her. "You know Giacomo Bonavillagio?"

She flushed under his scrutiny and the change in his tone and manner. "I-I believe so."

"Did you know him well?" asked Tomaso.

"Yes—no. I suppose I didn't really," she said. It seemed the truth at this moment. How much did she really know about Barnabas? And she certainly knew next to nothing about him as Giacomo.

"Giacomo once mentioned a young girl he knew in England. Would that be you?" asked Niccolo his tone enthusiastic.

"He mentioned me?" Alys didn't know what to think. The flash of joy gave way to caution and scepticism. "It most likely wasn't me." She forced a trace of humour in her voice. "There are many girls in London."

"And you are certainly no girl," said Tomaso, eyeing her breasts. He raised her hand and gave it a long and lingering kiss.

Alessandra came up beside Tomaso. "I must greet you most particularly, Tomaso. It has been some time since you have graced us with your company, but I am glad to see you are discovering the charms of my protégé. I hope that will help make you less of a stranger."

Tomaso turned, bowed and gave Alessandra a lazy smile. "I was under the impression you found someone else's card playing more amusing."

Alessandra cocked her head. "Tomaso, you couldn't be jealous, could you? But you see it isn't necessary. Look around you. Are you not the best card player here?"

He bowed again. "You're correct. Equilibrium has been restored."

"But I must claim you now and let others spend time in our little Virgin Madonna's company," said Alessandra.

She led Tomaso away into the throng. Niccolo gave them hardly a glance before focussing on Alys again.

"Your name, madonna, it is Maria?" he asked.

She forced a smile and nodded. "Yes, that's what they call me."

"Maria, it's beautiful. It's a shame that Giacomo isn't here to meet you and then you could see for yourself if it is the man you knew. Though, I cannot be too sorry, because I would rather not have him to compete for your company."

"Where is Giacomo?" she asked.

"Gone with the blackamoor to Egypt, I think. Alexandria. It's where Giacomo's father and brother are. Giacomo was reluctant to go, but his obligations demanded it."

"Will he be away for a time?"

"He said he wouldn't be very long, but it seems he has been kept there longer than he'd hoped. I thought he would have returned by now."

Alys sorted through his words. What did this information mean to her now? It was undoubtedly Barnabas if he was in the company of a blackamoor. It was too much chance to be otherwise. But Alexandria? That seemed an impossible place to journey to, even if she could in her present situation. A place so foreign she had no notion of what she, a woman of Christendom, would face there.

A heavyset man with dark eyes and thick jowls approached her and bowed. His rich silk and velvet robes testified to the wealth that was also displayed on his various gem encrusted rings on his fingers.

"Madonna, I meet you at last," he said.

Niccolo bowed, murmured a greeting and the man acknowledged it.

"Madonna, I would like to introduce you to Signore Luigi Bembo," said Niccolo.

Bembo took Alys' hand and she smiled at him. She kept her eyes on his nose so that she wouldn't have to see the jowls and beady eyes that stared back. Alessandra had described each guest and Alys remembered that Bembo, as a member of the Doge's inner council, was a very important man. She could feel Alessandra observing her even as she began a conversation with him. Soon she was joined by several other older men, all of whom were involved in some way in the governing of Venice, even Niccolo's uncle, Valentino, who'd joined Niccolo at her side shortly after Bembo had.

It was hours later, her head aching from the heat, and her fingers stinging from playing the lute with fingers sweating from nerves, that the evening drew to an end.

When the last guest had departed, Alys sighed and sank back against the chair where she was seated. Alessandra handed her a glass of wine. Alys shook her head.

"Drink it," Alessandra insisted. "It will calm you so you can sleep."

She eyed the glass doubtfully but accepted it from Alessandra's grasp. She took a sip and after a pause downed the rest of it. She sighed.

Alessandra stroked her head. "You've done well, *mia bambina*. None can deny what a triumph you are. Already I've had expressions of interest." Her tone was joyous. "They will pay dearly for your hymen. But I'll ensure they will pay even more than they now believe. Given a little time, they will think no price is too high."

Alys pulled away and stared up at Alessandra, trying to see her expression. She could see only a pale outline of the face under the dark veil. "You are selling my virginity?"

"Of course. What did you think was going to happen?"

Alys paused, fighting the anger. What had she thought? "I knew of course I would be entertaining men. And that at some point I would bed some of them. But you're having them bid for me?"

"Yes, you fool. Don't you see how much more valued you will be if it's done in this way? The money will be more, the notice will be greater and the wealth of the men who will vie for your attention will be huge in number."

Alys stared at the covered figure before her and searched for words. "Do we need so many?" She thought of the rich old men that had gathered around her. "Must they be all that wealthy?"

"They are your security," said Alessandra, her voice growing in anger. "They are my security."

She pulled off the dark veil and revealed a face livid with red scars and skin stretched over the remains of a nose and a misshapen mouth. The eyes, dark and glittering, flashed with emotion.

"Do you think any man would be charmed by me? Not so long ago I was the most celebrated courtesan in Venice." Her chest heaved and she fought for control. "We courtesans may be cultured and skilled in conversation and music, but without our looks we are nothing! We grow old and shrivelled, or, like me, fate takes a hand and we have suddenly no future and little money to keep us. So, to prepare against such events, we must create our own wealth, our own security that will see us through to our end. Just count yourself lucky that you don't have your whole family depending on you."

Alys said nothing for a moment, too stunned to reply to the tirade. Eventually, she lowered her head and nodded.

"You're right. I understand and ask your forgiveness for my ingratitude. You've done much for me and I forgot for one small moment."

"You're forgiven," said Alessandra. There was an edge to her voice. She draped the veil once more over her head. "And remember, the more you earn, the faster you'll be able to pay off your debts. Debts of money and obligation. For you are my security, as well as your own." Alessandra turned and went to the door. "I'll send Joanie to you to help you to bed."

Alys nodded and heard the door close. She studied her hands, wondering at the red marks that still remained on the fingertips. They would harden in time, she was sure, just as she would to the future she was facing in the next few months. She must remember that. And in that time she would try and find out more about Tomaso Cortini, for she had just remembered where she'd heard that name. It had been the signature on the letter she'd received when she'd first arrived in Venice and had inquired about Barnabas.

CHAPTER EIGHTEEN
Hüdavendigar, Autumn 1445
BARNABAS

I ran my finger along the curved blade carefully, testing the sharpness. The edge would cut through my finger without effort, I had no doubt about that. I balanced it in my hand, as I'd been taught, growing accustomed to its weight and handling. It was a fine scimitar and I was momentarily flattered that Umar had thought me capable enough to practice with it now.

"It's a fine blade," I said.

"See that you earn its use, Ahmed," said Umar in a mixture of Arabic and Turkish. He poked my padded vest and then tapped the metal helmet that topped my head. "These will only serve you so far, so be careful. I wouldn't have you cut your leg off by mistake."

I grinned, lifted the scimitar, and gripped it tightly in my hand. With my eye on the target, I sliced and slashed away at the side of skinned goat that hung from a suspended pole. It moved and twirled under my impact, but the cuts were nearly through to the other side. When the goat was butchered beyond recognition, I stopped, panting a bit.

"Very good," said Umar. "For your first time you have done well."

I couldn't help but feel delighted. "Will I be able to do it from the back of a horse soon?"

"You are still new to this, remember. It's best not to leap before you can even walk." Umar clapped me on the back. "You're doing very well, though, Ahmed. You're quicker than anyone else I've trained."

I felt a glow from the praise he'd given. By now I knew Umar didn't give it lightly. He meant every word. His approval meant more to me than I wanted to acknowledge after all these months, despite the fact he addressed me as Ahmed at every opportunity. I'd objected at first, refusing to answer to it. But it didn't stop him. He told me it was for my own good. To help me adjust to my new situation more quickly. As a tribute boy himself, he knew how best to leave the old life behind.

Umar slipped a wooden sword into my hand. "Here. We'll practice against each other now. Your arms are clearly strong enough."

I shook my head of the thoughts that forced themselves forward each day. I wouldn't dwell on my role as a "tribute boy." Though I was technically much older than was normal, I knew I was no different than those who were given to the sultan to be raised and educated to serve in various capacities.

Umar banged my sword with his. "Pay attention, Ahmed."

I focussed on his eyes and followed him slowly around the yard, both our wooden swords poised for action. Suddenly, he thrust his sword forward and the play began, lunging and parrying while we tried different forms of attack and defence. My mind cleared of all else and I sank into the enjoyment of the mock battle. Eventually, Umar called a halt and we sank down on the ground to rest.

"Good. You have improved. You remembered what I said the last time," said Umar. "You will be an excellent soldier." He grinned. "Maybe even better than me, someday. But probably not, if your archery doesn't improve."

I laughed. "Just how old were you when you came here first?" I asked eventually.

Umar shrugged. "Young. Much younger than you."

I looked at his brown curling hair, hazel eyes, and saw the skin that was pale enough, despite its tan. "Where are you from, then? Was your family upset when they gave you up?"

Umar shook his head. "I was born just south of the Danube. My parents were farmers, with many children, so they were happy when I was selected. It was an opportunity for me to be educated and possibly rise to a rank my family could only dream of. And so I have." He patted my shoulder. "There are many opportunities for you, too. You could go far. Perhaps even become a commander."

I glanced up at the palace window that overlooked the practice ground where often I would see Halil Pasha observing me. It was empty at the moment.

"I'm not certain that a soldier's life is what's planned for me," I said grimly. Since the first night I had been in Halil Pasha's company several nights a week. Nights that sometimes stretched into mornings that were only foggy in my memory because of the honeyed drink he pressed me to have and the heavy incense that filled the air, so thick it nearly choked me.

For the most part we conversed during these nights, or rather he talked to me, but there were times when he would stroke my arm, or my chest and murmur endearments, and no amount of washing afterwards could eliminate the crawling feeling on my skin. And there were a few nights that were lost to me, where afterwards I would lay fuzzy headed on my own mattress with no recollection of getting there, sore in body and in mind.

Umar knew what I meant and deep down it appalled me he knew. He'd been the janissary there at the door the first night. Now, he only shrugged. "*Insha'Allah.*"

I frowned. I wouldn't leave it up to Allah, or God. I was happy to learn these sword skills in the meantime, but I would make certain that I would find some way to escape. Nothing would change that.

I glanced up at the window. It was no longer empty. Halil Pasha raised his hand and motioned me to come to him.

"You're progressing well," said Halil Pasha.

I raised my head from the floor and looked at him. I nodded and adopted a neutral tone. "Umar is pleased, I think."

"And Habib, too. He says you have memorised more passages than he expected. He also says you're adept at Greek and have helped him with some translations."

I nodded, thinking about the Greek texts. Some were ancient, full of treatises on philosophy, and others of mathematics. I would spend hours over them, fascinated by their contents. Occasionally the imam, Habib, would debate with me. And in those moments I would forget myself and what I'd become.

Halil Pasha lifted a sweat-stained lock from my forehead. I went rigid. Even now his touch sent a wave of revulsion through me.

"Go, now. Prepare yourself for the evening," he said. "I'll meet you later."

I bowed low again, my head to the floor, and withdrew. The young slave, Usef, who attended me regularly, appeared outside my room and bowed his greeting. In what had become a nightly ritual, he helped me remove my clothes and slip on a robe and then followed me to the baths. There, he would wait patiently while I immersed myself in the steaming water and soaked away the sweat and grime from battle practice. Afterwards, he would towel me try and rub oil onto my body, massaging the muscles and create a sleek sheen on my skin.

When we'd returned to my room, he'd helped me dress in a robe and loose breeches selected by Halil Pasha. Once fully dressed, Usef would slip rings on my fingers, gold bands on my arm, or a gold chain around my neck. Finally, he'd rim my eyes with kohl and redden my lips. I felt like an ornament painted and decorated for show.

Now, it was no different, except for one detail. Tonight my robe was a vivid red silk, heavily embroidered with gold thread, with slippers to match and loose gold-coloured breeches. It was the richest outfit yet, and it made me wonder what it signified.

Usef nodded his approval. "The young master looks very fine." Usef's Arabic was difficult to understand at times and often he slipped in Turkish words. Like Umar and many in the palace, the tongue of the Turks was their native language. I was becoming increasingly proficient in it, but used Arabic when possible.

Despite Usef's words of praise, though, I could see that something bothered him. In the months since he'd served me I had found the formality between us had eased somewhat, to the point we could exchange a few pleasantries, but nothing beyond that.

"Is something wrong, Usef?"

Usef forced a smile and shook his head. "No, nothing. What could be wrong? The master pleases the Grand Vizier very much."

"And that's good?"

He muttered something in Turkish and I only caught a little of it. "The Grand Vizier is needed elsewhere?"

"Forgive me, young master. I have said too much already. It is nothing."

"Have you served the Grand Vizier for many years?"

Usef gave a wide smile, clearly glad for the change of subject. "Many years, yes. Since I was a very young boy. I travel with him wherever he goes."

I nodded and looked at him closely. Though there were traces of lines around his eyes and his skin was weathered I could see the handsome boy he'd once been. Was his remark borne of jealousy, or something else?

I stowed the thought away and steeled myself to the night ahead. After a nod to Usef, he led me from my room and down the hall to the spacious room in which I spent most evenings. Lamps illuminated the room and cast crenulated shadows along the carved screens and arches. Halil Pasha was waiting for me, resplendent in a long gold brocade gown. He dismissed Usef and I moved toward him and made my obeisance. When I rose he put his hands on my shoulders and examined me carefully.

I held his gaze for as long as I could, but eventually I glanced away. What I saw there was too much for me. It was the look that a man gives a beautiful woman he wants to bed.

"Yes. It is almost perfect. Just a few more touches," said Halil Pasha.

He reached inside his robe and withdrew a small velvet pouch. Carefully he emptied its contents onto his palm and held it out for me to see. A diamond earring.

"You are to wear this in your ear. It will be a mark of your rank, but also a mark of my connection to you."

"But my ear is not pierced," I said lamely.

He gave a small laugh. "I will remedy that now."

He moved over to a small table and took out a small gold needle from a box. He held it in the flame of one of the lamps for a moment and then came over to me. I braced myself as he pinched my right ear and then shoved the gold needle through. I said nothing, staring straight ahead. I felt him wipe the ear and place the diamond stud in position.

"There. It is done." He stepped back and nodded. "And now for the final step."

He clapped his hands and a man entered carrying a folded white cloth and a red cone. The man knelt on the floor, bowing low and placed the cloth beside him.

"Sit now, Ahmed," said Halil Pasha.

I did as I was told and the man came and knelt beside me. With great care and skill he placed the cone on my head and then wound the white cloth around it in the most elaborate of folds. When he was finished, Halil Pasha handed him a feather and a small jewel. The man secured them on the turban, bowed low and left.

Halil Pasha regarded me, a huge smile on his face. "Yes. Now it is perfect."

He took a seat beside me and patted my knee. "We have a guest tonight. A man who I have trusted for years. You will be gracious to him, I know."

I pushed aside any thought about what he might mean by the term "gracious." A short while later the door opened and a janissary ushered in a portly man with a large moustache and beard in a robe of silver and blue, his head encased in an oversized turban with a large red plume tucked in it. He bowed very low, and without kneeling, voiced a greeting to Halil Pasha.

"Please. Sit down, my friend."

"I thank you, lord."

The man took the place indicated on the thick carpet and offered a few pleasantries. Bowls of flat bread, stewed meats, and even sheep's feet were brought in, along with a spiced drink that was unfamiliar to me. The two men talked idly while I ate my fill, conscious of the strange glances the man gave me periodically. Eventually he spoke to me and asked me questions that concerned an array of topics including philosophy, geography, mathematics, and rhetoric, in Arabic, but also sometimes in Greek. I answered the best I could, aware that Halil Pasha listened carefully to everything I said.

Sweat beaded my lip and my tongue felt thick and dry. Nervously, I took a deep sip of my drink. The undercurrents heightened all my senses and I waited in dread for the end of the meal.

When the remains of the food were finally removed Halil Pasha spoke to the man, whose name was still a mystery to me. "Well, what do you think?"

The man nodded. "The resemblance is very striking. Uncanny, even."

"Yes. I agree. And he has the knowledge, too."

"He does. I think he is even more knowledgeable. But will his skills be enough?"

"They will," said Halil Pasha. "I'll make certain of it."

The man nodded. "When will you take the next step?"

"Soon, soon."

"I'm ready," said the man. "You need only send the signal."

"I thank you, my friend. I count on your support."

Halil Pasha nodded and the man took it as a sign to depart. He rose and after a deep bow and a few words of farewell, left the room. When the door closed Halil Pasha turned to me.

"You're no doubt wondering what that discussion was about. I will start by explaining what it was that drew you to my particular attention. You are of course unaware of it, but you have a very strong resemblance to the young Sultan's close friend who was sadly lost in battle."

"He was from the West, from Christendom, as I am?"

"He was a tribute boy, like you are. He had an aptitude for many things and was quickly selected to be a companion to the Sultan when the Sultan was but a young prince. Mehmet is still young now, too young, but sadly his father felt the need to step down and give the throne to him. But these are difficult times and it requires a man's wisdom and a man's strength, and I fear our young Sultan is incapable of such strength just yet."

"I'm sorry he's lost his friend, but I don't see how my resemblance to that friend can change the situation."

"Oh, but it can. With careful planning and timing it can indeed. And it must be done."

I looked at him mystified. "Did you want me to influence him? Surely I cannot convince the Sultan that I am his friend come back from the dead."

"No, you mistake me. Mehmet means me harm and I think nothing you can do will change that."

"You're certain of that? You want me to spy on Mehmet to warn you of danger?"

Halil Pasha laughed. "Nothing so innocent as that. No, Mehmet will never change, I know him too well. And your reading in the showstone only proved that. He will lead the armies of the Ottoman to disaster. He must be stopped. With your help we can do that."

I gave him an uneasy look. I had no doubt what he meant now. "You want me to take his life."

"I knew you would grasp the situation once it was explained. Yes, you will gain the Sultan's trust, and when you have sufficient access to him, you'll find an opportunity to poison him."

My eyes widened. "Poison? Do you really think I would be able to find such an opportunity? Why would he take as a companion a complete stranger, even though he might bear some resemblance to his dead friend? It doesn't seem possible."

"Oh it's possible. You have the looks and with the strong resemblance he will be unable to resist you. You will succumb sweetly to his advances, for haven't I groomed you well for such a thing? Then you build his trust, and when you can arrange it, slip the poison into his food."

I shook my head in disbelief. "But they would suspect me, surely. I would be killed. You're mad if you think I would agree to this."

"My dear Ahmed. You behave as if you have a choice."

"I won't agree. I'll tell him of your plans."

Halil Pasha laughed. "And they will kill you. Is that what you want?" He studied his nails. "Yes. Yes you will agree. Shall I tell you why? You will do it because I own you, but you will also do it because you are bound to me in more ways than you think."

I stared at him, puzzled. "I don't understand."

"No, you will, though." He reached across and wiped his fingers along my brow and then across my lip picking up the tiny rivulets of moisture that were trickling down. He held up his wet finger. "You are sweating, I see. And your heart beats fast, your tongue feels thick and dry and there is a slight cramp in your stomach, is that not correct?"

I frowned at him, cursing the truth that he spoke. I'd noticed the symptoms beginning earlier, but at their mention now, they seemed that much worse.

"You must have observed that I haven't given you the honeyed drink, or filled the room with incense as I have done every other night?"

I nodded, not trusting myself to speak.

"The drink you so obligingly quaffed every night and the incense were full of opiates. And over the course of these nights to come you'll find that if you don't have these nightly drinks and exposure to the opiates you will suffer."

I recalled the missing hours, the clouded thoughts and befuddled heads. "You've drugged me so that I would help you in this?"

"It was not only for this task. In addition to the immediate pleasure of your languorous cooperation each night, it has the added benefit of heightening your senses, making your abilities with the sword all the more keen the following day and your intellect that much sharper. That is if the doses are correctly administered."

"And you're saying I must continue with the doses if I'm not too suffer. Well, I will suffer, then."

Halil Pasha laid a hand on my shoulder. "I admire your courage, Ahmed. And I will give you an opportunity to test it, but I fear that you have a stronger master now that won't allow disobedience."

"Give me this chance, then," I said. I could feel the cramps growing stronger, but I ignored them. "I will do this."

"I'll strike a bargain with you. If you do resist the pull of the opiates, I'll let you go free. Is it agreed?"

I nodded only, too afraid to speak. The nausea that suddenly gripped me was so strong I was afraid I might empty the contents of my stomach at any moment.

CHAPTER NINETEEN
Hüdavendigar, Late Autumn 1445
BARNABAS

I repeated the phrase the Habib had given me listlessly and watched him nod his approval. I had little energy and would rather spend the time in my room, rolled up on my mattress, than sitting here reciting sections of the Koran. I licked my lips, now dry and cracked. Usef would tend them later, I knew, but I cared little.

I had lasted two days, no more, before the need for relief became so overwhelming, I'd begged Usef to take me to Halil Pasha though it was still night. Later, when relief came in the form of the honeyed drink, I cried piteously in my bed. By morning I could only feel disgust and anger at myself. Such emotions had dulled and I became, in only a few days, what I was now. Indifferent.

The small fire in the brazier in the room did little to warm my feet, chilled from sitting still and cross-legged for so long. My slippers were thin, though the carpet on which we sat was thick and soft, so that it wasn't the chill from the marble tiles beneath them that made me cold. It was more the constant watchfulness that drained my energy and the heat from my toes and fingers.

"Repeat all the phrases now," said Habib.

His beard seemed to have greyed even more since he'd taken on my instruction. I was a difficult student, there was no doubt. I repeated the whole passage as instructed, but took no pride in my accomplishment. I started to rise.

"Wait, my young student. We haven't quite finished this section."

I nodded and sighed. The remaining passages were recited, explained, and recited again. I repeated them obediently. I had no problem remembering them, I'd found I was quick enough with it. The Koran had many ideas that were familiar enough, and though the phrasing might be a little strange to me, it wasn't complicated.

Habib folded his hands. "Before you leave I have something for you to see." He reached over and pulled a wooden box towards him. "You asked me some time ago about the manuscript that al Qali had requested. The one regarding Prester John. Well here, in this box, I have a list of the manuscripts in our valued collections."

My interest stirred. "May I see the list? Is the Prester John manuscript named?" I looked at the box. "Does it say anything about what's in the manuscript?"

"I'm not certain if there is any detail about that particular manuscript." Habib paused. "Or if it is in the collection."

He let the words hang in the air and I swallowed the question that rose to my lips. Whether in actual fact if al Qali had received the genuine manuscript and if not, was it ever in this collection? Recalling the details that had brought us both here I realised it was entirely possible that the manuscript could be elsewhere. If it really existed.

"Do you know what it was that al Qali wished to find in the manuscript?" I asked.

Habib shook his head. "He disclosed very little about the reason for his search. But I can guess. You know the tale of Prestor John?"

"A little. I know that the legend has him a Christian priest and king who ruled over a vast wealthy empire somewhere."

"Yes. I see he has told you the main points. Did he place Prester John in any location?"

I thought. It was true that al Qali had mentioned Prester John, but only once, in passing, when I was discussing with him the manuscript I'd seen at the Duke of Burgundy's. The one by Rusticello da Pisa recounting Marco Polo's journeys.

"Was his kingdom somewhere in the Orient? Persia, or Cathay?"

Habib gave me an odd look. "Perhaps. Others think it might be in Africa."

His phrasing caught my attention. "They think it still exists?"

He sighed. "There were many rumours for centuries about this kingdom. They still persist. Who can resist a tale of a place with great riches?"

"And you think that al Qali was after its riches."

"It seems the most likely explanation. Though he might be seeking a place where there are fellow Christians of his kind."

I was stunned. "Christian? But al Qali isn't Christian. He is of your faith. I've seen him at prayers."

"Truly? Well, that is interesting," said Habib. "I understood that he was raised in Egypt and his mother was a Nestorian Christian from Syria and his father from somewhere in the heart of Africa."

I sat a moment and tried to make sense of the words and realised I knew very little about Master al Qali. Even less than I'd thought. His dark skin had always made me wonder about his background, but his ease with languages and his vast knowledge of so many subjects convinced me that the skin colour was more of a quizzical happenstance than a geographic location. But now I was determined to find out more, and the key seemed to be the manuscript.

"May I look at that list?"

Habib smiled and patted the box. "Of course. That's why I brought it to you."

He opened the lid and removed a large sheaf of papers and placed it in front of me. I stared at it in wonder. There were at least twenty titles on each page. And perhaps two or three hundred pages.

"This is a large collection," I said.

"No. It isn't. It's small in comparison to other libraries, I assure you. This is the Grand Vizier's personal collection."

I scanned the first page and saw that the titles were listed in a variety of languages, not just Arabic. It would take me some time to go through it all. In any case, would I know the Prester John manuscript by its title?

Usef applied the kohl stick to my eyes and stood back in satisfaction. "Even without a smile you are a handsome young man."

I suppressed the urge to scowl at him. It wasn't his fault that I was being dressed up like a doll once more, the turban man ready to perform his skill on my head. Already my blood sang in anticipation of the honeyed drink and the drug-laced smoke and I despised myself for it. For a few hours, in the quiet of the imam's study I had been able to forget all of this and lose myself in the joy of discovering the contents of the library, speculating on the titles, as I searched for one that might be linked to Prester John. When the tap had come at the library door and Usef had appeared to usher me back to my room, I sank once more into the depression that had lain heavy in me at the day's start. That I'd only managed half of the list and found nothing, didn't help my poor humour.

Usef now led me along the wide corridor to the familiar large room. I nodded to Umar who was standing guard. He gave me a reassuring smile and opened the door for me. I entered, walked slowly to Halil Pasha and made my obeisance. Incense hung in the air, thick and heavy with the drug and as I lifted my head I felt it fill my nostrils. I started to quiver, hating the very thought of what it was doing to me, but at the same time I couldn't stop inhaling it deeply and have it spread through my body in delicious relief. Was there any point in fighting it?

"Ah, good," said Halil. "I see that you understand your position now." He ran a finger along my chin and lifted it, looking into my eyes. "Even now your eyes dilate."

Without thinking I moved my head away and shut my eyes, hating that he could read my body so well. He gripped my chin and moved it back.

"Come now. There is no need for petulance. You shouldn't be worried. The dose you have is manageable. There will be no impairment. Haven't I told you that already?"

I glared at him. "I recall nothing about some evenings. Though I'm certainly grateful for that."

Halil Pasha gave me a slap on the face that was just hard enough to earn a red mark. "Nonsense," he said. "It was your body that failed to keep your mind sharp, nothing more."

He ran his hand again along my face and caressed the place he'd slapped moments before. I flinched at his touch.

"Come, come. Let us put aside this acrimony. We're here to enjoy the evening. Tonight I'll begin to teach you the proper etiquette for the Sultan's court, though we won't make you too polished. Mehmet prefers his companions a little….raw." Halil Pasha gave a short laugh.

I sat cross-legged across from him as he indicated. He poured the honeyed drink and offered it to me. "Don't worry, I haven't forgotten."

I took the goblet from him and sipped it. The taste was sweet and it coated my throat as it slid down. For a brief moment I thought I might drink half only, and in the coming weeks, wean myself off this delicious and dangerous drink. I took another sip and another and drank half, before I could stop and put it down. I was like a man parched with thirst after days without water.

Halil Pasha patted my hand. "Glad to see you enjoy your drink."

I strangled the sob that rose up. My humiliation couldn't go any deeper. I lowered my head and remained quiet during the meal, but Halil Pasha didn't seem to notice, and he filled the silence with instructions and descriptions of the Sultan's court at Edirne. I listened with half an ear until he began to question me about what he'd said.

"Pay attention to my words, Ahmed. Remembering everything I'm teaching you now could mean the difference between life and death."

I looked at him stupidly. The drug had erased the early sullenness and now I could only nod. His words made sense, I thought. Perhaps it would be best to concentrate. He quizzed me some more and I managed to satisfy him most of the time. After one question to do with the Sultan's food preferences a thought struck me.

"What will happen if I succeed in this task?" I couldn't bring myself to state the nature of the task.

"Why, as I said. Mehmet's father will have to leave his theological contemplations and resume his throne. Things will be as they were before Mehmet."

"And what of me? What will I do? Will you let me leave, return to my people?"

Halil Pasha gave me a peculiar look and squeezed my thigh. "Of course you will be free to choose what you will do. I want to see you happy. Don't you know that yet?"

A chill went down my spine. The look and his words had done nothing to reassure me.

~~~

I was near the end of the list and had only three possibilities. There was nothing in the title or the notation beside it that contained the name Prester John, though. They were only accounts of travellers. It was possible one of them mentioned Prester John. It was a small hope but it was the best I could see.

When I finished going through the list and had added only one more possibility to my own, I asked Habib if it was possible to look at them. He nodded and disappeared. While I waited I considered my findings. With no specific listing of a manuscript that included Prester John in its title, what manuscript did al Qali receive? And where did he go? Would it matter if Habib looked through these possibilities since al Qali hadn't seen them anyway? If only he knew what manuscript al Qali had been given.

An hour passed and the time for prayers approached, and still Habib hadn't returned. Finally, just as the call came from the muezzin, Habib appeared with a couple of rolled parchments and one bound manuscript in his arms. I smiled at the sight and took the bundle from him gratefully. I reached for the first and he stilled my arm and shook his head. I sighed and rose from the sitting position. I followed him out of the room to the small mosque where I would perform the ritual washing, unfold my rug and begin the prayers.

"There is one manuscript missing," he told me when we returned.

"Could that be the one that was given to al Qali?"

"It's possible. It was Halil Pasha who gave the manuscript to Master al Qali. He retrieved it and he alone knows which one he gave to al Qali, other than your friend, al Qali."

"He isn't my friend," I said flatly.

"No. I suppose he isn't."

I looked at the three manuscripts that were in front of me. I unrolled the nearest one and studied it. It was, as listed, a travel account of one Ben Izr across the deserts of Africa in the wake of the nomads who traded in salt. The language was vague and his account full of religious overtones. I soon tired of its rambling sentences and overblown phrases.

The second one proved even worse. It was an account of a journey, as was stated, but the journey was a magical one, filled with sea monsters and terrors that could easily have been in the mind. I discarded that one and took up the final manuscript, the one sewn with a soft leather binding. The account was specific enough and was a land journey followed by a sea journey described in excruciating detail. It spoke of the food that was eaten, the animals and fish that were observed and finally the dress of the people the narrator had encountered. No names were mentioned and despite the detail, there was no indication where the journey was made. I looked at the title again, trying to find a clue, but there was none.

I sighed and set it aside. I consulted my list of titles to find the one that was missing for any clue that it might hold. It was called *An Account of the Travels of Guillaume le Franc*. It hardly seemed relevant.

"Do you know this manuscript at all?" I asked Habib. I pointed to the title.

He studied the name for a while and then picked up the thick sheaves of paper that had all the titles. He flipped the pages and, finding the one he wanted, ran his finger along it until he stopped at the title. There was a small mark beside it.

"Yes," he said. "I thought as much. There are a few manuscripts we copy, for various reasons. Some are so valuable we ensure that only the copy is used for study. Others are copied and given as gifts to distant scholars or libraries if they request it. This manuscript has been copied, I see. Because it is so valuable."

I felt a flicker of hope. "Can I see the copy?"

He smiled and held up a hand. "You may, of course. For are you not a scholar?"

I let that thought echo in my head while I waited for Habib to retrieve this final manuscript. Was I a scholar? I gave a bitter laugh. At one time I would have taken delight in the notion. Felt flattered. Now I knew it was a lie. I wasn't a scholar, or a soldier. I was a slave, an addict, and worse. Soon I was to be a murderer, if Halil Pasha had anything to say.

"You are fortunate, my young friend," said Habib when he returned, puffing gently from the exertion. "The manuscript was there, on top of its box." He placed it on the table. After a moment he frowned. "Wait, this isn't a copy. It's the original."

I touched the parchment, sewn carefully at the side to form a slim codex. The first page was blank except for the few words written in some nondescript ink, now faded with age. The title was exactly as noted in the holdings list.

"You're certain?" I asked.

He nodded. "Yes. The ink, you see. And the parchment. It's sheepskin whereas our copies are made from goatskin. Cheaper and not as fine." He made his way to the door. "I must look and see if the copy is there. It's a serious matter if someone has put this back incorrectly."

I nodded and Habib left. I turned to the valuable manuscript and carefully opened it. It had been copied from a French document which could have easily been lost centuries before. The words, in Turkish, rang out in a curt and careful language, the language of a soldier, I thought. Like the other authors, he wrote of his travels, a soldier who had begun with the crusades and, the battles over and lost, had journeyed on to other lands. He described the countryside, his manner detailed enough that you would understand his progress, and he also described the people he'd encountered. One such meeting led to an exchange of tales that were so fantastic, so unbelievable, the narrator felt compelled to note them down, but added his own words of caution about their truth.

It was this exchange that caught my particular attention, because the man he encountered claimed to have been to the kingdom founded by Prester John. A Prester John who claimed descent from the third Magi and of such holiness that everyone he met immediately fell into a state of grace. He had even converted the grand king of a vast empire who had handed over his wealth and people in the hopes that they would be similarly blessed.

I felt a tinge of excitement. Was this what al Qali had sought? I searched for more clues that might reveal the kingdom's location. There was little enough information, except there was abundance of vegetation and heat in this place.

The door opened and I looked up. "The copy is missing," said Habib, frowning. "I'll try and discover how it came to be so."

"At least your valuable manuscript is still here. You can always copy it again."

Habib gave a grim smile. "Yes, that is so."

"I will copy it for you," I said. "I can begin now."

Habib nodded vaguely. "I will see that you have the necessary supplies."

"Thank you. I would consider it an honour to copy a valuable work from such an exalted library."

Habib waved his hand. "Yes, yes. I thank you, also. If you'll excuse me I'll make the arrangements."

Habib closed the door, his manner very distracted. I scooped up the manuscripts that I'd looked at previously and pushed them aside. One manuscript, Ben Izr's description of the nomad's journey along the salt route, rolled off the table. I bent to pick it up. On an impulse I rolled it up tighter and stuck it inside my tunic. Something exotic, as Alessandra requested? The thought surprised me, because it assumed that I would escape this prison alive, an unlikely event. I started to remove the scroll from my tunic, paused, and tucked it back in.

CHAPTER TWENTY
Venice, Winter 1446
ALYS

Alys swirled the ground pigment in with the oil, taking pleasure in the way the colour gradually emerged. It was Crivelli's preferred method of creating paint and she could see why. The colours retained a rich vibrancy that mixing with egg white didn't always achieve. It might not be the best choice for painting friezes on the walls of churches and palazzos, but it was perfect for working on board or canvas.

She'd come to appreciate the difference just in these last weeks in the few times she was allowed to assist Crivelli at his studio. Even now she was supposed to be sitting for Crivelli for a new commission from a Signoro Portelli who'd seen the other painting in its new home. It was another religious scene; this time she was St Catherine posing as a graceful martyr amid a sumptuous swirl of fabrics, while in the distance the cross on which she was to be crucified stood starkly. The background was completed with its azure skies and wind-blown clouds that topped the hill seen through a large window. The interior and her position were only blocked in on the board. Crivelli had sketched in her various poses earlier, but the real work was beginning.

She picked up a brush and ran it along her palm. Crivelli had allowed her to apply the raw sienna underpainting that gave the painting its golden hue. She'd loved every moment of that, even though it was simple enough. Now she itched for something more complicated, like creating the undercoats of the rich crimson cloth.

"I've finished making the paint," she said.

Crivelli looked up from the table where he was studying his sketches. He stared at her blankly for a moment and then a slow smile spread across his face. "Good. Very good."

He rose from the table and went over to inspect her work. Great blobs of colour rested on the wooden palette on the table near the large board that held the painting.

"*Bene.* You have a good touch. That's perfect." He leaned over, brushed her hair aside and kissed her neck.

Alys manoeuvred away from him and looked at Joanie, sitting in the corner patiently. Joanie frowned at her and shook her head.

"Crivelli, please. You mustn't. Madonna Alessandra would be cross."

He caressed her cheek with his hand. "Ah, but not for long, *mi bella amore*. Soon you will be plucked, and then she won't mind so much."

Alys went cold. "What do you mean? Has someone offered a price?" She couldn't bring herself to say it all. She knew that Alessandra had good reasons for trying to get as much money as she could for the price of Alys' virtue, but it didn't stop the deep feelings it created, even though she couldn't name those feelings. It wasn't horror, it wasn't exactly despair; all she knew was that it pained her deeply.

"Many have offered prices for you, little one, but the bidding is closed now."

"And who is it that won?"

Crivelli sighed and nibbled her neck, suddenly drew her into his arms and kissed her soundly. She allowed it and for a moment felt the enjoyment of it.

"Who is it?" she asked again. Was it so terribly bad that he felt he had to make love to her himself?

"Alas, my lovely one, I only know that it isn't me. Wish that I had the funds to be the one to deflower you."

He bent over to kiss her again, but Alys pulled away firmly. "I'm sorry, Crivelli. I must go, now."

She snatched up her cloak and nodded to Joanie, who followed her out of the studio and down to the street below. It was then Joanie gave vent to her thoughts.

"That woman. It's disgraceful the way she's 'aving all those dirty old men sniffing around you and then bidding for you like you was some 'orse they wants to buy."

Joanie was breathing heavily, her anger fierce. Alys winced under her tirade. She'd done her best to explain the reasoning behind what Alessandra was doing—what she, Alys, was doing—but Joanie found it difficult to accept.

"If you must go through with this, Alys, at least get the money from that woman first. She can't be trusted."

"She has spent a lot of money on me, Joanie. On the both of us. The doctor, my leg, my clothes. All costly things."

Joanie shook her head. "I knows that if it was me, I'd at least be asking 'ow much."

Alys sighed. It wasn't the amount she was being sold for that she wanted to know but the identity person who was paying the money.

❧

When Alys arrived home she headed directly for the *sala* in the hope that Alessandra might be there, Joanie trailing behind her. She knocked and waited for permission as she always did. Alessandra preferred it, and Alys knew it was to give her time to put her veil into place, rather than any strict adherence to manners or privacy.

Alessandra's voice issued the words of permission and Alys entered the room. Alessandra was sitting at her small desk, writing. A dim light filtered in from the long windows that were shut tight against the cool breezes of winter that blew in from the canal.

Alessandra looked up when Alys entered, limping slightly. "Ah, my little madonna. She returns early. Is the painting progressing well?"

Alys gave a small curtsey. "Yes. I think you'll be pleased." She paused a moment before continuing, taking a deep breath. "Crivelli mentioned that you have received bids. That it had finished."

Alessandra nodded slowly. "Yes, there has been much interest, I'm pleased to say. And the highest offer is beyond my expectation."

Alys tried to hide her annoyance. Was she to have remained in ignorance? "May I ask who the successful person is?"

Alessandra laughed. "Oh, you mustn't fret, Maria *mia*. I intended to inform you today when you returned. You will be pleased, I think, when I tell you who it is. Though I must say that I'm surprised myself. Who'd have thought it, eh?"

Alys tensed. Pleased? Crivelli had already said it wasn't him. "Who is it?"

"Tomaso."

"Tomaso?" she asked, startled. It was true that Tomaso had paid her much attention in these past weeks and she'd found him very charming and entertaining. He'd kissed her hand a few times in a lingering manner and had once brushed a few stray hairs out of her face, but she'd no idea he was that enamoured of her.

"But I didn't realise that he... that he wanted me in that way."

Alessandra shrugged. "Some men enjoy deflowering women. Though I have to say that Tomaso never struck me as one of that kind. I also didn't realise he had that kind of money. He must have had some very successful nights at cards."

Alys considered Alessandra's words. What could a man possibly like about taking someone's virginity? Suddenly she didn't feel as relieved as she first was when Alessandra had told her.

"Was his offer very large?" Alys asked.

"Very large," said Alessandra with real joy in her voice. "The offer was so handsome that it will of a certainty cause great attention. And that will beget more interest in you. It is all good, child."

Child. That's what she felt like at the moment, though it was soon to be a laughable endearment.

"When will this assignation take place, Madonna Alessandra?" asked Joanie asked in Italian. "I think of the young madonna's gown, you see, and the care of her skin and hair."

"That isn't your concern. I'll see to her dress." Alessandra waved her hand in dismissal.

Joanie gave Alys a reluctant look and departed. Alys turned to Alessandra expectantly. Despite the dark veil, Alys could feel Alessandra studying her carefully.

"You know what goes on between a man and a woman?" asked Alessandra, her tone careful.

Alys flushed, though she had no idea why she should feel embarrassed at this point. The time for pandering to sensibilities had long since passed.

"I have some idea," she said.

"It would be best if you had more than an idea." Alessandra rose from the desk and made her way to the cushioned strewn high backed bench. She patted the place beside her. "Come, sit here. It's time you learned the more intimate ways of pleasuring a man. I wouldn't have you so awkward that you will cause Tomaso impatience. And you will see, in the end, that it's better for you and your partner if you are skilled. Better for me, as well, for I wouldn't have Tomaso or anyone think I wouldn't pass on my knowledge to anyone I sponsor."

"Madonna, there's no need. I'm sure I'll manage."

The thought of Alessandra discussing frankly her artful ways with any man was more than Alys could bear at the moment. She looked down at the small leather bracelet that still hung around her wrist and picked at it. Her life had taken a shape she would have never imagined when Barnabas gave her this all those years ago. She'd worn it constantly since then, but now it seemed wrong. The pledge it symbolised to her was broken, or as near to being broken as ever it could be. Alys felt a hand grip her arm.

"This isn't the time for feminine blushes." Alessandra's tone was sharp. "You'll pay attention. We're in a business that requires certain skills. And the quality of our skills contributes to the price we can demand."

Alessandra squeezed her arm tighter. "Do you understand my meaning?"

"Yes, madonna."

"Good. Now, for your first time it's fitting that you should be a little shy and awkward. Men like that."

"Men like it?" asked Alys.

Alessandra gave a throaty laugh. "Oh, yes. It gives them a sense of power, that they have found territory where no else has been and that somehow makes it special for them. Believe me, I know. I saw it often enough when I was playing the virgin."

"Was it painful?" Alys blurted out. It was something that she'd wondered for a while now. She couldn't bring herself even to ask Joanie, for fear of bringing another tirade down upon her.

"For me it was. Only because it was my mother's lover who took me first, in secret, when I was but fourteen," she said bitterly.

"I'm sorry," Alys said. The words seemed feeble enough but it was all she could think to say. "You weren't a courtesan then?"

Alessandra snorted. "Oh, I was being trained for it. My mother was planning it carefully, so that I might have as many high bidders as you and that my name would be entered on the Register of Courtesans with praise even before I started. When she'd discovered what had happened, she paid off her lover and pretended that I was still untouched. At the time of my official deflowering by an appropriately high bidder, who was a lump of an old patrician, she consulted an herbalist beforehand and made it seem as though I was a virgin." She shrugged. "The man never knew the difference."

"Your mother trained you to be a courtesan?"

The thought hadn't occurred to Alys. Though she'd met a few of the other courtesans at the parties she'd attended, she'd never conversed with them in any depth. She'd never imagined a mother would train her daughter to be a courtesan. It seemed unnatural to her.

"Of course. My mother had great skill. She'd learned from Francesca, a woman renowned for her beauty and poetry. My mother's family couldn't afford a dowry for her and they needed the money she could provide as a courtesan. It's not uncommon, you understand. The cost of a dowry is high, and not every family can manage it if they have more than one daughter. It's either this choice or the church, and my mother would certainly not have chosen to spend her life secluded in that way."

The bald manner in which Alessandra had recounted her story took Alys aback. She'd wondered what had made Alessandra make the choices she had, but Alys had always imagined it had been something desperate and tragic, like the fire that had ruined her face and body.

"I see," said Alys, attempting calm. "I had no idea it was such a practical decision."

Alessandra shrugged again. "It is a choice that has its benefits." She gestured around her. "I have my comforts, I'm able to have a household, to play my music and to enjoy my entertainments. I have no cause for complaint. Besides, I have other ventures that are becoming just as lucrative. Once you are well established, I may even allow you to buy my share of my investment in you."

Alys gave her a weak smile. She supposed she should be grateful to Alessandra for what she knew was a generous offer, but somehow she took no joy in it.

"Come now," said Alessandra. "There is much to learn in five days."

"Five days?"

"Yes. Didn't I say? Tomaso and I have fixed a date for the meeting in five days' time."

Alys' mouth opened in a perfect 'o.' Five days and then she would be launched into a life from which she knew there was little hope of return. Was it what she wanted? But then there was little choice, so there was no use mourning about it. She picked at the leather bracelet on her wrist.

❧

Alys fingered the silk ribbon that tied the long sleeveless blue silk robe closed just beneath her breasts. Underneath, she wore nothing but the sheerest linen shift that left nothing to the imagination. Her hair was caught up with a few pearl-encrusted combs and there was a small braid at either side of her head. Blue silk slippers covered her feet. Alessandra had chosen blue because she thought it made Alys look ethereal and her hair even more golden red. Now she examined the results and gave a nod of approval.

"*Molto bella.* Tomaso will be pleased. He loves beautiful things."

Alys tried not to show her agitation and murmured a few words of thanks. Her hands were clammy and her heart was beating at a pace she was certain would be noticeable. Her damaged leg throbbed and she tried to ignore it. She glanced around her, noting again the effort that Alessandra had made to create a luxurious setting for an intimate evening. A table was placed in her bedroom, near the window, the rich curtains now drawn across it. Only one candelabra was lit, but it was set so that it illuminated the rich food on the table covered with a soft Persian rug. A deep red wine filled a pair of goblets made from the finest Murano glass. Alys knew without checking that the wine was Tomaso's favourite. Flowers perfumed the room, specially obtained and at great expense, blending perfectly with Alessandra's scent, which had been sprinkled liberally on Alys' skin.

Alessandra's lute lay against the arm of one of the chairs. Alys moved over to it, trying not to limp, and picked it up, glad to have something to keep her occupied while she waited for Tomaso to arrive. Before she could strum even the first chord she heard voices below.

Alessandra laughed. "He is early, the scamp. He is either eager or he doesn't want to give me time to finish my work."

Alys fiddled nervously with the pegs on the lute. The door opened and one of the servants announced Tomaso as he followed her in.

"There is no need," he said. "Madonna Alessandra is expecting me."

He bowed with a flourish. His speech was slurred slightly and his fine velvet cloak and doublet were a little dishevelled.

"Oh, Tomaso," said Alessandra, humour in her voice. "You've been celebrating already?"

"Merely fortifying myself against the dazzling beauty of your protégé."

Tomaso examined Alys carefully for several moments, then made his way to her, took her hand and kissed it, first on the back and then in her palm.

"But I see it has been to no effect. I am dazzled beyond reason," said Tomaso.

Alys blushed and lowered her head. "You do me a great honour with your compliments, signore."

"Tomaso. You must call me, Tomaso. For aren't we to have a night of heavenly bliss together?"

Alessandra laughed. "Oh, you are a rogue. Don't be so heavy with your compliments. You will scare the child witless if you're not careful." She offered her gloved hand to Tomaso who took it and kissed it lightly. "Now, I'll excuse myself and leave you two to a perfect evening." She lifted her skirts and made her way to the door. "The servants will be within call, should you need anything."

Alessandra's tone had been light, but there was a hint of warning behind it for Tomaso. Should he by some reason take it upon himself to behave badly, there would be consequences. Alys took small comfort in that.

Left alone with Tomaso, Alys stared at him a moment, speechless. She was just about to offer him something to eat when he spoke.

"Shall we play cards, then?"

The suggestion surprised her. "Wouldn't you rather eat something? Or have some wine? I'm sure it's your favourite. Or perhaps you would like me to play for you?" She held up the lute still clutched in her hands.

"No, I think not. I prefer cards. They relax me."

It hadn't occurred to Alys that Tomaso might be nervous as well. She smiled and nodded. She made her way over to the table and started to move the plate of food and bottle of wine aside. Reconsidering, she took the wine bottle and poured herself a glass. She offered him wine again and this time he nodded.

A few moments later they were seated at the table and ensconced in a game of cards. He laughed at some of her choices and explained better selections and strategies.

"I'll make a good card player out of you," he said. "It's clear that Giacomo taught you nothing of card playing."

Alys blinked. "Giacomo plays cards?" She knew she shouldn't be surprised. In the years since she'd seen him he could have changed beyond recognition for all she knew. But something inside her told her the Barnabas she remembered would always be there. The funny, impish boy, who was too clever by half and full of courage.

A dark look passed across Tomaso's face. "Yes, he plays. Too well, I think for it to be anything but tricks, but he had Alessandra's blessing, so who would challenge him? Not I, even though none could beat me before that."

"He played cards with you, then?" Alys tried to keep her voice calm. It was clear that Tomaso had no liking for Giacomo, but she needed to find out what he knew. She hadn't realised that he'd known Giacomo so well. She'd thought only Niccolo was acquainted with him to any large degree, and she'd not seen Niccolo since her first night in public.

"Not often. I had my fill of him after the first time, when he partnered Alessandra. He pretended to have only a passing knowledge of the card game, but that was soon proved wrong when we were deep in play. It wasn't honest, I say."

"And you play honestly?" she asked, her voice innocent. She knew from Alessandra that Tomaso was as full of tricks as anyone who ever sat at a gaming table. "I am glad to hear it, signore. I hear that so many are not."

Tomaso gave her an odd look, but let the remark pass. "Let us speak no more of the man. I would have nothing good to say about him." He gave her a warm smile, reached for her hand and kissed it. "Except to say that he has exquisite taste in women."

She forced a smile and cocked her head prettily. "Thank you, Tomaso. But rest assured that it is you who fills my mind at present."

Tomaso drained his glass and took up her hand once again, kissing and caressing the palm. He pulled her up and drew her into his arms and pressed his lips hard against hers. He placed kisses along her neck and ran his arm along her back to her buttocks. She could feel the heat of his hand through the thin silk fabric and linen. With effort, she suppressed the nervous shaking that threatened to overtake her. Instead, she took his hand and led him to the bed, Alessandra's instructions echoing in her head.

Tomaso fumbled with the tie on her robe inexpertly. She took it from him and loosened it from its simple bow. She removed the robe slowly, watching Tomaso's eyes, which seemed to look past her. Perhaps he was still nervous, an ironic thought considering her state. She remembered Alessandra's guidance regarding the nervous and shy, and with a deep breath took Tomaso's hand and placed it on her breast. His palm was sweaty and it lay flat and unmoving for a few moments before he removed it.

Trying another tack, she unfastened the laces of his doublet and helped him to remove it, and then applied herself to the ties on his pourpoint. He stopped her a moment and placed a hand at his crotch. There was little evidence of the erection that Alessandra had described as necessary. Tomaso suddenly caught up her hands and turned her around so that her back was facing him. He pressed himself against her and began rubbing hard against her buttocks. It was then she felt his erection. A moment later he'd lifted her shift and took her then and there from behind. Pain ripped through and she cried out. Tomaso kissed her neck and made soft soothing noises in her ear. The pain continued as he thrust against her, clutching her around the waist. She could think of nothing but the pain.

It was later, lying on the bed, her bloodied thighs rinsed and dried, the pain subsiding, that she allowed herself to think about what had happened. It wasn't as

Alessandra had explained. Not fully. She'd not mentioned this amount of pain. She could only hope that in future there would be less.

Tomaso's arm was draped across her waist. Carefully she turned on her side, so that she faced away from him. A tear slid down her face and she brushed it away. This was the life she'd chosen and she must live with it, there was nothing else to be said. Like Alessandra she must enjoy the comforts it brought, like her painting.

In the late morning, after Tomaso had departed, Alys slipped into a metal tub filled with hot water and allowed it to soothe her. With Joanie's help, she carefully rinsed and washed out her womb with the preparation Alessandra had given her to prevent any chance of conception.

She was still soaking in the tub, her eyes closed when Alessandra entered and began to quiz her about the evening. After Alys described the manner in which Tomaso took her Alessandra gave a murmur of surprise.

"I'm sorry," she said. "I didn't expect him to behave that way. But it seems to confirm what I had always suspected."

Alys waited a moment but Alessandra remained silent. "What did you suspect?"

"That Tomaso preferred men."

"Preferred men? But then why choose me? Why pay all that money to have my virginity?"

Alessandra shrugged. "Fame. To acquire more notice and invitations to card games. Who knows?"

Alys frowned. Was that the reason? She wasn't certain it was that simple. But there was no doubt in her mind that her first sexual encounter had been in no way enjoyable. But as she reminded herself, she would take

233

her pleasure from painting and the rest would be business.

CHAPTER TWENTY-ONE
Venice, Early Spring,1446
ALYS

Alys' laughter rang out as she climbed the stairs to the front door of the palazzo, forcing her damaged leg to keep its pace. Three men trailed behind her. Reflections of the torch flames shimmered brightly in the water and added to the festive feel of the party. The men shoved each other and spouted bad poetry. Alys faltered on the steps, her leg still weak. One man broke away and came alongside Alys, offering his arm. It was Valentino, Niccolo's uncle, ever the gallant in public. She patted his hand gave him a light kiss on the cheek.

"Sweet madonna, can you not send these young knaves home early so we can begin our night together that much sooner?" he asked.

"It gladdens my heart to see you so eager, signore, but I assure you there is plenty of time for all manner of pleasure."

Valentino gave a small groan. "Is it not bad enough that I only get to see you once a fortnight?"

"I only wish it could be every night, I do," said Alys with a small pout. "But you know I have other engagements that I'm not able to break." She squeezed his arm. "We'll just sing a song or two and then send Niccolo and Pietro away."

"One song?"

She laughed again. "Two. To do otherwise would be rude. And I cannot have that."

They entered the palazzo, Niccolo and Pietro railing behind, and made their way to the *sala*. Alessandra was there, clad in her usual black, holding a basket.

"Ah, you've returned," she said. "And brought some fine friends with you, I see. Welcome Valentino. So good to see you as always. And your nephew as well. I don't think I know your other friend, though."

Valentino made the introductions and nodded to the basket she held. "You've just returned from the market?" he said in a humorous tone.

A scrabbling noise could be heard from inside the basket and Alessandra laughed. "Perhaps it is a fine plump chicken. No, a messenger just brought it from Signore Fabriano. He said it was a gift for Madonna Maria." She presented the basket to Alys.

Alys took it from Alessandra and looked at it curiously. Carefully, she opened up the lid and a furry head popped out and gave a little yip. It was a small dog, with large sad eyes that stared dolefully out at Alys.

"How dear it is," she said. "I must write a note at once to tell Signore Fabriano how delighted I am."

Niccolo came over and stroked the soft fur on its head. "What will you call it?"

"I don't know. Is it a bitch?"

Niccolo pulled the little dog from its basket and examined it. "No, definitely not."

Alys placed the basket at her feet and took the dog from Niccolo. She held him up and looked into its small, flat face and once again noticed the large sad eyes. The dog gave a small yip.

"Barnabas," she said. "I think I'll call him Barnabas."

Niccolo exchanged a glance with Pietro and Valentino looked puzzled.

Alessandra laughed. "What a curious name. But perhaps you have an affinity to that saint."

Alys nodded and pulled the dog in under her arm and fondled his ears. "His feast day is special to me, it's true. I like the name."

Valentino shrugged. "Whatever name you give him, you look most charming together."

Alys laughed. "We will be inseparable, I think."

"Not too inseparable, I hope," he said.

Joanie poured the water into the large bowl and turned to help Alys off with her thin silk chemise. Valentino had gone at the first sign of light and it was time for what had become a ritual washing away of her night's activities. She remained still while Joanie ran the wet cloth down along her body. The water was cool and refreshing. Even the thorough dousing of her womb with vinegar and herbs gave her a sense of peace at the end of it.

The little dog raised his head at the sound of all the activity. All night he had remained curled up underneath her bed after Valentino had thrust him there. A few whimpers had tugged at her heart, but eventually he'd settled down to sleep. Now he emerged from the bed cautiously and made his way over to Alys. She patted his head affectionately.

"He's a lovely little thing," said Joanie. She bent down and stroked his head. The dog licked her fingers and she laughed. "Well, this little mite is gentle with his attention." She frowned and eyed Alys' arm, where a small bruise was beginning to form.

Alys shrugged. "The dog doesn't pay for the privilege of my attention."

It happened on occasion, especially with Valentino, who would grip her arm or perhaps clutch her buttocks so tightly bruises would appear that she would have to conceal with carefully applied powder.

"That may be so, but there is no call for marking your beautiful skin, no matter 'ow much he pays for it."

Alys shrugged. She'd grown used to it, thinking there were far greater things that could happen.

"Don't pass it off, Alys. It ain't right. The sooner we can quit this place and go back to England, the better."

Alys patted Joanie's arm. "I know you want to go soon, but it will be some time before we can even consider it."

"It's not for me, Alys. I worries about you. You mustn't forget who you are, now. Promise me."

"How could I forget with my dearest friend here to remind me?" She kissed Joanie on the cheek.

Later, she fondled and stroked Barnabas' fur, thinking about the source of this gift. Cosimo Fabriano came every week since he'd first made the arrangement with Alessandra months ago. Alys knew he'd paid a hefty price for the pleasure of it, and since then, he'd given her a necklace, and when the weather was cold, a fur muff. She found his manner hesitant and kindly when he was alone with her, and often all she did was sit on his knee while he stroked her hair and talked about his long dead wife. Now he'd given her this little dog. Whatever had made her name it Barnabas? It had come to her in a fit of pique and longing, but now when she considered it, she realised it was foolish. She caught sight of the worn leather bracelet around her wrist. With a sigh she untied the bracelet and put it away in the small wooden case that held her few jewels.

She bent down and kissed the little dog. "I will call you Bitty, because you're a small little thing."

***

She climbed carefully from the gondola, Joanie in tow, and made her way along past the church of St Simon and turned down to the street where Crivelli lived. She stopped short when she saw a figure slumped across the steps. It took her a few moments to recognise Crivelli. She rushed forward and knelt at his side. His face was a mass of bruises and his right arm hung at an awkward angle. Blood trickled from his mouth.

"Quick, Joanie, help me get him inside." The two of them lifted Crivelli and supported him up the steps. He groaned loudly with the pain. Joanie pounded on the door and the owner, Signore Barberi, answered.

"It's Signore Crivelli," said Alys. "He's badly injured."

"Here, give him to me," Barberi said. "I'll get him to his room."

Barberi took Crivelli from Joanie and Alys and hoisted him against his side. Crivelli cried out.

"Have a care, signore," said Alys. "He appears to have injured his arm."

Barberi grunted and made his way back through the door and up the narrow stairs that led to Crivelli's room, Alys and Joanie in his wake. Eventually, Crivelli was settled in his bed and Alys could begin to examine him.

"I'll call my servant," said Barberi. "We'll see to him. You can go, now."

"We'll stay," said Alys firmly. "If you could have your servant bring some hot water in a bowl and some cloths, I would appreciate it." She began to remove her cloak.

Barberi gave her a hard look. "It isn't right that a lady be in a gentleman's room, let alone tend to him." He eyed her up and down and then looked across at the painting of her propped on an easel by the window. "But then I guess you're not a lady, are you."

It wasn't a question, Alys knew that. It was a statement of fact. She flushed nonetheless, but a moment later, set her shoulders firmly.

"There is no time to discuss niceties, signore. My friend needs help and I'm here, so that's all there is to it. I would appreciate it very much, though, if you could ask your servant to bring the water and cloths. My own servant will assist me, and should anything more intimate be required, I'm certain she can manage. Otherwise, if we need you, we'll let you know."

Barberi frowned and gave a short nod. "Very well. I'll see it done." He gave one last glance down at Crivelli, who lay pale and sweating on the bed, and left the room.

After he'd gone, Alys turned once again to Crivelli. His clothes were ripped, one boot was missing, and there was no sign of a hat. Never the most fastidious of dressers, Crivelli had nonetheless carried an air of dishevelled elegance about him. There was nothing of that evident, now.

She removed Crivelli's remaining boot with Joanie's help and then began on his clothes. His tattered doublet was undone, the laces slashed, and they managed to remove it after some struggle and groaning from Crivelli. It was then that Alys saw the tear in the thin pourpoint vest and the blood seeping from it. Joanie gasped.

"Crivelli, were you stabbed in the side?" asked Alys.

Crivelli opened his eyes at the sound of his name. "Madonna," he murmured. "Or are you an angel saint from heaven to take me off?"

Alys heard the trace of humour and took heart from it. "Not an angel, certainly, but here to help you. It seems you've been stabbed. Are there any other wounds we should know about?"

"No," he said weakly. "I don't know."

She frowned. "You'll need to help me, Joanie. We have to examine him fully."

"Let me, Alys. It makes no odds to me what I see."

Alys shook her head. "It matters not which one of us does it. And it's likely I've seen more bare flesh on men than you."

The two of them worked slowly, taking care for Crivelli's bruises and other potential injuries. Halfway through their efforts the servant came with the water and cloths. When Crivelli was lying naked in the bed, Alys saw that it would take more than wet cloths to help him. His arm was broken and she thought a rib might be broken, but the blood that had trailed from his mouth was only from a badly bitten lip. There was only one knife wound, though, and she was thankful that it didn't appear to be very deep.

"I'll go talk to Signore Barberi," said Joanie. "See if they have some salve for the knife wound and something to bind and strap his arm with. If not, we'll have to return later."

"Thank you," said Alys.

When Joanie left Alys began to wash Crivelli the best she could, wiping first the blood from his side.

"All my secrets are bared to you, now," said Crivelli.

She smiled at him. "Ah, I always knew you had hidden treasures."

His laugh turned into a groan of pain. "You would kill me with your wit?"

"Someone tried to kill you, for it was clear you had little to rob," she said, her tone serious. "Who would do such a thing?"

He gave a small shrug and winced. "There a few possibilities. But you're right, it wasn't theft. I had only a small purse on me, a little enticement to take on a commission. I was on my way back from the meeting last night when they attacked me."

"Last night?"

"Yes. Well early this morning. I did a little celebrating." He frowned. "I was lying there for some time, unable to move. Finally, I was able to make my way back home and then collapsed on the steps where you found me. So much for celebrating my commission."

"Another commission?" she asked.

"The second offer this week." He attempted a grin. "Word is spreading. I'm a genius."

"You are a genius," she said.

"No, not after this." He gazed ruefully at his arm. "I can't even lift a paintbrush."

"It's only temporary. You'll be back painting soon enough."

He shook his head. "The commissions. And your painting still isn't finished. I'm late enough, now. Fabriano is grumbling. There are more commissions coming in and I won't be able to do anything for a while. They will go to other people in the end."

"They will come back to you for the next painting."

"That's not how it works. I am fashionable, now. Everyone speaks of me, so everyone wants me. They'll move on to someone else and he will become the fashion. I will merely be a 'painter who was once promising.'"

She stared at him for a moment, an idea forming in her mind. "If you'll let me, I'll help."

A spark of hope appeared in his eyes and then faded again. "No, I think not."

She pursed her lips but let it go. There would be time later to reason with him, when he was feeling better. She wiped the cloth along his chest again, careful of the wound and the rib. It might just be bruised, she thought.

"If I help you," she said, "will you sit up, so I can wash your back? I don't think it's wise for you to roll over on your side."

"I'll try, my angel."

Carefully, she sat on the bed, leaned forward and eased him towards her. She felt him stiffen with pain but he relaxed after a moment and kissed her ear lightly. Surprised, she pulled back and looked for the joke, but his face was serious and his eyes searched hers.

"You can't be having amorous thoughts, now, Crivelli," she said in a deliberately light tone.

"Carlo," he said. "Call me Carlo." He gave her a faint smile.

He leaned over and gave her a soft kiss on the mouth and this time she didn't pull back. With his good hand he stroked her hair.

"My own beautiful and pure madonna," he said.

Tears came to her eyes. "I'm hardly pure, Carlo."

He put a finger to her lips. "Hush. I won't listen to such talk. You're pure of heart and soul."

She shook her head. His words touched her deeply and suddenly she wanted to lay her head on his chest and feel his arms around her. Up until now, she had deliberately kept their relationship from becoming anything more than friends. In part because he was the only man that was just her friend and that she could trust.

She'd received his quips and innuendos as the banter she thought he'd intended them to be, but now she wasn't certain what she wanted from him.

"This isn't the time for any talk," she said finally. "I need to finish this and get your wounds dressed."

She continued washing his back and then his arms. Joanie entered soon after her with a basket full of linen, salve and wood for a splint, as well as an herbal mixture for Crivelli to drink. Her arrival relieved Alys of the decision about washing the rest of him. Suddenly, she felt uncomfortable with the idea of even more intimate contact with him. She hid her unease by fashioning bandages and preparing the salve.

Crivelli remained silent throughout the rest of their ministrations, except for an occasional grunt or grimace when they caused him pain. Eventually, he lay back in the bed, with only a few drops remaining in the cup containing herbal draught.

"Thank you both," he said.

His eyelids drooped and lines of exhaustion etched his face. Alys hoped that they'd done enough for him and that his wound wouldn't fester. The break seemed clean enough, according to Joanie, nothing like the severity of Alys' that still caused her pain. Despite its debilitating limp, her injured leg hadn't deterred any of the men who came to see her. In fact it seemed to have created an added attraction, a frisson that she couldn't understand. The imperfect perfection. Alessandra had only laughed about it and put it down to men's unnatural curiosity and attraction to the deformed. Alys had refrained from mentioning Alessandra's own deformity.

"Will we leave now?" asked Joanie.

"No, Joanie. I'd like you to go to Madonna Alessandra and tell her that I shan't be home tonight. There's no one calling, so she shouldn't mind."

Joanie frowned. "If you're staying 'ere tonight, then I will too."

"If you insist. But go deliver the message first."

Joanie sighed but did as she was told. The door shut behind her and Alys turned back to Crivelli. He was sleeping now, but his breathing was a little ragged. Small beads of sweat appeared on his lip. It wasn't a good sign.

CHAPTER TWENTY-TWO
Hüdavendigar, Ottoman Empire, Early Spring 1446
BARNABAS

I stepped into the hall ready for travel, clad in a thick brocade coat, heavy loose breeches and soft kidskin boots. A sword dangled at my side and a carefully arranged turban with a small jewel affixed to it topped my head. I was dressed for the part I was meant to play—a potential companion at arms and friend to the sultan.

Servants bustled in and out, collecting the many chests, boxes, and sacks that lined the one side of the room to strap to the horses that would take us to the ship.

"Ah, good. You're ready," came a voice.

I turned and saw Halil Pasha stride towards me, the plume in his own turban so large it touched the ceiling. His moustache was freshly oiled and his coat woven with silver and gold thread shone in the morning light. He was certainly dressed for his rank today.

Behind him Usef hovered uncertainly. He was due to travel with us to act as both my servant and keeper on the journey. I gave him a bleak smile and he came to my side.

"Is Umar ready?" I asked.

"Umar isn't coming," said Halil Pasha. "It was decided at the last minute that he should remain with the small garrison here. He'll come later."

I suppressed my disappointment and tried to keep my tone even. "Will I be training with someone else in the meantime?"

Halil Pasha gave a small smile. "Perhaps I will take on that part of your training as well."

I kept my eyes steady on him and showed no reaction, though it was the last thing I desired. "If that suits you, lord, I would be privileged to have your sage guidance."

He cocked his head and laughed, satisfied. "You know, perhaps I might at that."

He turned to Usef and asked him to check to see if our horses were ready. I pulled on the leather gloves carefully, giving myself time to regain my temper. I glanced over at the chests. My eyes narrowed. In the corner, next to my own chest I spotted the familiar small carved chest that contained the showstone. I cursed silently. With any luck that dreaded stone would be lost at the bottom of the sea.

Under the small chest was my own and in that was secreted and wrapped in an oiled leather cloth, not just the manuscript I'd taken first, but a rolled copy of the manuscript of the account of Prester John.

In the weeks I'd painstakingly transcribed the manuscript, I'd devoured all the words of the account so that I could nearly recite it without fault. It had been fascinating to read it, and at times I'd had to remind myself of my purpose. It told of the narrator's encounter with a man, Alemdar Ibn Aziz, who had travelled far in search of riches both in stories and goods. On his journey he had followed the ancient salt route into the very heart of Africa. He described the gruelling journey through parched deserts whipped by brutal windstorms to finally arrive at a small oasis where the salt traders exchanged their wares for various goods.

It was at this oasis that he met a strange and richly dressed blackamoor, who'd emerged from the wild region to the north and east of the oasis and claimed to be a descendant of Prester John, the Christian king. Ibn Aziz questioned the man and found his story credible. The man wore jewels in his cap, around his neck, and on his fingers, flaunting them as if they were nothing to him. He spoke also of magical creatures, horses that flew, beasts with horns in the centre of their heads and other such things.

I'd read the manuscript avidly and pondered its impact on al Qali. Was this the manuscript he'd sought so desperately? And was it the home of Prester John that was at the heart of it all? The thought of al Qali getting any reward for his betrayal but death had me seething with anger. With this manuscript as a guide it was possible I could hunt him down and give him his just reward.

"Come, Ahmed," said Halil Pasha. "It's time to mount our horses."

I hated that I responded to the name automatically. Giacomo was gone and I no longer remembered what it felt to be Barnabas. I nursed the resentment and anger, glad for its presence, but my body was still sore enough from the rough usage of the night before. I loathed these encounters more and more. The drug that used to render me all but senseless no longer provided the release it had, and Halil Pasha would allow me no extra. And with no Umar as a friend to distract me on the journey ahead, I would be left even more to nursing my anger and thoughts of revenge.

I took a deep breath and walked out of the palace and mounted my horse. The wind was chill enough. A row of janissaries were already mounted and ready for the signal. I sized them up carefully, though I knew full well there was no hope of escape. My head would be sliced from my body before I could reach the gate below.

⌘

I watched the activity below from my position on deck. Languages like Turkish, Greek, Arabic, Italian, Spanish, and a smattering of Dutch filled the air as men loaded goods and others were chained to the oars of the single mast galley. All manner of skin and hair colour was evident among that group who'd been captured in war or just unfortunate perhaps, like me.

The captain appeared, clad in an immaculate red coat, loose white breeches, boots and turban. He approached Halil Pasha, who stood beside me, bowed low and made his obeisance.

"Lord, we hope to be off soon," he said in Turkish, his voice tight with nerves. "The last of the cargo is being loaded now."

Halil Pasha frowned. "We were due to leave an hour ago. What's the delay?"

"I'm sorry, lord. One of the men let the ropes slip and the cargo spilled on the deck. We had to clear it before we could load more."

"Seize who was responsible and kill him," said Halil Pasha.

The captain bowed. "Yes, lord, it is done."

He backed away and called out. Another man appeared, his clothes not so immaculate. The captain spoke a few words and the man nodded and left.

Halil Pasha turned away and looked down at the scene below. "They're a scrawny crew. They don't look as if they'll have the strength to row us out of the harbour, let alone across the Sea of Marmara."

"How long will it take?" I asked.

He glanced at me surprised, as if he'd forgotten I was there. "The captain will complete the journey quickly, if he knows what's best."

I nodded, understanding it was better to say nothing. "May I go to my cabin? I would like to study my lessons Habib set for me." It was the best excuse I could think of to leave.

He gave me a distracted nod and I bowed low, like he bid me to do in public. I reached my cabin relieved that I was away from his notice with his present precarious temper. The cabin was little better. Usef hovered over the chests filled with my belongings, attempting to open them so he could lay out garments for me for later.

"Leave them for now," I said. "Could you bring back a small bit of food instead?"

"Of course," he said, his voice full of reluctance. He bowed slowly and left the cabin.

I gave a sigh of relief. I wanted ample time to get my manuscripts out of the chests and hidden away from Usef's prying eyes. I scanned the cabin for a secure hiding place. The cabin wasn't large and barely contained room for my chests, a small table fixed to the floor and a cot. After much searching, I finally pried away a plank in the wall beside my cot. There wasn't much space, but it was all I could find. I stuffed them in and replaced the plank.

I waited for a while for Usef to return, but when he didn't, I decided to make my way on deck again. I opened the door and several janissaries passed me in the narrow corridor on the way to the decks below. When the last one had gone I made my way up the narrow steps to the main deck. As I emerged I bumped into large muscled man with fair hair, wearing a short jacket and ragged loose breeches that might have once been white.

"Sorry, lord," he said in Turkish and bowed. "Bleeding fancy men," he muttered softly in English.

Impulsively I grabbed his arm. "You're from London," I whispered in English.

He stared at me warily. "Maybe."

"How is it you're here?"

"It's a long story, lord."

"I mean you no harm," I said. "It's been years since I've met a fellow Londoner."

"Ye're from London?" His voice was disbelieving.

I nodded. "Near Queenhithe."

He blinked. "Nooo."

"It's true," I said.

"If yeh pardon me saying so, lord, but yeh don't sound as if yeh do."

"It's been many years. My speech has changed." I fell back into my old manner for a lark. "But it ain't left me for good."

"Whatever is yeh doing 'ere dressed like a Turk?" he asked.

I grinned. "It's a long story."

"I bet and all." He smiled suddenly. "Name's Hal."

I nodded and hesitated. "Jack," I said, eventually. It was close enough to Giacomo. "Though I'm called Ahmed, now."

"They don't call me Hal either. Just 'hey you' in Turkish."

I laughed softly, aware suddenly how good it was to speak English with someone who knew the places I did.

"Where are you from, Hal?"

"Queenhithe."

"Nooo," I said, suddenly light-headed.

A shout came from behind. Fear flashed across Hal's face. "I better get on. We're setting off, now. I gots to do the drum for rowers."

Before I could say more he was off, winding his way along the deck down the few steps to the deck below where the men sat at the oars. I watched him take his place at the large drum and take up a pair of mallets. A dark-haired Turk, his gnarled hands holding a whip, glared at him and spoke to him harshly in Turkish.

The man nodded to Hal and shouted at the rowers who raised the oars and began their strokes. Only about one third of them worked the oars, leaving the others to rest and take their turn later. Hal set the beat while the rowers worked the oars in time. The drum was almost mesmerising, until I saw what a strain the pace put on the rowers. Such a pace must be down to Halil Pasha.

I frowned, wondering what life on board would be like for me. Would Halil Pasha demand my presence as he had so often back in Hüdavendigar? I could only hope not.

～～

The warm wind stung my face and I stood there at the rail for a while, savouring its smell and licking the salt from my lips. The sun was sinking towards the horizon and was casting an orange glow across the water. I loved these moments at sea and tried to forget what else this voyage held for me. On the deck below, I heard the shouts of the guards who ensured the rowers pulled their weight. In the three days since the journey had begun, the stink from their sweat and urine had grown. There were no niceties for galley slaves.

Hal sat in a corner labouring over a sail, his needle plying the cloth with determination. I caught his eye and gave him a small wave and he nodded back, a grin flashing across his face. Though he was a slave, he'd held more privileges than the ordinary galley worker because of his shipboard skills and quick mind. That much had become clear to me since I'd taken to observing him at any opportunity. I'd only spoken to him once more, a brief exchange that was friendly enough, but he was too wary of his position and mine to risk initiating contact.

I became aware of the sweat beading on my lip and the slight cramping in my belly. With a sigh I turned away from the railing and made my way below. It was time for my honeyed drink. Hopefully Usef would be there waiting with it. Since I'd boarded the galley, Halil Pasha had been too busy to spend much time in my company and I was glad. Still, each day hung over me like a sword ready to drop as I waited for the evening hours to arrive, and with it, his summons.

I opened the door to my cabin and was relieved to see Usef was there. A second glance told me that he was sorting through my chests and withdrawing an elaborately embroidered coat that Halil Pasha preferred on me. The cramping in my stomach grew worse.

Usef lifted his head when I entered. "Ah, good, master. I was just coming to fetch you. Lord Halil Pasha requires you tonight. You are to attend him as soon as I make you ready."

I frowned and eyed the clothes set out. "Is the captain to be with us as well?"

"I know not what Lord Pasha had in mind."

His tone was even, but I could detect just a hint of the usual insolence that had seemed to grow worse since we'd boarded the ship. I waved my hand at the clothes and bid him begin. While he dressed me, I tried to reassure myself that Halil Pasha wished me only as an extra guest at the table. The captain and his second in command wouldn't be able to converse on the various topics that took Halil Pasha's fancy and after two nights of that limited company he'd decided to include me as well.

When I was fully dressed, Usef attempted to match the elaborate folds on the turban that I'd had the day of my arrival on board. The result was acceptable only and I took a small bit of satisfaction from his failure. It was with this little comfort that I knocked on Halil Pasha's cabin door and entered when bid. The captain was there, to my relief, and I moved forward and made my obeisance to Halil Pasha. I remained on my knees while the captain finished his explanations.

"It won't be long, lord. Tomorrow at the latest should see us in Yaliova," said the captain. "As I've mentioned, the wind has been against us and slowed progress."

Halil Pasha's face darkened. "I don't want excuses, just see that it's done."

The captain bowed low and took his leave, backing out of the cabin. Halil Pasha turned to me and nodded for me to rise. The cabin, I could see then, was spacious enough, and Usef and another servant had done their best to provide some luxuries, draping the large cot and cabin walls with silk hangings, and scattering large cushions on the thick carpets.

"Come. We will celebrate the beginning of our journey that will lead to great things," said Halil Pasha.

I said nothing and watched as he handed me a large cup filled with the honeyed drink. I tried not to gulp it down too quickly, in my desire to feed the greedy gnawing in my stomach and calm the pace of my heart. Halil Pasha drank from his own cup, though I'd no idea what dosage he gave himself.

"Will Usef provide me with this when I'm in Edirne?" I asked, holding up the cup.

"He will at the outset. But perhaps, in time, I will instruct you on how to mix it yourself."

"And the opium? Who provides that?"

"That isn't your concern," said Halil Pasha.

I nodded. Any control was better than none, for it might provide a way for me to escape.

"Will you remain in Edirne?" I asked.

"Of course. Though the sultan and I may not agree, I am still the Grand Vizier. Besides, I would want to ensure that nothing hinders you in your task."

I concealed my disappointment with effort. It was foolish to have hoped that he might leave me to it. At the very least I could allow the possibility he might be too busy to insist I visit his bed.

Already I could feel the effect of the drug seeping into my body, fuzzing my thoughts. I looked at Halil Pasha. Whatever would be, would be.

Later, after we'd eaten, Halil Pasha spoke. "Go over to the corner and retrieve the small chest there."

I looked over where he indicated and frowned. It was the chest containing the showstone. With reluctance I rose and did as I was bid. When I'd placed it in front of him he opened the chest and withdrew the showstone. I gave it a resentful look.

"Now, I ask that tonight you look in it and see if you can tell me what outcome this plan of ours will have."

"I'm not sure I will be able to, lord."

He gripped my hand tightly and placed it on the showstone. He gave me a hard stare.

"You will do as I say."

"It's not that I don't want to—"

"You will do as I say."

The voice held menace and I knew there was no arguing. I doubted how much of my own future I could see, but I resigned myself to try. I placed my other hand on the showstone and closed my eyes for a moment to compose myself. When I felt calmer I opened them and gazed into the showstone. It felt cold and hard under my fingertips. Hatred of this stone and everything associated with it filled me. Would this cursed stone follow me around all my life?

There was nothing there, not even my fogged brain could manufacture an image or some idea that I might pass on to Halil Pasha. After a while I lifted my head and shook it.

"Nothing, lord." I licked my lips. Would I dare say what had just occurred to me? "It might be the drug, lord, but it's no use."

He raised his hand and slapped me across the face. "You will look into it until you see something."

Would I make something up? Could I be convincing if I did? At this moment it mattered not to me.

I shook my head. "I have no control, lord. The visions come or they don't. And tonight, they don't come."

He raised his hand to slap me again and I turned my face instinctively. He stopped and lowered his hand.

"Well, if we cannot make use of you in that way, we must make use of you in another way."

I paled. There was no doubt of his intention. He replaced the showstone in the box and closed the lid with a bang. He shoved it aside and pulled me to him, his hand gripping me painfully.

It was a night that he spared nothing in ensuring I experienced pain while giving him as much pleasure as he desired. When it was over, I screamed silently in rage and humiliation. The only saving grace was that when he was finished with me, I was allowed to go to my cabin rather than spend the rest of the night with him.

I crawled into my bed, sore and bruised, cursing the man and al Qali, who betrayed me and gave me into his custody. My mind raced with thoughts of revenge, unable to sleep.

A while later, still awake, I heard my cabin door open slowly. I laid unmoving and opened my eyes slightly. A dark shape moved to the bed. I saw a flash of a knife. The shape loomed over me and put a hand over my mouth. I started to struggle.

"Sshh," came a voice, whispering. "It's me, Hal."

I stopped my struggle and he spoke again.

"Someone wants you dead," he said. "Come wiv me and do what I say, got it?" I nodded. "Now get on some clothes and we'll go. Quickly, now, we ain't got much time."

Escape. It took a moment for understanding to sink in and then I moved quickly. I rose from the bed and drew on a pair of the loose breeches and a simple linen shirt. I grabbed the two rings that were gifts from Halil Pasha and shoved them on my fingers. The diamond in my ear would count for something, too I hoped, if we made good our escape.

I looked over to the plank that hid the two rolled manuscripts. After only a slight hesitation I prised it away and removed the two rolls in their oiled leather wrapping and shoved them into my breeches. I looked up and Hal, knife in hand, grabbed my wrist and made a quick cut across it. He held my wrist over the silk covering and the blood dribbled out onto it.

"This'll frow them off. Make it look convincing," he said.

I nodded and without a backward glance, I followed Hal out of the cabin. Once on deck he led me aft and bade me wait a moment. I huddled there, casting my eyes out to the horizon. To my relief, I could see some flickering lights that signalled that shore was close. Below me, oars splashed in the sea rhythmically. It wouldn't be long before the ship reached port.

Hal returned bearing a large plank and placed it on the deck. "You swim?"

I shrugged. "A bit."

"You reckon you could swim to shore?"

I look at the distance dubiously but steeled myself and nodded.

He lifted the plank and slid it into the water. "Just in case," he said. "Don't know if I can make it myself."

Without further words he slipped over the side of the ship. I heard a splash a moment later and looked around quickly for any signs of detection. I took a deep breath and followed him overboard.

The water was so much different than the Thames where I'd had my previous dousing and experience, tossed off the wherry, or the docks at Queenhithe during some great lark with Tom or Black Jack. Still, my heart beat quickly and I thrashed wildly until I surfaced and was able to get my bearings. Overhead, there was no sign of alarm, and with a little more hope, I began to paddle towards the plank and Hal.

CHAPTER TWENTY-THREE
Sea Of Marmara, Early Spring 1446
BARNABAS

We pulled ourselves up the ladder at the dock, the light beginning to break overhead. It had taken us more time than I could measure to make it, but we had in the end, thanks to Hal. He'd kept the effort up, kicking and paddling the plank and me towards the shore. My strength, so much less than I'd imagined, had given out three quarters of the way. Now, I expended my last bit of energy to get myself up the ladder to solid ground.

Hal hauled me up the last step and the two of us weaved in and out of wooden crates, crouching low lest someone be guarding the docks. I could feel the bundle of manuscripts heavy inside the waist of my breeches. Luckily, despite everything, I'd still managed to hang on to them.

Breathing heavily, I followed Hal away from the water and towards the buildings that collected near the docks.

We dodged down a street and after a little while he pulled me into a deep, recessed doorway.

"We'll wait 'ere," he said. "Rest a while and then I'll see if there are any ships going. We need to leave this place fast. Afore they 'ave time to start searching for us, in case they don't think we drowned." He looked me up and down. "Do you fink you can pass for a seaman?"

Still panting, I nodded. "Of course. I used to help out on a wherry at Queenhithe."

Hal snorted. "Well I s'pose that's somefink. We'll just 'ave to 'ope they's desperate for men, is all."

We sat for a while in tense silence and I tried to catch my breath and clear my head. Already, I could feel the familiar gnawing in my stomach. I tried to shove the thought away. I started to shiver, my wet clothes in the cool morning air and my exhaustion catching up with me. Soon my teeth joined the rhythm and I folded my lips under to keep them from making any sounds. The last thing I wanted was for Hal to think I was unfit to make the journey.

"Thanks," I said and forced my teeth to still.

"Tweren't no bovver. When they told me to kill you I knew I'd be done for once I'd done the deed. Best I seize the chance and escape wiv you."

I nodded and managed to mutter, "grateful," before my teeth took up their own beat again.

Hal looked over at me. "Ah, don't worry, you'll be dry soon enough. Get some sun on yeh."

When the sun finally did pour into the doorway, I was physically shaking and I raised my head to catch as much warmth as I could. By this time my heart was beating rapidly and my stomach was clenching so hard I knew I would be vomiting soon. It only took short while before the sweat beaded my forehead and upper lip. I knew it wasn't a chill caught from my night's dunking that was causing it.

Hal looked over at me and frowned. He put a hand to my forehead and stared into my eyes. I tried to look away but his hand held me firm.

"You've got it bad, 'aven't you." It wasn't a question.

"What do you mean?" I said, though I knew exactly what he wanted to know.

"Opium. You're one of them ain't you? Don't say you ain't, cause I've seen 'em before."

I only nodded. "It wasn't my choice. Halil Pasha forced me."

Hal shook his head. "Well, we can't undo what's done." He picked up my hand. "'Ere. Give me one of those rings."

I stared at him a moment, but did as he bid.

"Wait 'ere, I'll see what I can do."

"Where are you going?" I asked.

"Why, to get you some of the stuff, if I can. It's clear we can't go any further without you 'aving some of it."

I knew he was right and made no protest, though I loathed myself for such weakness. With one last glance at me, he rose and left, walking quickly down the street, turning off at the end. I drew myself further into the doorway, glad now that it was deep. Already I could hear the bustle of people nearby and knew the place was waking up, everyone beginning their day's chores. I looked up at my doorway and hoped that its weather beaten and decayed look meant that no one lived here at the moment.

It was later, after I'd been shooed away from two different doorways, that Hal finally returned. I was hovering at the opposite end of the road, leaning on a ramshackle building, my arms clutched around my stomach. Already I'd vomited twice. After a few quick glances, he spied me and hurried towards me. I could see he clutched a small sack and I reached out for it eagerly.

"You got it? Give it here, quickly," I said. I couldn't help my manner though I was ashamed of it.

"Steady, now," he said when he reached my side. "Let's go somewhere we can't be seen."

He grabbed my arm and pulled me along until we came to a small alcove. It stank of urine and worse, but I cared nothing for that. He pulled me cautiously to the ground and withdrew a pouch and then a small leather flagon.

"How much?" he asked.

"How much what?"

He gave an impatient snort. "How much of the stuff do yeh take?"

I gave him a panicked look. "I don't know. It was in a drink. Not that much, I don't think."

He removed the stopper from the flagon, put a pinch of the powder in it, looked at me hard and then added a bit more. He handed me the flagon.

"It's some kind of fermented milk drink. It's the best I could do. Drink it quickly and yeh won't taste it. Well, not much."

I lifted the flagon to my mouth and downed the drink. Hal was right, it was awful, but I was past caring. When I'd finished I wiped my mouth and waited. It wasn't long before the soft feeling came over me and the cramping faded.

I smiled. "Thank you, Hal. It has helped."

He gave me a dubious look. "Well yeh might feel on top of the world now, but yeh can't keep at that stuff. It'll kill yeh."

"I know. And as soon as I get back to Venice I intend to do something about it."

"Venice? Is that where ye're aiming for?"

"If I can. Did you have other plans?"

He cocked his head. "Aw, why not? Venice it is, eventually. For now we just want to be on the first ship out of here that will take us. We can't risk anyone recognising that ring I just sold."

"Did you find out anything?"

"I 'eard about two possibilities. There's a Genoese galley leaving tonight for Modone and then Genoa and a Dutch carvel leaving tomorrow for Bruges."

"A Dutch carvel? Maybe we should try for that." For a moment I considered the carvel, if only that it would take me so far away from here and to a place I knew.

"We'll try for whichever one will take us, Jack." He leaned over and touched the diamond in my ear. "And you best 'ide this, an all. And the ring."

I nodded and removed the ring from my finger as well as the stud from my ear. I held them in my palm, and on impulse tore a small bit from my shirt and wrapped them in it.

"What've you got stuck in your breeches?" asked Hal.

"Manuscripts. Old ones. They're very valuable. Probably worth as much as the ring, if not more."

Hal raised his brows. "Give 'em 'ere, then. We'll put it all in this small sack and get a few clothes with the money that's left over and put them around it."

I rose and scooped the flagon and pouch back into the small sack. I would have to take great care with that sack.

~~

It was easy enough for Hal to be taken on, but when they looked at me they weren't as certain I was a proper seaman. My clothes certainly didn't fit the part and the

265

smeared khol that was almost certainly around my eyes probably made me look sicklier than I was. In the end, Hal convinced them to take me on the Genoese ship, Hal serving as all round hand, and me to serve my turn on the oars. There were few questions about our presence in Yaliova when seamen were in demand and the port serving ships from so many different places.

The thought of rowing hours on end was almost more than I could bear, but the alternative was less appealing. It meant that I could at least keep my sack at my feet when I was at the oars and take it with me when I was allowed to sleep. It was only until Modone, I told myself. Then we could sell either the ring or the stud and find passage to Venice. In Venice I would collect my money from Alessandra and then begin my hunt for al Qali to kill him. I wouldn't settle for anything else. It was that thought which kept me rowing.

❦

I looked at my hands and spat on them. They had long ago lost any of the soft skin that had marked me as a scholar and had pleased Halil Pasha. Raw and bleeding in places, they'd had no time to heal in the small breaks from oars since we'd left Yaliova. We were nearing Modone, now, and I counted myself lucky to have survived the voyage this long.

Over by the sail rigging Hal gave me a quick wave and smile of encouragement. It was really down to Hal that I had made it, truth be told. He'd made sure that I'd had plenty of breaks in the beginning, even spelling me on the oars himself at one point. I promised myself not to allow him to do that again and I worked hard to grow accustom to the strain, though my arm and back muscles screamed under the effort.

The man cried the change of rowers and I gave a grim smile in relief. Now I could slip away and take my dosage. The pinches of powder had grown smaller as the days passed and I worried if I would have enough to last the voyage. I refused to consider whether I'd be able to get more in Modone.

I grabbed my sack and followed the ten or so others to the side and sat down. Glancing around I opened the sack and removed the small pouch. I reached in with my fingers, took a pinch and put the fingers in my mouth. I rubbed the residue along my gums and licked my fingers. I closed my eyes and after a short while the familiar aching eased. The raw pain from in my back from the few times the lash felt it eased as well.

When I opened my eyes, I saw that Hal was looking at me, pity in his eyes. He gave a little shake of his head and I looked away. I couldn't bear it. Soon, I promised myself. Soon, I would do what it took to give it up.

I was still resting when I heard the lookout give the cry for land. My spirits lifted. I had made it and in a few short weeks, maybe even less, I would be back in Venice. Modone was on the Venetian trade routes and there were sure to be ships heading that way.

The wind was with us and it was only a few hours later that the port was looming close and the orders were given to weigh anchor. An impressive rock dominated the harbour edge and a fort rose up from the town. It took some time but eventually Hal and I were standing onshore, a few coins in our hand, at liberty at last.

Overhead, the sun shone in all its strength and heat for a day in early summer. At least that's what I'd calculated, though in truth I'd lost track of the days since I'd left the palace.

Hal turned to me and draped his arm around my shoulders. "Well, it won't be long afore we're 'ome free. This is a Venetian trading port, so no one can claim us 'ere. Still, best be careful, eh?"

I flinched under Hal's touch. Not because of any pain, but a reason deeper than that which I refused to name. I forced a smile and agreed with him.

"Let's see if we can find some rum. Drink away the 'ard work and dirt."

I let him lead me away in search of a tavern, though the small sack with its dwindling supply of the opiate burned in my hand. That was my first need, said a little voice inside me.

He located a small house, not far from the docks and drew me inside. There we found a small rough table and bench in the corner and slid into it. I clutched the sack tightly in my lap and Hal saw me.

He frowned. "Don't fret. I knows what you want. 'Ere is a good a place to find more and at least we can enjoy ourselves while we do it."

I nodded and tried to appear calm. Hal rose and went in search of the rum and hopefully my own requirements while I cast my eye around the tavern. It was crowded enough, unshaven men in mismatched clothes of no discernable fashion or nationality, with skin of varying shades and backgrounds. The stench of sweat combated with odour of various bodily contents emptied on the floor in the past few days. The smell was familiar enough after days at sea on the galley and I found it hardly bothered me. It was the lack of motion, that unsettled me, I guessed. I leaned my head back and closed my eyes against the noise.

"You look as though you need some company," said a voice in Greek.

I opened my eyes and looked up to see a woman taking the seat next to me. Her hair was a dark tangle and her face was streaked with dirt. Her dark eyes glittered at me. An ample breast was shoved against my arm. I flinched and tried to calm myself.

"Thanks, but I don't think so," I said in broken Greek.

She smiled wider and the gaps in her teeth showed. "Ah, come. I can see you've just been at sea. And no one as handsome as you should spend their first hours on shore alone."

She stroked my arm and gave me a quick peck on the cheek. I pulled away instinctively.

"I-I have a friend. He'll be back in a moment."

"That's no problem. I have a friend for him as well." She pulled away and studied me. "Unless you're one of those."

"One of those?" I asked.

"You know. The ones who prefer men."

A huge rage flared up inside me. I wanted to hit her but clenched my fists instead. "I'm nothing of the sort."

"Relax," she said in a soothing voice. "I meant nothing by it. I didn't think you were."

"What's this? A pretty maid come to join us?" asked Hal, two cups in his hand. He set the cups on the table and grabbed the woman's hand. "Come, 'ere Sally girl, and give us a kiss."

Though it was said in English there was no doubt to the meaning. The woman was happy to oblige. She left my side and allowed Hal to pull her onto his lap. He gave her a smacking kiss on the lips and fondled one of her breasts.

"I can see you are appreciative of what a girl has to offer," she said in Greek.

"Always, my duck," Hall answered in passable Greek. "But do you have a friend for Jack? He's been away an awful long time and could use company as well."

I frowned. "I'm fine."

Hal shook his head. "You ain't. Trust me." He turned to the woman and gave her an encouraging smile. "Come on, a friend for Jack?"

She hesitated a moment and slid off his lap. "I won't be long. Promise you'll still be here?"

Hal grinned. "Of course. Why wouldn't I be with your charms to look forward to?"

When she'd left Hal turned to me. "I knows what you're finking. But don't worry. I gots it all arranged with the tavern keeper. 'E'll 'ave what we need afore the day's out."

The sense of relief lasted only for a moment before my previous anxiety returned.

"Hal, I don't think the woman is a good idea."

"Why not?"

"I'm not up for it."

"But she's willing, and we 'ave the time."

"No," I said, anger in my voice. "I said no. I'll hear nothing more about it." I knew I was behaving unreasonably, but I couldn't help it. The words just tumbled out. "You go ahead, though, Hal," I said, trying to find a pleasant manner. "I'll be fine here."

Hal shrugged, his manner cool. "Whatever you say."

And so it was, with sour amusement I watched Hal go off with both woman, an arm around each. I turned to the cup of rum I'd been nursing, lifted it to my lips and downed the rest in one gulp. Venice. When I got to Venice I would make it up to Hal.

CHAPTER TWENTY-FOUR
Venice, Summer 1446
ALYS

Alys leaned over and stroked Crivelli's cheek. "Your arm is nearly healed, *mi amore.* Soon you'll be holding your paintbrush all day and creating masterworks."

Crivelli, pulled her head to him and kissed her deeply. "Soon I will have the money to be able to make love to you beyond just kisses and fondles."

She laughed and glanced over at Joanie who sat primly by the window pretending to mend one of Crivelli's shirts. At her feet Alys' dog, Bitty, lay curled up in a ball.

"Ah, dearest Carlo, there is no need for that. When you're well enough I will pay for you to come to my bed."

His eyes sparkled. "I know you only say that because I've let you start painting those commissions."

He nodded to the canvas and board over by the window. One was propped on an easel and two boards leaned against the wall. The boards were the subject of a diptych, one showing the wedding of St Cecilia to

Valerian and the other, her martyrdom. The canvas was another Annunciation.

It was the diptych that was Alys' favourite, for the scope of the narrative was larger and the opportunity to learn more had been thrilling. Under Crivelli's guidance she had put on the underpainting, blocked out the figures at the feast celebrating the wedding, and then the figures of those who stoked the fire of the baths that caused her death.

Alys had made Valerian in Crivelli's likeness, spending hours sketching him while he sat in his bed. She also sketched herself back in her room in the palazzo while she sat at the polished mirror. Together they had planned the painting, he guiding her strokes on occasion with his splinted arm, until gradually he was able to hold the brush for only a short time.

The paintings progressed and she took great joy in their advancement, glowing under his praise and striving to do better at his criticisms. The paintings were nearly finished now, and needed only his touch for the finer features as working the light that made his paintings so special and delicate. She owed him much and loved him for his trust in her abilities.

She leaned down once more and gave him a lingering kiss. He slipped his hand inside her bodice, out of sight of Joanie's scrutiny. Joanie had said little enough and Alys knew she would never tell Alessandra what passed between her and Crivelli while she was here under the guise of a model. She wondered if Alessandra would even care. The promise of a portion of the sale would surely be enough for her to accept whatever means was used to complete the painting.

She passed a hand along his cheek again. "You know I care for you more than I can say," she murmured. "And it's not just the painting."

He gave a rueful smile. "Soon your fame will be such, *madonna mia*, that I will have to make an appointment a year in advance just to see you."

"Never for you, Carlo."

There was a certain truth to his words. Her afternoons and nights had ceased to be her own, except on the odd occasion. Her mornings were given to sleep, or visiting Crivelli to paint. Except this last week, when she had pleaded a bad head and upset stomach to her patrons so that she could complete her work here in order that Crivelli could give the paintings to his patrons, as promised, at the end of the next week.

In truth, it was as though her excuses had come to haunt her, for her head hurt and her body was aching a little too. Perhaps it was the fumes from clearing the paint from the brushes, or the miasma from the canal that seeped in the windows in the heat of the last few days.

She rose and began the process of cleaning the brushes. Joanie helped her, just as skilled in ensuring they were thoroughly free of paint. Alys was running late and she appreciated the help. She'd told Alessandra she'd return by early evening and already she could see the light was fading outside. But her lateness couldn't dampen her high spirits at Crivelli's approval of what she had accomplished.

She swept out of the room a while later with one last kiss to Crivelli and a check that he had all he needed for the night. He was able to walk around with little pain, now, but she still enjoyed fussing over him.

Joanie followed her down the stairs, carrying the basket containing Bitty. They made their way down the street and along to the canal. Alys' leg ached badly and her limp was even more pronounced than usual. At the water's edge Joanie, noticing her distress, quickly signalled a passing barchetta. It was late and she would bear the press of others in the boat, if only to make speed.

"Oh, Joanie, just think," she said quietly once they'd boarded. "My paintings will be hanging on the walls to be admired."

Joanie gave her a weak smile. "I'm glad you're pleased. Shame it can't be your own name that's on it, though."

"It doesn't matter. It's more than I ever hoped for and I'm grateful."

"Yes, but just think, that money could be all yours. Instead of promising it to Madonna Alessandra."

Alys sighed. "Just be happy for me, please."

"Of course I'm 'appy that you've been learning painting like you wanted. But I do worry."

"There's no need. We'll be fine. I'm as popular as ever and more money is coming in. Eventually we'll be able to leave."

Joanie pursed her lips. "I'm glad to hear you're still thinking we should leave. The way you talk to that Crivelli, I was beginning to wonder."

Alys forced a smile. She hardly knew herself what she meant when she talked to Crivelli. She found him deeply attractive and compelling, and she knew in some way she cared for him. She owed him much and his admiration of her and the interests they shared made him seem perfect in so many ways. What other man would allow her to learn to paint, let alone teach her? She had no idea if there was a future with him, but it seemed more tangible than any she could imagine back in England.

She entered the palazzo, Joanie and Bitty in tow. Lucia rushed to greet her.

"Madonna Alessandra says you are to go straight to your room. She will meet you there to explain."

Puzzled, Alys frowned and made her way up the steps and across the hall to her bedroom. She entered and saw Alessandra standing in front of the large window. It was open and a gentle breeze ruffled the veil that covered her head. Her gloved hands fidgeted nervously.

"Ah, you've finally come. I was about to send a servant to collect you."

"I'm sorry, I'm late. The painting was at a critical point and Crivelli wanted to finish it."

Alessandra waved her hand impatiently. "Never mind that. You're here now."

"Is something amiss?" asked Alys.

"No. It's only that I have a special guest who arrived unexpectedly."

"A guest? I thought it was agreed I could be released from my obligations for the week."

"As I said, this guest is special. He's been away on a gruelling journey and now seeks some pleasure to distract him from it."

"You would have me entertain him. Tonight?"

Alessandra nodded. "I want you to apply all your charms. Play music, sing to him. Have a game of cards if he wishes. And most of all, give him the most pleasurable time in bed possible."

Alys sighed and nodded. Her limbs ached almost as much as her head at the moment, but she knew she had little choice in the matter.

"And wear the kermes silk dress."

"The one I wore when you showed the painting?"

"Yes. And I will send jewels to you and have Lucia dress your hair. Be as quick as you can, though. My guest is here and waiting in the *sala*. You can join us when you're ready."

Alys stared after Alessandra as she left the room, too stunned to reply. She admitted to a certain amount of curiosity about this man who had aroused Alessandra's emotions in a way Alys had never seen in her. That Alessandra cared for him seemed plain, but it was still curious. She was to provide the pleasure it seemed, almost as proxy for Alessandra, whom she knew would never consider doing it herself.

She was still musing while Joanie helped her into the silk gown, lacing up the back so that it fit her snugly. This time there was no question about any linen lace to hide her breasts. They shone pale as milk in the fading light. Her hair was swept up and dressed elaborately in braids and ropes of pearls to reflect the gold in her hair. Pearls hung at her ears and a matching large pearl hung around her throat. As a final touch, Lucia doused Alys in Alessandra's scent, convincing Alys that her insight about her role tonight was correct.

Her toilet completed, Alys gave Joanie a little kiss of dismissal and swept to the door.

"You looks beautiful," said Joanie. "More beautiful than anyone I've ever seen."

Alys gave her a faint smile and left. She let Joanie's words fill her as she walked to the door of the *sala* and opened it. Entering, she sank into a curtsey and murmured an apology for her tardiness.

In the brief moment that his back was turned to her, she took in the broad shoulders, covered in a blue silk doublet woven with silver thread, and the well-muscled legs in matching hose. Tousled curls, the colour of corn, topped his head. He turned and her heart stopped.

"Barnabas," she whispered faintly.

"I hope you left that dog in a basket in the kitchen," said Alessandra with a laugh. She turned to her guest. "It's a little plaything that was given to her, but he can be too playful at times."

"And it's called Barnabas?" he said. He studied her carefully without any hint of surprise or recognition.

"Silly name, really," Alys said. The words came out of nowhere, cold and protective. "I call him Bitty for short. He does no harm really and can be good company."

"Giacomo," said Alessandra. "I am being remiss. Let me introduce you to my protégé, Maria. Maria, come meet Signore Giacomo Bonavillagio."

Barnabas came forward and bowed. "Maria, is it? I'm most pleased to meet you, Maria."

Alys sank into another curtsey and rose to look up into his face. His eyes seemed distant and still betrayed nothing. He gave her a lazy look.

"I am indeed pleased to meet you, Signore Bonavillagio."

"Giacomo, please."

"Oh, but that name is reserved only for intimate friends, I'm sure, signore. We've only just met."

He gave a small laugh. "Ah but I am told you are skilled in making all strangers seem friends in a very little time."

Her head whirled. There was something unreal about what was happening. She cocked her head and forced a laugh. "Madonna Alessandra praises me too much, I think."

A loud chitter from the corner of the room caught her attention. A small monkey wearing a little cone-shaped hat on his head squatted on a cushion. Around his neck was a collar and a golden chain hung from it. Her heart tightened a moment as she recalled a young lad on Queenhithe dock capturing an escaped monkey.

"You have a friend, signore?" Alys asked.

"Ah, yes. He attached himself to me in Modone. It seemed a shame to abandon him, so I brought him back to Venice with me. I call him Tomaso."

A small laugh escaped her as the thought of what might be concealed in the little wicked joke struck her. Could it be he was naming it after his former teacher, Father Thomas, who had drawn him into all the events that had gotten him into trouble in the first place? Or perhaps a Tomas of more recent acquaintance.

"That's an apt name for a monkey," she said.

A flash of humour crossed his face but it was so quick that Alys couldn't be certain she saw it. He gave her a nod and took a seat next to his monkey.

"Come, Maria, play something on the lute for Giacomo and show him your skill."

Alys looked across at Alessandra and tried to read her. Her dark gown and veil were the same as ever, but she sat taut with tension. Alys nodded and went over to the chair that held the lute. She picked it up and strummed it for a few moments, searching for an appropriate piece. Her usual fare consisted of love songs and bawdy ballads. In the end she settled for bawdy, for she felt it would lighten the tone and help her humour. She made her way through the verses, but to her dismay found herself colouring in embarrassment. In the end, she omitted the last verse.

"Most entertaining," said Barnabas, a half smile on his face. "I can see you're nimble fingered enough. I assume you practice plucking strings often."

The remark irritated her and prompted her to retort, "Oh, I'm well plucked, signore."

Alessandra gave her a severe look and rose. "I'll leave you two then. Giacomo, we'll continue our discussion soon. We have much to resolve."

Barnabas stood up. "Of course, Alessandra, *mi amore*. But my decision will remain unchanged."

Alessandra made her way over to him. "Let's see if Maria can persuade you otherwise. Her charms and beauty are widely known."

Barnabas glanced over at Alys. "I can well imagine. But your charms were and are beyond compare, madonna."

Alessandra held out her gloved hand to him. He hesitated a moment and then took the hand and gave it a perfunctory kiss. She raised it to his cheek and he pulled away the slightest fraction. He murmured an apology and a word or two of reassurance that Alys couldn't quite hear. The tone made her throat catch. Alys turned away. Alessandra clasped her hands, opened the door and left the room with a final nod. Alys took a deep breath and clutched the lute tighter.

"Shall I play another tune?" she asked, her heart beating fast. She continued to speak in Italian, for all she could think to do was to maintain the charade that had begun moments before.

"If you like," Barnabas replied in the same language. He took his seat again and pulled the monkey onto his lap. "It seems to soothe Tomaso, if nothing else."

She stiffened. Everything he said appeared to contain a hidden insult. Was her music only suitable for a monkey?

"How nice to know that there is one beast I can tame. Tell me, did you encounter many wild beasts on your travels? I understand you've been journeying for some time."

His eyes darkened and anger flashed in his face briefly. "Beasts of all kinds and many that you cannot imagine."

She nodded and looked quickly down at the lute. Would he ever say anything to her beyond these surface comments?

"Another humorous song, perhaps?" she asked. She tried to keep the bitter tone from her voice. "Or would you like to play cards? I understand you're good at gambling."

"There are some times when it's best not to gamble. I think this is one of them."

"A song it is, then. Perhaps some wine, first?" She rose from the chair, setting the lute on it, and made her way to the table slowly, making every effort to minimise her limp. At the table she lifted the flagon of Alessandra's best wine and poured it into the expensive glasses, attempting the best she could to still her trembling. She could feel his eyes on her and she allowed herself some steadying breaths. Lifting the glasses, she handed him one and raised the other.

"To a safe return," she said.

He raised his glass and held her eyes. "A safe return."

She closed her eyes and drank deeply. The wine slipped down and warmed her. Ordinarily she would only sip a glass throughout the evening. But tonight was different. Tonight she promised herself she would even have another glass and one after that, for the night would be long and she had no idea what it would hold.

It was after the third song, a light air of no real consequence that spoke only briefly about love, that she lowered the lute and asked if he would like a plate of figs or slices of beef. He accepted the offer of figs and she assembled some on a small gold plate and brought it to him.

He took the offered plate and the monkey, still seated in his lap, picked one up and popped it in his mouth. Alys laughed, caught off guard. Barnabas looked up at her, his eyes speculative. He fingered the sleeve of her gown.

"The gown. Is that your own, now?"

"It was Madonna Alessandra's, but I wear it on occasion, when she instructs me to."

"And tonight was such an occasion?"

She nodded. "In truth I've only worn it once before, my first appearance in public."

He raised his brows. "Is that so?" He rubbed his hand along the sleeve and frowned.

"Is there a problem? You don't like the gown?"

"It's not that I don't like the gown, so much as what it represents."

"And what is that?"

He sighed. "I fear that it reminds me of my obligations."

"Obligations?"

He nodded and rose, setting the plate beside the monkey. "You have a room?"

She nodded, her heart racing again. "You wish to go there, now?"

"But of course. Isn't that what Madonna Alessandra desires? That you entertain me in all manner of ways?"

She turned and walked to the door. Barnabas followed her, leading the monkey with its golden chain. She entered her room and saw no trace of Joanie, only a small array of candles on the table near the bed.

The monkey chittered and Bitty popped his head from his basket. Spying the dog, the monkey scampered towards him, pulling the chain out of Barnabas' hand. The dog barked and the monkey went for the dog, the two biting and nipping each other. Alys ran to Bitty and struggled with the two animals, reprimanding the pair of them. Barnabas grabbed the monkey and separated him from Bitty.

"A definite quarrel of a serious nature," said Barnabas.

Flushed with anger, she gave him a hard look while she stroked her dog and made soothing noises. "Your monkey attacked. The quarrel, if that's what you must call it, is down to him."

Barnabas shrugged. "I'll tie him up for now but I daresay the two of them will grow accustomed to one another eventually."

Alys looked at the monkey dubiously. She went over to the basket and placed the dog inside, closing the lid this time. "It's for your own good, Bitty," she murmured.

She rose and backed away, watching the little eyes through the weave of the basket. She bumped into the table, tipping over one of the candles.

"Watch out!" said Barnabas in English.

She turned, and before she could do anything, he'd grabbed her and shoved her away from the table and she fell to the floor. The candle, once it had tipped over, sputtered out and no flame remained. The other two still burned brightly. She looked up at Barnabas, bewildered.

"I'm sorry," he said in Italian.

He hesitated and then offered her a hand. She took it and he pulled her up with such strength that she fell against him, clutching him for balance. He looked at her, his eyes virtually unreadable. For a moment the two stood locked together holding each other's gaze. He raised his hand to her cheek and a small smile played at his mouth. She closed her eyes and waited, holding her breath, not daring to move.

Lips pressed against hers, tentative at first and then firm, demanding. She opened her mouth slightly and the kiss deepened. Inside her something loosened and unfolded slowly. She slid her arms around his neck and he pulled her closer to him. They kissed hungrily, and he slid his mouth down her neck and to her breasts, her skin burning at their touch. A small groan escaped and she arched against him. They pulled at the laces of her gown and his pourpoint and shed their clothes quickly. He pushed her gently back against the bed and for a moment she was lying naked while he stood watching her. She could feel the warmth of the pearl necklace lying against her breasts, the heat of her body absorbed into the gem. She held out her hand to him. A glimmer of fear crossed his face. Did he think her too brazen? She lowered her hand and turned away, suddenly embarrassed.

A moment later his body was pressed against hers and he was covering her with kisses. She enfolded him with her arms, kissing his ear and running her hands along his body. She savoured the feel of his body, his muscled frame and the taste of his skin. With a skill she'd not experienced before, he wooed her body in return, stroking, kissing, and plying his fingers so that she bloomed under him, finally fully wakened, each petal spread gloriously wide. All her wiles and arts remained unused as she caressed and moved in an instinctive rhythm that was completely new.

Later, she lay beside him, full of wonder at the manner and joy of the lovemaking she'd never thought possible. She turned and ran her hands along his chest, afraid to say anything, lest the feeling disappear. He stroked and fondled her back, praising her beauty, her soft skin, her full lips and her silken hair. Carefully, he released the ropes of pearls, removed the earrings and necklace and loosened her hair so that it fell to her waist in thick waves. He buried his face in it, murmured things in a language she didn't understand and then held her face in his hands, tears in his eyes. When she tried to speak, he put a finger to her mouth and kissed it instead, his tongue searching deeply, until they began all over again the joyous coupling like before.

She couldn't have enough of him, and it seemed he of her, and she wished that the night would never end, that they could go on loving each other, locked in each other's arms forever. Finally, when the first rays of light were coming through the window, she fell asleep.

☙

She awoke and felt the heat of the sun on her legs. Over in the corner where Barnabas had chained him, the monkey chittered away and then gave a little screech. She smiled. The poor mite was probably hungry. As she was certain her dog was, too. She could see his little nose peeking out through a gap in the wicker.

She rolled over and saw the space beside her was empty. She scanned the room. His clothes were gone. Had he dressed and gone in search of food? Or Alessandra? Most likely that was the cause of his absence, because the monkey was still there. She lay back on the bed a moment, suddenly feeling dizzy. After a while, when the room stopped spinning, she rose, wrapped herself in a robe and called at the door for Joanie. She came a moment later, a jug of water in hand.

"That was some night," Joanie said. "You haven't slept that late in a long while."

"Oh, Joanie, it was wonderful. I can't explain it, but I've not experienced anything like it in my life."

"Well you certainly do have a glow." She put her hand to Alys' head and frowned. "You're even a bit feverish."

Alys swatted away her friend's hand. "I feel fine. In fact I feel wonderful. Is Giacomo with Alessandra in the *sala*?"

"That the man you was with last night? If you mean 'im, he's gone."

Her heart sank. "Gone? But he will be back."

"I don't think so. Leastways, that's what Alessandra said. Apparently 'e's got to go away again. She's cross about it, too. Says 'e should stay here, but 'e says no, 'e has things to do."

Alys stood there, the words floating above her, refusing to penetrate her mind. Finally a rage rose inside her, the bloom that had filled her earlier shrivelled and dead.

"He's gone," she said flatly.

"Yes. You mind that 'e's gone? Why? What's 'e to you?"

She eyed Joanie. "Maybe long ago he was something to me. But now, he's nothing."

She went to the small wooden box where she held her collection of jewels and opened it. She withdrew the leather bracelet and stared at it, breathing rapidly. She walked over to the window, opened it wider, and tossed the bracelet out into the canal. Behind her the monkey chittered and screeched.

CHAPTER TWENTY-FIVE
Venice, Summer 1446
BARNABAS

I sat in the chair by the table, looking at the manuscripts on the desk. They were still legible, though the ink in the one was smeared in places and both were stained badly. They would both still fetch a large sum. The account of Prester John I had no intention of selling, and the other would perhaps do well in Alessandra's safekeeping.

I took up the cup filled with my honey mixture and drank deeply. Last night had taken much of my energy. More than I'd imagined. I thought of Alys, in all her beauty, such beauty that had allayed all my fears and made me whole again. I wished once more that things could be different. Why had she followed me to Venice? I felt ashamed at the situation my choices had forced her into. I only wished I could make it up to her, give her all that I'd promised those many years ago. But it was too late now. I gave the cup a baleful look. I was damaged. Besides, now my life was given over to other matters that must take precedence.

I gazed miserably around the room. The books that al Qali had gathered still lined the shelves. I'd arrived from Modone and went to our rooms only find them empty, the servants gone and no sign of al Qali's whereabouts. In the days to come, with Hal's help I would find out all I could and plan my course of action. I knew al Qali would be compelled to retrace the journey recounted in the manuscript. I just needed to find out where he'd begun it. I wanted to follow every footstep, so as not to miss him.

The door opened and a ragged man appeared, crouching low.

I blinked, hardly believing what I saw. It had been years since he'd last appeared. "Sam?" I said softly.

He edged forward and shook his head. I was stunned. Limping Sam. Here? I blinked again. What did he want? Was he here to warn me about something?

Behind him Alys appeared, limping just like Sam, dressed only in her shift, her hair loose about her shoulders.

"Alys," I said. "Sam. Is something wrong with Alys?"

I rose and went toward her, reaching out. My arms grew increasingly longer until they became snakes writhing in the air. I pulled back and more snakes came from my head, twisting and turning. Limping Sam wrapped his arms around Alys and pulled her back from me. I cried out and the snakes turned towards me, twisting, wrapping themselves around my body, suffocating me until I lost consciousness.

I woke up in a fading light, my face buried in my arms, leaning on the table. My cup had fallen over and the drink pooled near my nose. I lifted my head warily. I rubbed my face and tried to focus. Perhaps I'd had too much of the opiate this time. My mouth was dry and my tongue felt too big. I frowned. I must seek some advice. Hal would be back soon. He'd find someone for me. I knew that now was not the time to be rid of this addiction, but I could at least find the best way to manage it.

A thump sounded behind me. I turned and saw a book lying on the floor next to the shelves. I stared at the empty space where it had rested moments before. How had that happened? Curious, I went over and picked up the book. It was one of the volumes I'd had with me in Paris. I opened the cover and saw a folded sheet of paper inside it. I opened it, even though I knew its contents. A drawing of a young boy stared back at me. Wide-eyed and full of mischief, but innocent all the same. The boy who had pledged to protect Alys. The boy who had promised to return.

I replaced the book on the shelf. That boy no longer existed. The man who lived now was full of demons and I would never visit them on Alys. I was the only one who could exorcise them. She'd suffered enough already. I folded the paper once more and went over to the candle and lit it, watching the flame catch up. Calmly, I held the paper over the flame and waited for it to light. It took only an instant and before I'd drawn my next breath the paper had burned completely.

HISTORICAL NOTE

Venice in the time period in which this novel is set was a vibrant city, on the one hand, filled with merchants profiting from expanded trade opportunities and proud of its republic standing. They were generally a sober lot and the women of their class and the nobility were seldom seen in public. When they did, they too were soberly dressed, in dark colours. On the other hand, Venice was filled with people who worked at the shipyards, at the fisheries, the glassworks and other manufacturers in this blossoming commercial centre. There was faction fighting between the workers- sometimes fought desperately over bridges like the Rialto. Enemies of any class could be despatched in a dark alley and tossed in the canal.

Poised between the two sides of Venice were the courtesans. They were seen as cultured women who provided entertainment for wealthy noblemen and merchants. A man wouldn't be expected to marry until well into his thirties, so it was best that he take his pleasure with someone who would be cultured and unlikely to be diseased. An older man might feel the need of a mistress when his wife was more than likely raised in a convent-like atmosphere. It wasn't unusual for a courtesan to come from a merchant family or noble family when there was more than one daughter and the dowries were a huge financial burden. Some courtesans supported their families, who might have been in straightened circumstances. I am indebted to Margaret Rosenthal's work, The Honest Courtesan, for insight into this world.

Women artists were also rare in the Renaissance which restricted women's activities so much, despite its flourishing art world. Artemesia Gentileschi was one of the few who managed to paint for a living and achieved recognition, but she was trained in her father's workshop and had a tragic life, including being raped by one of her father's students. Her work is now admired greatly and one of her paintings is hanging in the Uffizzi Gallery in Florence and is the only female artist represented there, I believe.

Halil Pasha and Mehmet are real figures in history. Halil Pasha was made Grand Vizier under Mehmet's father. Mehmet was given the throne for two years and Halil Pasha opposed him and conspired to get the father to return to the throne. Mehmet lasted two years in the political intrigue that swirled in the court and was deposed and the father brought back. When the father died a few years later Mehmet came to the throne and Halil Pasha was slain. Mehmet went on to be a powerful ruler who expanded the Ottoman Empire exponentially. He took Constantinople in 1453.

ABOUT THE AUTHOR

Originally from Philadelphia, Kristin Gleeson lives in Ireland, in the West Cork Gaeltacht, where she teaches art classes, plays harp, sings in a choir and runs two book clubs for the village library. She holds a Masters in Library Science and a Ph.D. in history and for a time was an administrator of a large archives, library and museum in America. She also served as a public librarian in America and in Ireland.

Kristin Gleeson has also published *The Celtic Knot Series*, in addition to this series. This book is the second volume of *The Renaissance Sojourner Series*. There is a free novelette prequel, *A Trick of Fate* and volume one, *The Imp of Eye* published so far, all of which are available at online retailers.

She has also published a commercial biography on a First Nations Canadian woman, *Anahareo, A Wilderness Spirit*, published with Fireship Press and available on Amazon.

Look for *The Hostage of Glenorchy*, the first book in a new series, The Highland Ballad Series in April 2016 and available now.

If you have enjoyed this book please post a review on Amazon. It helps so much towards getting the book noticed.

If you go to the author website and join the mailing list to receive news of forthcoming releases, special offers and events you'll receive a **FREE prequel novelette** to *Along the Far Shores*.

www.kristingleeson.com

CPSIA information can be obtained
at www.ICGtesting.com
Printed in the USA
LVHW111303080319
609985LV00001B/93/P